THE COUNCIL OF NINE

INDRASHISH MITRA

This book has been fully funded by the Wordit Art Fund.
Wordit Art Fund helps deserving authors publish their work by providing
monetary support. To apply for funding, please visit us
at www.BecomeShakespeare.com

First published in 2017 by:
Becomeshakespeare.com
Wordit Content Design & Editing Services Pvt Ltd
Unit - 26, Building A-1, Nr Wadala RTO, Wadala (East),
Mumbai 400037, India
T:+91 8080226699

Author photograph by © Sagar Jeswani

©
ISBN – 978-93-86487-37-7

ACKNOWLEDGMENTS

This book would not have been in your hands if not for Mrs. Malini Nair, Senior Acquisitions Editor at LeadStart Publishing who secured a place for me in this Art Fund where my book could be published. I would also like to thank Mr. Sameer Ambildhok and Mrs. Amrita Jagtap, my project managers for working so hard, seeing to it that every doubt of mine was answered before later steps took place.

I would like to thank my dear parents who were responsible for my passion for reading and hence writing. They have always been an unparalleled source of support and motivation.

I would also like to thank all my friends and teachers who have known about my dream of becoming a published author and have been encouraging me all along. If not for your motivation, this honestly wouldn't have been possible.

Last but not the least; I would like to thank you, my dear reader for picking up this book. I hope this book lives up to your expectations and all my future books do too!

Wishing you my best!

'The truth is not for all men, but only for those who seek it.'

- Ayn Rand

'Among the tens of thousands of names of monarchs accumulated of the files of history, the name *Ashoka*, shines almost alone, like a star.'

'Outline of History' – HG Wells

PROLOGUE

Dauli Hills (Kalinga – Present Day), Orissa, India 261 BC

Ashoka the Great emerged slowly out of his tent, to greet the rising sun. The garish orange sun shone with breathtaking brilliance, shining in its golden glory. Ashoka looked at it; squinting his eyes and he inhaled the cold misty morning air. He gazed up at the partially visible moon and folded his hands into a formal *Namaste*, and sent up a silent prayer to the gods. He thought over the plans for the day of battle. He had never thought of the consequences of the battle at but now his face now betrayed a sense of foreboding. This was going to be the last day of battle. Hopefully. This battle was supposed to be a quick in and out operation, conquering the rich land of Kalinga. But the battle had stretched on for days together, mounting number of casualties on either side. This had been the only city that remained independent outside the Mauryan Empire under him. It was also a matter of pride; his grandfather had been unable to conquer this land. He, the grandson would have to do it as it would permanently secure his position as king forever. Soon, he saw soldiers rising, one by one at first then the multitude. Within an hour, his commander-in-chief reported to Ashoka, "*Maharaj*, the soldiers are in position. Should we go into battle?"

Ashoka gazed towards the north, his eyes grim, facing the land of

Kalinga. He nodded his brow in a tight furrow. Ashoka then donned his silver chainmail over his steel breastplate and placed his crown on his head. He strapped on his pure leather belt attaching his gold scabbard to his waist. He pulled out the sword out of his smooth velvet scabbard, holding it from the bejewelled hilt and swung it gracefully, cutting the air with a whistle. He sheathed his sword and gazed into the distance. Soon his army assembled in front of him, dressed in their regal attires, looking resplendent in the sun.

Soon, they rode into battle, with him on the lead. The battle wore on as the sun glided over the sky towards the opposite horizon. The piles of dead bodies rose higher and higher as the hours passed by in the relentless brutal political murders of kinsmen, brothers and husbands and sons from people sharing the same land, just different kings. The clangs as two swords met in all ferociousness, the gurgle as a sharp arrow pierced the fragile human body, trumpets of the huge war elephants as they stampeded through the ranks of the enemy trampling them beyond recognition, the sound of explosions as mortars blew resounded for miles around, striking fear into the hearts of one and all.

Soon, as the day came to an end, so did the battle. Rotten carcasses, mutilated underfoot lay here and there, waiting for the vultures to feed upon. Blood of those slain soaked into the earth, and turned nearby rivers crimson. Soon an unfamiliar noise rose from among the bloody mess. It was the collective wail of pain and loss from thousands of women all across the land.

'Oh! What have I done?' Ashoka exclaimed, amidst all the rejoicing around him, letting his sword drop to the floor of the chariot he was in. It clattered loudly, diverting the attention of those rejoicing around their king.

Ashoka got down from his chariot, walked some distance and kneeled down in front of a woman wailing, clasping her dead son's head in her bosom. As he approached and kneeled down, the woman spoke up, her voice broken by the sobs, 'Oh king! Your war has taken away my brother, husband and son. Now what do I have left to live for?'

Tears sprang forth from the great king's eyes as his eyes caressed the dead son. *I might have won a great war but I have lost something far more valuable,* Ashoka thought, *love.* The weight of the hundreds of thousands of lives lost fell upon his bare shoulders. His body felt heavy, his mind balancing on the brink insanity, almost tipping over. He could feel the penetrating and boring gazes of the mothers and wives, young sons and daughters pierce through him wordlessly like a sword through their tear rimmed eyes, curse him through their voices, choked with emotion.

On that day, the king underwent a change in heart. Never again would this king kill and subdue others in order to acquire. This was the birth of a new king, a king whose deeds would be proudly documented in the annals history as the greatest monarch to have ever lived in the entire history of the human race.

And on that day, he took a decision. A decision that would change his entire life and the course of history for the entire nation and the world for years to come.

Couple of years back

This was it!

This was the moment he had so longed and waited for!

The forty five year old man shifted his weight. He, along with a huge congregation of men and women stood in the dark chamber lit up by over a hundred candles perched upon the high walls. All the candles in the room, the man noticed, were festooned in the exact same way. All of them had a particular snake like design winding its way up. As was the two millennia old tradition, he had begun his journey into the brotherhood, wearing nothing but a white *dhoti*, which symbolized purity in its highest form. He had progressed through the hierarchy, now wearing a silk *dhoti* but purple in colour, revealing his ripped six feet physique. Nobody has ever been able to guess his age correctly, his strict fitness routine took care of that. He also had the customary jewel hilted sword sheathed in pure leather rimmed and velvet body scabbard wound around his broad waist.

There was a man, dressed in a similar fashion, standing on a raised platform in the middle of the cavernous room. He was tenderly holding an unrolled piece of laminated parchment with gloved hands and singing out the contents. The entire congregation stood staring at him, as if transfixed and hypnotised by some mystical power that the singer wielded.

The initiate, however, felt no such thing.

The congregation of men and women around him were too adorned in similar regalia. Most of these men and women were people who wielded enormous influence and power. The collective strength of the congregation in the room could easily topple entire

11

nations, both in terms of financial resources or political power. Yet the man knew these materialistic power and influence in the outer world had little significance within the four walls of this chamber. In here, they were nothing but brothers and sisters, united to protect a cause.

Four years had passed since he had been brought into his secret community as an initiate. And not even a day in those four years had he been admitted into this room. The room was cavernous, the walls rose straight up to fifteen feet of height, and six monolithic pillars were placed perfectly in the shape of a star, one of the most ancient of all symbols, made from two oppositely ended overlapping equilateral triangles to support the weight of the immense ceiling. The initiate, for a moment, caught a whiff of claustrophobia with the idea of imagining the several tons of rock debris that could crush all the scurrying human worms in a fraction of a second. But the feeling soon subsided.

After all, this place has endured two millennia under the ground. It could take on the burden for at least a few more hours. The initiate cared very little for what might happen later to the ancient fortress. He inhaled deeply and waited for the moment. He could feel the air in the room tighten, as the musical crescendo rose both melodiously and ominously. Though he couldn't understand what was being conveyed, he knew that it was the old almost forgotten language of *Pali*.

A quarter of an hour later, the song ended and nine people from the front row of the congregation ascended the raised platform and encircled the singer. They too were dressed in similar apparel as his. Their heads were low and were murmuring something, almost praying. Suddenly, all the nine men took four measured steps back, placed their hands on the hilts of their swords and drew them with the hands of a practiced swordsman. A fraction of a moment later, their swords clanged in the air. The entire congregation erupted into a roar of praise and applause.

Soon the nine men parted, revealing the singer in the middle, gently holding the rolled parchment in his hands. The clamour died a little later, everybody waited with baited breath for the final event of the evening. A minute later, when complete silence ensued in the room, the man with the parchment pronounced his name. The initiate could feel glances turn towards him and crowd parted in front of him, clearing his path to the platform. He took another deep breath in and started walking towards the platform in slow measured steps, ignoring the stares of the people around. He gracefully climbed up the stairs and stood, facing all the ten men in front of him. He gazed intently at their faces and even recognized one's face from the cover of some famous business magazines and investment journals he so often saw at newspaper stalls in the mornings. It was unnerving to see him up close suddenly but it didn't surprise him. A minute later, the man in the centre walked a step forward and held up the rolled parchment to the initiate.

The initiate's heart began to flutter. This was the moment he had been waiting for years. Quietly steadying his nerves, he raised his hands and clutched the two red velvet rimmed, gold encrusted ends of the parchment. It was time for the oath.

'Are you, in your full consciousness, willing to take the oath of utter secrecy and devotion to the brotherhood's purpose and endeavours? Are you willing to leave behind all traces of your old life and join the secret ranks of this community and serve it with your life? Will you preserve the secrets that will be bestowed upon you?' the old man asked.

The initiate took the parchment with his left hand and unsheathed his sword with his right, held it up high in the air and spoke, 'May this sword that I now hold so proudly be at my throat should I ever knowingly or willingly violate the sacred vow of secrecy and protection of this community.'

His voice echoed through the cavernous room. Pin drop silence ensued.

The initiate exhaled heavily as he kneeled down to hand back the parchment to the man in the centre. Then he looked up at the man and smiled.

You have got no idea what's coming for you.

1

The man stood before the intricately designed doorway of the mansion, going over his plan for one last time. The way he saw it, there wasn't any flaw in the entire scheme. If everything went well, nobody would even suspect him. He entered through the door and walked along the princely hall of the mansion.

The others in the family had gone out for a party, which was going to end abruptly. And he had ordered the servants to take an early day off so the entire house was completely devoid of human presence except for an old man lying in his bed in a corner of the mansion, attached to several life support systems and several bottles dripping nutrition directly into his bloodstream. This man was *being* kept alive. There wasn't any use of doing so; every person had his or her time to enjoy the pleasures of this materialistic world. Then it is time for them to leave.

He tightened the latex gloves over his hand, rubbing his fingers with fierce anticipation. He walked over the tile carefully, not to make any noise even though he knew his rubber soled shoes would take care of that. He walked up the steps, careful not to bump against anything here and there. He patted his sweatshirt pocket to ensure the filled syringe was still in there. He soon reached the top of the stairs and stood in front of the door where his victim lay.

He rubbed his fingers yet once again, placed his right hand over the doorknob and turned it ever so slowly. A little squeak cut through the quiet house and he just stood there, paralyzed, wondering if the noise had woken the old man. He peeked through the little crevice and heaved a sigh of relief as he saw the old man under his sheets, a contended smile on his face. One of the bedside lamps was switched on, but the old man's eyes were closed, a gently snoring away.

The man walked inside and went up to the nutrition IV bag. It was half way done dumping its content into the old man's bloodstream. He pulled out the pre-prepared syringe from his pocket and uncapped it. He then pierced the thin plastic of the bottle and pushed the back of the syringe, emptying the colourless liquid into the bag. He then recapped the syringe, placed it back in his pocket and smiled.

No one would be able to suspect anything until it was too late. Toxicology results took at least a week to come out. And even if, by chance the little hole was noticed, there wasn't anything that could be done to save the old man. One of the world's best kept secrets would die with him.

He cast a glance over the peaceful old face of the man lying on the bed.

All hell was about to break lose.

And he would be there to witness it all.

2

Aditya Tiwari sat at his table at the Taj Hotel, Mumbai, drumming his fingers impatiently against the table. This was his first date he had ever attended in his lifetime of twenty years and he was excited. He had enough reasons to be so. He gingerly fingered the exquisite Bormioli Rocco wine glasses laid out in front of him, impatiently waiting for her to arrive.

He had a hundred questions bouncing about in his mind and he absentmindedly checked his watch.

8:45 pm. She was supposed to have come by 8:30 pm.

He slipped his phone out, fingered it for a minute or two, unable to rest on one object. He slipped the phone back inside and straightened the collar and cuff of his shirt, shyly wondering if she would like his choice of colour. He toyed with the cold fork placed tangentially to the white plate in front of him.

He finally pulled his phone out for the second time and dialled the familiar number. The line was busy and it went into call waiting. Frustrated, he hung up and was about to leave when suddenly his phone rang. His spirits lifted as he pulled out his phone for the third time out of his pocket in an interval of five minutes. But almost immediately, his spirits dampened.

It wasn't her. It was his uncle. Crestfallen, he picked up the call and said, 'Hello?'

'Aditya?' replied an urgent voice.

'Yes, uncle, what is it?'

'This is an emergency. Your grandfather has passed away. Come here as quickly as possible!'

Aditya's own parents, both father and mother, had passed away long before, just after his birth when their plane had crashed when they were arriving back from a business trip from Australia. His grandfather had taken on the responsibility of fathering him and had become their godfather. He had brought him up like his own son since he himself had lost his son. And for Aditya too, he had become his world, catering to each and every of his whim and fancy, never letting him feel the loss of his parents.

'I'll be there in a minute, uncle.' Aditya promised.

He got up from his table, paid a little tip for occupying the table for so long and dashed out. A chauffeur brought out his Audi from the parking lot and stood in front of him. He jumped inside, kicked the throttle and burst out of the place, closely evading one of those horse drawn rides along the Arabian Sea coast. He shifted to top gear as he wound through the narrow streets of Colaba in central Mumbai. He nearly dashed into another man who jumped aside and before he could even think of his abuses to hurl, Aditya was out of earshot.

Soon he reached his home and saw that he was a little too late. Over ten police vehicles had surrounded the gates; security had been tripled in the past half an hour. He was immediately granted entry into the vast estate of the Tiwari family. He got out of his car and ran inside. His uncle was waiting at the door. He pushed him aside and stepped in when his uncle grasped his arm from behind.

'I do not think you will want to see it.'

Aditya was horrified. 'Why wouldn't I?'

His uncle left the grasp over his arm and said, 'It is too horrible.'

But Aditya had made up his mind. He shook his head and said nothing. He turned around and ran towards his grandfather's bedchamber. He pushed open the door and burst in. An unfamiliar stench had begun to spread throughout the otherwise perfectly ventilated air conditioned room. His grandfather lay there on the bed, completely immobile in his bed, unlike the usual enthusiasm he usually was welcomed with by his grandfather. His grandfather's face had become pale, drained of his usual cheerful pink colour and his lifeless eyes wide open staring at the ceiling. It was as if his body had shrunk down, had Aditya almost felt like he was looking at a different man.

There were half a dozen men milling about in the room. There was one taking high resolution photographs of the scene. Forensic experts were snooping around for any traces that the murderer might have left behind. A doctor was busy fiddling with several IV tubes. Two more policemen were talking to each other when they noticed Aditya in the room. One of them came up and gently tried to push him out of the room saying, 'Official investigation is underway and we don't want any intruders. It would be appreciated if you could stand outside.'

This ticked Aditya off. 'He's my grandfather for God's sakes and you are pushing me out? What do you think of yourself, huh?' Aditya whipped back ferociously, pushing the police officer back. 'I will stand here all night if I have to and you just shut up!'

His uncle huddled into the room and gently coaxed him, 'Aditya, it is okay. He doesn't know who you are. Please forgive him and come out, there are more important things to be talked about than fighting uselessly here.'

Aditya left the room and sat down on an intricately carved mahogany sofa, burying his face into his palms, barely able to control his tears. His uncle sat down beside him and laid an affectionate arm over his shoulder.

Aditya sat up suddenly, his eyes red. 'Why is the police force here instead of the doctors?'

'We suspect murder. The doctors initially were sure of a cardiac arrest but on further inspection of the surroundings, the doctors noticed a small puncture on the IV nutrition bag hanging beside his bed which led us to believe that he might have been murdered, thus the presence of the police. The doctor says that it was very quick, with minimum amount of pain. So at least the murderer was considerate enough.' Aditya's uncle wiped a tear from his face.

Aditya buried his face into his palms. A minute later, he sat up. The gaze of his eyes was painful. 'I am going to find him and I am going to make him pay.'

He jumped up from his seat and stormed out of the place.

3

The killer smiled inwardly as he saw the grandson jump up and stomp away from the place. He could feel for the young lad. He had lost the only man he loved most, the one who had brought him up; the old man was the only parent he had known. So it was only natural to be distressed. There were also a multitude of far and distant family relatives that had come in at such a short notice.

But it also made him a threat. If he became too determined, things might turn sour and he might have to do something. But the killer didn't want to do anything to the lad. He had no antagonism against the boy, but against his grandfather.

Such men had no rights to live. They deserved to die.

To keep such a secret from the world, is a heinous crime and punishable by death, if not anything mightier.

His plan was slowly and steadily starting to fall into place. Killing the old man had been his first step. Others were yet to die in his intricately woven plan. But they wouldn't die in vain. Their deaths would bring him glory beyond this world.

Only if the boy stayed out of this, everything would work out just fine.

4

Aditya jumped up through the stairs of the mansion, skipping three or four steps at a time. He reached his own room and dashed in and banged the door behind him. He glanced up at his wall clock and noticed that a little over had hour had passed since the last time he had glanced at the time. He slumped down on the luxurious queen size bed that he had all for himself and again buried his face into his palms to hide his freely flowing tears.

Woe and heartache soon transformed by stronger emotions of frustration and wrath. He balled up his fingers and punched whatever was in front of him. He was seething with rage as he mowed down several expensive household appliances in his room. It was a little shard of glass that punctured his skin as he punched through the mirror which brought him back to his senses. He rushed to the wash basin to wash off the freely flowing blood from the wound. He then carefully extricated the tiny fragment of glass sticking out between his knuckles, wincing in pain. He poured the cold tap water over the region for some more time before applied a band-aid. He then sat back on his bed and surveyed the mess around him. He pulled out his phone and flicked through it. Condolence messages had already started pouring in great numbers.

The time was 10:15 pm.

He placed his phone of the side table, kicked off his shoes. Just as his head was about to touch with the pillow, a thought crossed his mind. He jumped up from his bed and threw open the newspaper rack in the corner of his room. He hurriedly rifled through the papers, tearing up some in the process. Several minutes later, he found the one he was looking for.

It was an issue of the Times from a few months back, something that his grandfather had shown him personally that day and asked him to remember lest something happened and things went for a toss. The news had made the front page article.

City private investigator catches two murderers under a week!

City investigator Mubeen Roy tracks down two murderers under a week of their crime. City officials are now in charge of the murderers and are awaiting trial. Sources say there is no chance for the murderers to get anything under life imprisonment.

This was the man he had been looking for. Mubeen Roy.

He picked his phone up and dialled a familiar number. It rang twice before picking up. 'Hello? Fiona?'

'Yes?' replied a tired voice.

'I need a little help.'

The woman on the other side sighed and said, 'What is it?'

5

Mubeen Roy's phone rang loudly from his bedside table. His eyes flung open as the piercing sound of his cell phone reached his ears. Then, as he realised it, he sat up and took up the phone. The call was from an unknown number. He rubbed his aching temples. Frustrated, he picked up the call.

'Mr. Roy?' a woman's voice asked.

'Hey, whoever you are? You know, this is a really bad time to call. It's the middle of the night. I hope you understand this.'

The woman replied calmly, 'I understand that very well since I am standing just outside your hotel. I was going to come in straightaway but then I thought I would rather call. So, are you free right now?'

What the hell? Am I free? What kind of a question is that? Of course I'm not free! It's in the middle of the night! Anyway, where am I? He thought, his sleepy indolence shrouding his mind entirely. He stood up and looked about; he noticed the doorstep menu pamphlet bear the words *HOTEL MARINE PLAZA, MUMBAI.*

Slowly, realisation dawned upon him.

I'm on a vacation for God's sake!

'What do you need me at this hour? And who are you?' he asked, rubbing his eyes out of sleep.

'I have a case. Can I come in?'

This got him interested, even though he was on a vacation. A case always got him interested. 'Okay. Come on in.'

He looked at his bedside watch. 1:15 am. Barely an hour had passed since he had hit the bed. A minute later, a loud knock resonated throughout his tiny room. He clumsily walked up to the door and opened it. The woman was standing, wearing an elegant black tuxedo. *Who wears a tux in the middle of the night?* Mubeen thought. He noticed her hairdo was done pretty well too. They shook hands and Roy accosted her inside sleepily. The woman introduced herself as Fiona.

'I am really sorry to have disturbed you at this hour but we have something of interest for you. A man has been killed.'

'Hundreds of people die all over the world every day. What's so special about this guy? And, by the way, how did you locate me?' Roy asked, yawning.

'We have our ways and means to find you, Mr. Roy. And the name of this *guy* is Mr. Harish Tiwari. He was murdered a couple of hours back. In his bed.' Fiona replied, rather offended by the yawn right on her face.

This shook him out of his slumber. 'You mean THE Mr. Harish Tiwari?'

'The one and only.' she replied, shaking her head in affirmation.

'You really mean THE Mr. Harish Tiwari, don't you? One of the biggest, most iconic real estate mogul in the world, isn't he?'

'Yes. Now stop asking me the same question.' Fiona snapped.

'In Mumbai? His grandson is here too, isn't he?'

'I see you are well informed.'

'Well, in a job like mine, you always have to be well informed. Okay. Tell me more.'

'I've already told you a lot.'

'Come on. I would have eventually come to know about it tomorrow morning when the news channel reporters are going to go crazy with the news and the TRP's are going to reach sky high until the news becomes stale after a day or two. Thousands of so-called witnesses are going to drop in their tweets, giving rise to even more number of conspiracy theories all of which aren't going to reach anywhere. Unless of course, if you could tell me something... more revealing.'

'I cannot really say anything more about the investigation unless you officially agree to work for us. Also, when you do agree, I will not be the one to give you the details, Aditya Tiwari will be the one to do it. I have a vehicle waiting outside for you.' The woman replied, looking into her phone and typing something.

'Wait. I haven't given my assent as of yet.'

Fiona pursed her lips. 'Well, I assumed since you showed much enthusiasm and cooperation in talking about the case, you might as well want to solve the case itself. And by the way,' she continued nonchalantly, 'we needed an expert in the field who also values secrecy. Because the information you are going to be provided with isn't to be shared.' She raised her eyebrows, hoping that Roy might just nod his head in approval with the bonus praise. 'And the pay's good, I can assure you that. If you can solve this, you'll get enough cash to survive lavishly the upcoming year, unemployed.' He was sure of that. Wherever this Tiwari family was involved, there was sure to be some really good cash involved.

Roy brushed his hand over his hair and nodded his head. 'Okay. I'm in. But I don't have a good feeling about this.'

'Excellent!' Fiona exclaimed and rose. 'I'll be waiting in the lobby. Ready your stuff. We're leaving within half an hour.'

'Really? Half an hour?' he asked, glancing at the watch yet again and groaned.

'Yes.'

Twenty five minutes later, he looked out of the window as he shouldered his backpack, admiring the ferocious beauty of the Arabian Sea lashing on the shores. His heart told him to reject the very idea of accepting the case but his mind told him this was going to be a challenge. And he loved challenges. And the money was promising too, considering the fact that Mr. Harish Tiwari's grandson had hired him.

I'll be back for you, I promise. Roy promised solemnly to the dark seashore.

6

The car came to a halt behind the immense Tiwari mansion, in front of a smaller but equally royal door with several intricate designs etched over the surface. Roy imagined the door alone must have cost a small fortune. Fiona went up and knocked lightly. A moment later, the door swung open and a familiar face emerged. It took a moment for him to recognize but he finally realized that he had seen Aditya Tiwari's face on the newspapers a lot many times and thus it seemed vaguely familiar.

'Mr. Tiwari, I presume?' Roy asked hesitantly, raising his hand for a shake.

Aditya nodded curtly and turned to Fiona and said, 'Fiona, thank you so much. I don't know how much I will ever be indebted to you. But keep this a secret, will you?'

Fiona just smiled and nodded. Now as Roy compared her with Aditya, she seemed a little older than she had first seemed. But there was definitely something between them. He just shrugged and dropped his hand.

Aditya turned his attention to him and said quietly, 'Mr. Roy. Please come in. Forgive me for my ill manners but I am not in the mood, really. I presume you know the reason why.'

'No, no. It is okay. And that's perfectly understandable.'

'Okay. Come on in. And quietly.' Aditya moved aside and opened the door for him. Roy stepped into the room and closed the door silently behind him. Aditya motioned to him to follow. Roy followed mutely, treading silently over the exquisitely finished marble floors of the Tiwari mansion. His eyes had adjusted to the darkness all around and he could make out the several objects and paintings lined up against the walls. This was the first time he had ever entered the famed Tiwari mansion. And it was as beautiful as they claimed. He wondered how beautiful the place would look during the day.

Soon they reached another room and Aditya held the door open for him. Roy entered and Aditya came in, closing the door behind him and securely locking it. He switched on the lights and sat down on the bed. Roy took a seat near him.

'I'm so sorry I am forcing you to undergo all this in the middle of the night which I assume was the second day of your week long sabbatical, am I right?'

'Yes. But it's okay; a killer must never be let free, even if it costs a little vacation.'

'Right. So coming directly to the point, I want to hire you investigate into the matter for me, undercover.'

'Undercover?'

'Yes. Frankly speaking, I don't trust the police investigation systems and after this,' Aditya said, placing a news paper in front, 'I wanted nobody else.'

Roy smiled as he recognized the article when he had hit the front page news two months ago. It had been quite an achievement. And the process had been quite an adventure.

'Why don't you trust the police?' Roy asked.

'I believe my grandfather was killed because he was getting too powerful due to his business and to stay ahead in the competition, you must *eliminate* competition. And that is what, I believe, has happened here. And I know what the people in power are quite capable of.' Aditya said, stressing on the word.

'But what actually happened? How was he murdered?'

'My grandfather had recently undergone a knee replacement operation here in Mumbai and after which he was under medication. A doctor comes thrice a day to do the check-ups and changing nutrition bottles and other stuff I don't know much about. Initially we had assumed that he had died a natural death until one of the doctor's assistants found a tiny hole on the nutrition IV bag. He was poisoned. We do not know what it is for sure until the toxicology tests turn up but the doctor seems pretty sure. We haven't found anything else to suggest otherwise. The body has now been taken away for further inspection and for doing a post.'

'Any other wounds? Like, on Mr. Tiwari's body somewhere?'

'Nothing. The doctors have already inspected that. Nothing whatsoever.'

Roy's pinched the bridge of his nose and thought hard. There were a lot of things that could have happened that might have led to the murder of Mr. Tiwari.

'So do you want to investigate the case? Of course, there is no compulsion but I promise you will be looked after and also the financial matters wouldn't be a problem. If only you could catch this killer for me.' Aditya said, almost pleadingly.

Roy thought for a moment. Then he finally decided. 'Okay. I'll do my best.'

Aditya smiled and looked up. 'You'll need to do better than that.'

'So, what's next?'

'Okay. I want you to stay here with me now. A few hours later, I will familiarize you with the other inhabitants of this house and you can do your job. I do not want you to tell anybody that you're here to investigate the matter. Act as if you're my friend. That way I will be able to introduce you to everybody and you'll be able to do your job without anybody interfering. But the police officials might know you right?'

'As far as I know, I'm quite popular in those circles. But don't you worry. I'll handle that part.' Mubeen said with a smile.

7

Mumbai's December. A perfect mixture of cold with a hint of warmth. The mornings are the coldest, which graduated into moderately sultry afternoons and the relief of the evenings passing into the cold nights. The killer pulled the luxurious blanket over his body, enjoying the pleasant weather and the tingly warmth of his body under the blanket.

Today had been a great day. His plan had commenced with perfection. The first, most important player in the game had fallen. Nine others were yet to fall. The Corporation was happy with his job. The world wouldn't realize how much he sacrificed himself to serve humanity and bring knowledge out for everybody.

Suddenly he heard the sound of tyres crunching over gravel. And it was relatively near, almost just outside the house. He threw his blanket aside and jumped up with the catlike grace. He moved the dark curtains and peered out of the window. He saw just in time as a man and a woman stepped out of a Mercedes and the back door opened up. Though the man inside couldn't be seen, the killer had a strong suspicion that it was Aditya.

The man who had stepped out of the vehicle had an air of awe which suggested that he was new to this place. A few words transpired between the people and the woman left back with the car and the man entered.

The killer quickly ran to the door, placed his ear on it and waited. As expected, a few minutes later, a door closed faintly in the house, not enough to awaken the others but enough for him. He quietly turned the knob of his door and stepped outside and walked towards Aditya's room. He didn't mind walking fast; the plush carpeting of the floor would take care of any noise his feet would make. As he neared the door, he could hear muffled noises but couldn't make anything out of them. Aditya and his newly acquired accomplice were smart enough to realize that someone might be eavesdropping. Disappointed, the killer went back to his room, deciding further inspection would have to wait until the morning.

This was a new development. Aditya was beginning to suspect something.

But the killer was not perturbed. His plan was perfect. Nobody would be able to see through his scheme.

His trail was untraceable.

8

A few hours later, the sun routinely peeked out of the horizon, shining its warmth in the cold morning. Sunlight filtered through the glass window and fell on Mubeen's drooping head. He smiled unconsciously as immediately blood started refilling the vessels of his face, tickling him under the skin. A minute later, he opened his eyes and squinted in the light.

For a moment, he had forgotten what had happened last night. Then he saw Aditya on the floor, his back against the bed, his eyes closed and then it struck him.

Mubeen rubbed the sleep from his eyes and stood up. He went up to Aditya and gently nudged him awake. Aditya jumped up in surprise and a moment later remembered where he was and how he had gotten here. Mubeen shook his head groggily and went to the bathroom, closing the door behind him. He came out, five minutes later, fully refreshed.

Aditya performed his morning chores. Just as they were about to walk out, a slight knock on the door was heard.

'My uncle.' Aditya said under his breath. 'Remember the instructions.'

'What about my name?' Mubeen whispered back.

'Let it be the same. I doubt anybody in my family has the time to read newspapers, let alone remember one particular name from a cover page article two months back.'

Aditya went ahead and opened the door. As expected, his uncle was standing outside, his face glum.

'Good morning uncle. I'm sorry I didn't talk to you too much last night.'

'That is okay, son. But who is he?' he asked, his expression highly suspicious.

'Oh, him? Remember I had told you about a really good friend of mine from college? This is the guy. Mubeen Roy. He is my best friend and he came to town yesterday night looking for a job. Now as soon as I came to know about that, I couldn't let him stay in those pathetic city hotels, could I? So I called him here.' Aditya lied smoothly.

The uncle's face immediately relaxed. 'Oh! Nice to meet you, son. I'm sorry I didn't greet you properly in the beginning. Welcome to our abode.'

'Thank you so much for welcoming me so warm heartedly even in such perilous times. If I had known about this, I would never have agreed to intrude the family. Aditya hadn't told me about this earlier. It is I who should be sorry for intruding at such a delicate time.' Mubeen said, as politely as he could.

The uncle just smiled and nodded and Aditya beckoned to him. They walked out of the room and for the first time in his life, Mubeen's jaw dropped at the astounding beauty of the interior of the Tiwari mansion. Beautiful golden chandeliers hung from the high ceilings, marvellous masterpieces adorned the walls, an elegant stairway that led upstairs and the mahogany banisters had been etched with intricate designs, and several lush Kashmiri carpets lined the marble floorings. He couldn't believe his eyes. By rough estimate, the net worth of these antique articles could easily cross a million, if not more.

This... is how the upper echelon lives. Mubeen thought ruefully.

If all these items could be sold, even at fifty percent loss, it would be enough to support an entire village for one whole year.

They walked down the stairs. He couldn't believe that he had missed all this when he had sneaked in along with Aditya in the middle of the night. He knew he was going to have a hard time adjusting to this. Aditya introduced him to the rest of the family and Mubeen shook proffered hands politely and soon they all soon sat down to have breakfast. Waiters began streaming in, each one of them carrying a different delicacy. Everybody became very busy about it, probably forgetting that there had been a murder in the house last night. Mubeen also dug in, realizing that this was a hundred times a better breakfast than what he would have received back at the hotel.

Suddenly, the doorbell rang, the loudly resonating throughout the house, momentarily quietening the hubbub.

'I'll get it.' Aditya said, getting up quickly.

He reached the door and opened it. A man stood at the gate with a little box in his hands with his name written diagonally across. The box was apparently for him yet the man didn't look like the everyday delivery man.

'Are you Mr. Aditya Tiwari?' the man asked.

'Yes, I am.'

'This is for you. Your grandfather had instructed me to give this to you if something happened to him, worst case scenario. Just make sure only *you* see the contents of this box alone. This box was meant to be yours and yours alone. Don't tell anybody about the source of this, tell them I just delivered something which you had ordered and forgotten.' The man said, holding out the box for him.

Aditya gingerly took the box held out to him. The man at his door turned around and began to leave when Aditya asked, 'But who are you?'

'You'll know soon enough.' The man smiled warmly and left.

9

The killer arched his back to get a view what was happening at the door. He could see a man standing at the door but his face was obscured. Something was given to Aditya. He took it and said something to the man who replied very little and completely inaudible. He saw Aditya shake his head self-consciously and look at the object in his hands with curiosity.

What was happening?

Aditya balanced the box in his hands and closed the door behind him with his leg.

Somebody asked, 'What is it, Aditya?'

'Oh, this? This is just something I had ordered a few days back online. I'll just go and keep this in my room and be right back.'

'Okay.'

The killer frowned but didn't say anything. He couldn't say anything right now. It would do more harm than good.

10

Aditya walked up the stairs and opened the door of his room. He looked around, trying to find a place to hide the box till he had the time to examine the contents alone. He moved about his furniture, and suddenly remembered the safe which his grandfather had insisted him to install in his room. It would be just about the right size. And it was away from prying eyes and even if it was found, the code was known only to him. His grandfather only knew the location of the safe but not the combination.

He set the box on the bed and pushed it slightly to the left. He lifted the carpet from the place and felt about for the familiar line in the wood. He swiped his hands over the flooring until he finally found it. He pressed the region slightly and a small metal ring popped up. He grasped the ring and tugged. An entire section of the floor came out, revealing the reinforced steel safe hidden underneath. He smiled as he remembered his grandfather's ingenious idea to put in that fancy wooden cover. Nobody would be able to guess its presence. He typed out the combination and a small section smoothly slid out. Aditya placed his finger on the biometric sensor. A moment later, the machine pinged in recognition and a glass display bar burst to life. It displayed a welcome message and the door clicked open. He quickly slid the box into the safe and closed it. He slid back the safety trap back in place and replaced the carpet on top.

He stood up, brushed himself and walked out towards the dining hall. As he neared the hall, he could see Mubeen getting along pretty well with the remaining members of his family. That was a good sign. Then, when the time was right, Mubeen would subtly start questioning them and soon the perpetrator would be out. In the meantime, he would have to look into his grandfather's mysterious box.

'Hey, what took you so long?' his cousin sister asked, her streaked hair falling right over, obscuring her face almost completely. 'Here your friend is quite interesting and told us a story. You missed it.'

'That okay. I can catch up on those later. Right now, I am ravenous.' Aditya said.

'What did you order recently?' Aditya's uncle asked.

'Nothing. Just a bunch of t-shirts. My old ones were getting stretchy and worn out, that's why.'

'Oh, okay.'

Aditya turned his attention towards his food and dug in. He picked up his favourites from the array of dishes laid out in front of him. He then poured himself a glass of orange juice from a glass jug and took a sip. He set the glass down and began pondering over the mysterious delivery.

Mubeen took another long sip from his glass of orange juice and looked around. By this time, he had formed a fair character analysis of almost everybody around the table and to him none seemed to fall under the category of a cold-blooded murderer. He saw Aditya deep in thought, especially after the delivery and his lie was quite clear when he said it was something that he had ordered online. Mubeen had dealt with a lot of hardcore liars to see through Aditya's lie. But nobody around the room seemed to give a second thought to his answer. Everyone had gone back to their eating and talking. Aditya was occasionally poking at his food absentmindedly. He was surely hiding something for all of them. Even though Aditya himself had asked him to find the perpetrator, Mubeen couldn't rule him out of the list of possible suspects.

Soon they all finished their food and the waiters streamed in to pick up their plates and dishes. Mubeen was about to protest against the unacceptable amounts of food going waste but then bit back his comment. That would have to wait. He had something more important at hand.

To find out what was in that box.

11

Aditya cleaned himself up after the breakfast and retired to his room as quickly as he could, without arousing suspicion. He didn't want to alert anybody of his motives. Just as he closed the door behind him, a small knock sounded. Aditya sighed and opened the door. It was Mubeen.

'You need to tell me what's in that box. And please,' Mubeen whispered, 'don't give me that lie.'

Aditya looked here and there and finding nobody lurking nodded him inside and locked the door behind him.

From the drawing room below, the killer sat, obscuring his face with a newspaper but watching everything that was happening in Aditya's room. He saw him quickly retire and then Mubeen walked up immediately after that who was let in without a second question, which undoubtedly would have been a no for anybody else in the house, stating some lame excuse.

Something was seriously up.

'What is it?' Mubeen asked quite loudly.

'Shh. The walls have ears.' Aditya said, 'It is a box sent by my grandfather, specifically for my eyes only.' He stood up and went towards the Sony stereo system installed in his room. He absentmindedly selected some random song and raised the volume.

Mubeen ignored the last part and said over the noise, 'You said your grandfather has been murdered and then now you're saying he sent you a parting gift after he died?'

'No, no! Another person delivered it to me saying that my grandfather had instructed him to do so.'

'Who was the person who delivered you the box? Did you know him? How can you just take gifts from total strangers whom you've never even seen if your life? It might as well be a bomb in there, ticking away to glory.'

Aditya thought for a moment and then said, 'I am sure I have never met that man before. But one thing struck me as strange. When I asked the same question to him, he simply smiled and replied that I would come to know of it soon enough. That's it. Nothing else.'

Mubeen took a seat and rubbed his chin. 'Shall we look at the contents of the box?'

'Yes, let's do that.' Aditya said. He jumped up from the bed he was sitting on but a moment later sat down again, smiling. 'Guess where I might have hidden it.'

Mubeen accepted the challenge and looked around. He scrutinized every corner of the open wall, trying to find a crevice that might give away the location but couldn't find any. He imagined the box in Aditya's hands and did a rough calculation to gauge its size. After that, one look at the cupboards told him that box wouldn't fit in those. The walls looked perfect. He looked down. He saw many things strewn across the room but the carpet was perfectly laid out all over, except in one corner, near the bed. He stood up and walked to the place and jumped lightly over it. A hollow thud resonated over the music.

'Found it! Though I cannot say if this is a trap or not.' Mubeen exclaimed.

'You're really as good as they say you are.' Aditya said, admiringly.

Mubeen sat down on his knees and shifted the carpet. He found the little metal knob and tugged at it. It came out smoothly, revealing a small safe. Aditya typed in the key and swiped his finger on the biometric scanner while Mubeen looked away and it opened, revealing the box within. Aditya took it out and handed it to Mubeen.

'Shall I?'

Aditya nodded. Mubeen gently tore open the white plastic covering and opened the seal of the box. Inside was an envelope. Mubeen handed the envelope to Aditya and set the box aside. Aditya tore open the envelope and pulled out a sheet of paper. Aditya breezed through the letter and tears welled up in his eyes. He handed it to Mubeen who read through it carefully.

Dear Aditya,

If you are reading this letter, it means that I am no more and this has been delivered to you and you only as per my instructions. Do not be sad. You are now going to be entrusted with a secret and a journey that will change your life dramatically, in a way you could never have imagined. But do not worry. Whatever your choice, your life will be in great peril from this moment on. There are forces out there that plot to obstruct out path and stop us from achieving our objective and they will kill to do so, if necessary.

In the box along with this letter lies a secret that I am going to entrust you with. This secret will bring along with it a lot of risk. But you will have to promise me that you will guard the secret with your life. If you follow the trail I have laid out for you, you will be a part of something only a few hundreds have had the privilege to be a part of in the history of a little over two millennia of its existence. Make sure nobody knows the existence of this. I have cared for nothing more than you and I do not want to put you in any harm's way but you are the only person I can blindly entrust with the secret. I will be there along with you throughout your journey; I will help out wherever I can. You might not realize how but you will in due course of events.

But you and you alone will have to finish this journey; this will be your walk through fire, through ice and snow.

Yours lovingly,

Grandfather.

Interesting. Mubeen thought.

Below the letter was a well known gold *dharmachakra* insignia engraved deeply into the paper. Mubeen's investigative mind sparked off and it began analyzing the sheet. The sheet was a lot thicker than the usual everyday paper. There was a yellowish tinge to the edges which suggested that it was probably quite old. The stiffness of the paper also suggested that it hadn't been handled by hand in very recent past. Conclusion? Maybe, it was late Mr. Tiwari who had touched it for the first and last time before it was boxed up and kept away.

This meant that late Mr. Tiwari had known that there was a threat to his life and had taken precautions to ensure that his grandson got his message. But why now? Why after his *death*? Why not take precautions to protect one's own life? Mubeen exhaled heavily. This was going way too deep already. But it wasn't like he didn't like difficult cases. His mind craved constant pressure and thinking to solve a situation.

'What would you like me to do?' Mubeen asked quietly after a few moments.

This was going to be a very important decision for Aditya, Mubeen realized. His grandfather's strict instruction to not let anyone into the secrets that lay concealed within the box. On the other hand, Mubeen had come to know about the existence of the box which was again, a liability from his point of view. And there was no way for him to convince Aditya that he would keep his mouth sealed.

Aditya stayed silent for a few more moments and finally spoke up.

'Okay. Let's open this together.' Aditya whispered.

'Okay. You go ahead.'

12

The killer stood near Aditya's door, keeping an eye out over the horizon of the staircase for an intruder alert while he pressed his ear to the warm mahogany of the door and tried to listen to the conversation going on inside. He heard the new guy say something out loud but a minute later, a song began from within the room. Aditya had switched on his stereo system.

Damn! The killer thought. Aditya loved to listen to music and he knew there was no point in staying back to listen to anything. All he would be able to hear would be old Shashi Kapoor romantic song from the seventies.

Just as he was about to leave, something struck him. Aditya listening to 70's romantic songs? Change in taste? Highly unlikely. Trying to hide something, under the cover of sound so that nobody may be able to eavesdrop? Possible. So just in case, he decided to hang around. Over the noise, he heard words like delivered, grandfather, box among others. These words were enough for him to piece the story together.

Aditya had received a box from his dead grandfather, but how could that be possible in any way? *I killed him personally. There is no way for him to be alive.* But the person who had delivered the box had been somebody else, he was sure of that. Also, the grandfather's body was still at the morgue, there was no way he could be alive. The funeral rites were to be performed a little later.

The killer nodded to himself. Things would have to wait until further developments. Aditya and Mubeen might be on to something but he was sure, they were nowhere near the truth, his steps had been carefully concealed.

He wanted to remove Aditya from the equation. He hadn't expected Aditya to change into something like this.

But things would have to wait.

13

Aditya gingerly pried open the cardboard lid of the box. Both of them carefully peered in, not sure what they were going to see. Inside they saw yet another folded sheet of paper along with a small dusty old photo frame. Patches of golden foil were falling off from the wooden framework. Inside was a photo of two people, Aditya and his grandfather, when they were a lot younger. The picture quality wasn't great but it was clear that the two people were posing on a beach. The frothy navy blue waves crashing against the deep golden sands of the beach. Aditya was in his grandfather's arms, waving animatedly at the person taking the photograph. The only odd feature in the picture was that it had a black coloured statuette rising right in between the faces of the two. Mubeen could clearly gauge that it was quite far away but the face of the statuette wasn't discernable.

'Do you remember when this picture was taken?' Mubeen asked over his shoulder.

'No. Not really.' Aditya replied, handing the photograph to Mubeen and picking up the sheet of paper from within. This sheet of paper was even older, yellower than the previous one. Aditya gently unfolded the paper and read the contents. It was in his grandfather's neat cursive.

To a certain temple you need to go,

Where the angry goddess hath waited for days long,

Where the three waters converge unbound,

Where, like the goddess, the waters around are virgin,

Where, the father of a great nation such as this, rests,

At the foot of the eastern gate you shall find what you seek.

'Now, what is that supposed to mean? Find what?' Aditya murmured.

'One thing is clear. Your first clue lies near a confluence. And that is related to a goddess somehow. There are three hundred and thirty million gods and goddesses in the Hindu mythology. What would be the best place to begin?' Mubeen said.

'I don't know. You tell me.' Aditya said, staring hard into the sheet of paper.

Suddenly a knock resounded over the loud music. Both of them fumbled with the box and the objects they had brought out. They replaced everything back where it all had been and replaced the box in the secret hole in the floor under the carpet. Another knock was heard. Mubeen nodded to Aditya who briefly nodded back and then Mubeen opened the door. Aditya's second aunt was standing at the door, 'It is time dear. We must go now.'

The plump old lady looked kind and hearty but her cheeks bore stains of continuous tears and her expression, overcast and she had a genuine expression of sadness.

'Okay.' Aditya said.

After the woman left, Mubeen turned and asked, 'Go where?'

'Funeral rites.'

'Have the post mortem reports come in?'

'Those should be with the police, I believe. Come, we'll go together.'

14

The killer cursed under his breath. The arrival of Aditya's aunt had spoiled everything. He had been able to hear little snit bits of their conversation and out of those snit bits, he probably could have worked out what both of them were up to. But in the nick of time, he had noticed the aunt ambling up the stairs, swinging her plump body here and there. He had quickly moved out of the view.

The killed glanced at his watch. It was time for the funeral rites.

Something strong was cooking up that he had no idea about. That was a sensation he was unfamiliar with and did not wish to remain with that feeling for very long.

But the time was not right yet.

What he was doing for the betterment of all humanity. Not like those old scheming fools who kept such knowledge a secret from mankind. Discoveries and inventions should be made free for every human being to enjoy. And he was a part of something that was working to make such knowledge available to everybody.

The killer pulled out his phone and dialled a familiar number. The line rang twice and then it was picked up and a hoarse voice spoke from the other side, 'Any new news?'

'We must tread carefully. I tried overhearing them but they were smart enough to play loud music to discourage eavesdroppers. They probably have begun suspecting something; though I'm sure it is nowhere close to us.'

There was a pause from the other side. The killer stared out of the window of his room, which overlooked the massive garden of the Tiwari estate. Several gardeners were watering the neatly trimmed and lined plants. There was a tiny little pond right in the middle of the garden with a fountain at its centre. An assortment of red, yellow and white roses lined the circumference of the pond, giving it a beautiful look, especially in the afternoon. The colours shone in contrast with the green backdrop.

'Okay. Here's the thing. You keep a close watch on the new guy. Keep a track of every move he makes. In the meantime, I will look after Aditya myself. If you have any new developments, call me immediately and keep me updated, is that clear?'

'Perfectly.'

'Good. Now go. I believe it is time for the funeral rites, isn't it?'

'Yes.'

'And I have some work to do.'

15

Mubeen donned a white shirt and a cream coloured trouser for the funeral, since it was the closest colour to white that he had. Things moved pretty fast. Over a hundred men dressed in white had crammed into the tiny place along with a dozen media channels had flown down just to witness the burning pyre of late Mr. Tiwari. Media debaters had a new topic to debate upon – the death of Mr. Harish Tiwari, was it a murder or an accidental drug overdose? Several famous people from various fields had also come in to click a few selfies and update their twitter accounts. Some politicians had also turned up to show their mourning faces for free publicity and to stand a chance in the upcoming elections. And apart from all those, an entire army of onlookers had assembled outside the place just to see what was up.

The priest, fortunately oblivious to the hubbub and chaos all around, continued with his chanting complex mantras and hymns while some other workers systematically placed logs of wood over the body to prepare the pyre.

Soon it was all ready and the priest motioned for Aditya to come up, the only direct descendant of Mr. Harish Tiwari to perform the rites. Mubeen could see the strain on Aditya's face has he tried to keep himself from breaking down completely. He wore nothing but a white *dhoti* and the sacred thread over his lean physique. His body was so perfect that Mubeen wondered for a moment whether the reporters were filming the event or his physique. If the situation had been anything apart from a funeral rite the latter would certainly have been the case.

Aditya performed the rites and lit the pyre. A few minutes later, a huge flame surged forth from the pyre, spewing several gallons of dark black smoke into the clean evening air. Mubeen tried hard not to cough through the smoke and covered his mouth with his handkerchief. Within the span of a few seconds, two things happened. A sudden gust of cold wind swept in, thankfully blowing away a major portion of the smoke and just as the smoke cleared away, he saw Aditya's body swing back violently, and a swirl of crimson around his shoulder. Mubeen was one of the first ones to rush forward; all the others were just too stunned to react. He squatted down beside Aditya and noticed a hole in Aditya's forearm, and deep crimson blood seeping out incessantly from the wound.

Thinking quickly, Mubeen quickly unlatched his belt from his trouser, glad that he hadn't forgotten to wear those and wound it as tightly as he could above Aditya's wound in the fashion of a makeshift tourniquet. He also checked for his pulse and at the same moment he heard the wail of an ambulance. Thankfully someone had the presence of mind to call in one. A few minutes later, the crowd shifted, and two paramedics jumped into the scene. Mubeen moved away a little, to let the professionals do their job. The paramedics methodically checked while a third brought a stretcher from the ambulance. They carefully lifted Aditya's prone body and gently placed it on the stretcher. Aditya was coming around from his shock as was looking around, befuddled. Finally, the pain reached his brain and that pushed him back into unconsciousness.

The ambulance sped from the area and Mubeen along with the other family members followed it to the hospital. Aditya was quickly taken into the emergency ward followed by a bunch of doctors clad in official doctoral whites. Several of Aditya's cousin siblings were weeping, the older ones trying to console them. Mubeen stood in one corner, lost in thoughts.

The things are getting out of hand. First old Mr. Tiwari is murdered and now an attempted murder of his only direct descendant. Something big is going down. Mubeen had seen enough of gunshot wounds to know that what Aditya had suffered was going to cost nothing more than time to heal. It wouldn't be a threat to his life, unless he loses a lot of blood.

About an hour later, a senior doctor emerges from the room, and the older men folk of the family rushed forward. They seemed to know the doctor, probably their family physician. Mubeen again realized how lavishly the rich lived. They had a bunch of doctors, just for themselves.

The doctor spoke slowly and deliberately, 'Aditya is fortunately out of risk. He will survive,' the doctor paused for a while when all the family members collectively heaved a sigh of relief and the doctor continued, 'and this was possible due to the immediate application of, what I believe is a makeshift tourniquet. Whosoever did that, saved Aditya's life.'

All heads turned to Mubeen standing alone in the corner. *Oh come on! No need of those teary eyed stares.* Mubeen shifted uncomfortably on his feet.

'Thank you, Mubeen. We will never be able to be grateful enough to you.' Jaina, one of Aditya's younger siblings said.

'Oh, it's okay. Anybody in my position would have done the same.'

'But you were the only one to actually do it' she replied.

Thankfully for Mubeen, the doctor broke in and said, 'The wound isn't really bad. The bullet had missed his bone by just a fraction of an inch. A little more to the inside and it would have smashed his bone. Aditya should be up in about a day and back to the gym in a span of a few weeks.'

'Thank you, doctor.' Jaina's father said.

When all of them left, Mubeen went up to the doctor and spoke to him under his breath, 'Excuse me, doctor but could you do me a little favour?'

'What is it, son?'

'Is the bullet still in the wound?'

'Yes. The doctors are working on removing it as we speak. Why do you ask?'

'Now, I'm going to tell you something and I need you to keep it a secret okay? The Tiwari family does not know this but I am actually a detective hired by Aditya himself to investigate his grandfather's murder. The entire family knows me as one of his old childhood friends. I need the bullet to track down from where it was bought and who perpetrated the act. I am quite sure that whoever murdered Mr. Tiwari also has a hand in the attempted murder of Aditya.'

The doctor thought for a moment then replied, 'That explains your quick reaction of making the tourniquet with a belt. Okay. I will hand over the bullet to you but what will I say when the police come to investigate?'

'Tell them that the bullet had passed through. They do not know whether Aditya had an exit wound too. Only you and I along with the other doctors know this. I hope you will comply with secrecy. I require this kind of secrecy because I believe the ones after the Tiwari family aren't some petty killers. Something big is going to go down very soon.'

The doctor nodded gravely and asked, 'May I ask your name?'

'Mubeen Roy.'

The doctor's eyes widened in recognition of the name. 'So, you are...'

'Yes. Now,' Mubeen quickly scribbled down his phone number on a little piece of paper and slipped it into the doctor's hands, 'there you go. Don't forget to mention this to the other doctors.'

'I won't.'

16

The killer pulled out his phone, locked himself inside his bedroom. He dialled the familiar number and listened intently. It rang thrice this time and was finally picked up by the same raspy voiced man who seemed slightly out of breath.

'What have you done?' the killer asked.

'Why, I did the right thing. Aditya was beginning to be an obstacle to us achieving our goal and I tried to eliminate him, quite literally. Fortunately for the gust of wind, he didn't die but I'm sure the injury would keep him in bed for at least a month. If he continues, the next doctor he would see would be a coroner, I'll make sure of that.'

The killer flew into a fit of rage, 'But he hadn't done anything yet. Let me make this very clear. I had agreed to work along with you only on the condition that Aditya would not be touched until it was the only way left. And you attempted to kill him on the very first opportunity you got!'

'This was the only way left. A tiny little flaw can bring down the entire mechanism of our plan. Since I knew you wouldn't be able to do it, I decided to do it myself.'

The killer felt like throwing his phone out of the window but he resisted the urge to do so. The person he was talking to over the phone could literally kill anybody anonymously with a mere flick of his fingers. With a lot of effort, he calmed himself down and spoke, 'From now on, you will not touch Aditya. I will personally make sure Aditya stays out of all this. I do not want him to get hurt because of his grandfather's faults and mistakes.'

It was a long time before the person on the other side replied, 'Alright. I trust you to do the right thing. But are you sure *you're* taking the right decision? Ask yourself that.'

'I already have. And it is a yes. Aditya shouldn't be needlessly involved in this mess. He stays out of it and I will make sure of that.'

'If your decision turns out to be wrong, you could jeopardize us including yourself along with our mission. And I will not tolerate that.'

'I can promise it won't get to that. I know Aditya. I have known him from when he was a kid. I know how to contain him.'

'You'd better. Else the next time he might not be so lucky.'

'Okay.'

The killer hung up and threw the phone on his bed. He kicked off his shoes and socks and slipped himself between his sheets. Things were still under control. The plan was still in motion.

Tomorrow, another member of the brotherhood was going to fall.

Mr. Harish Tiwari was just the prologue.

The story was yet to begin.

17

Mubeen was sitting alone in the guest ward of the hospital. There were very few people about, he noticed an old man trying to get up on his feet with the help of his young son who could barely balance himself along with his father. Mubeen jumped up and ran to help the duo. With the extra support, the old man finally stood up firmly on his feet and smiled like a child who first learns to walk. A little later, his left leg began shaking violently and both of them sat him down.

The old man still had a contented look of his face. Mubeen looked inquiringly at the son who immediately replied, 'Paralysis. My father's left body had been paralysed after an accident at home when he slipped and fell. He has been undergoing therapy for a few months and this was the first time he stood on his own two feet after almost a year.'

That explained the childlike bliss. He bent down to face the old man and said, 'Congratulations! Does it feel good?'

'Yes, it does! Thank you so much.'

'What is there to thank? Come on. Let's try that one more time.' Mubeen said brightly.

'Okay. Come on. I have a trip that I have to go to.'

'Really father? Do you think you can manage it?' the son asked.

The old man turned to Mubeen and said, 'I am fit as a horse, aren't I? I can survive a trip to the *Triveni Sangam*. I must go there and take a dip in the confluence before I die.'

'Oh, please.'

Both the son and Mubeen firmly hold the man as he tried to get up. After a few attempts, he finally stood up and this time he could manage for a longer period of time.

Helping others does make one feel good, especially those in need.

Suddenly something struck him. *Triveni Sangam*. That was it! The confluence of three rivers!

Suddenly the doctor walked into the guest ward and slipped a little plastic packet into Mubeen's hands. 'You can meet him now if you want to. He has come around.'

'How soon will he recover?'

'He's a young lad and his body is in peak condition. His wound should completely heal away in a few weeks, a month at most.'

'Will he be able to travel in the interim, if need be?'

'Yeah, he will. But now he needs some rest. He has lost quite some blood and but for your tourniquet, he might have died on the way. A day or two and he should be up and walking.'

Mubeen followed the doctor through the maze of corridors into the room where Aditya was being kept after the emergency procedures. He walked in and exclaimed, 'Hey, how do you feel? I have some good news for you.'

'Apart from the feeling of a dead arm and a few bruises here and there, I'm perfectly fine. And hey, I have some good news too.'

Aditya replied, smiling.

'What is it?'

'I think I might have figured out my grandfather's riddle. It was simple really, if you come to think of it.'

Mubeen replied, '*Triveni Sangam.*'

'Correct!' Aditya asked, smiling contentedly.

'It is the confluence of three rivers in Allahabad, right?'

'Yes. It is the confluence of the three rivers, *Ganga, Yamuna* and the *Saraswati* Rivers. Did you know one interesting fact about the *Saraswati?* It is said that at the *Sangam*, the brownish waters of the *Ganga*, meets the slight greenish of the *Yamuna* both of which originate in the Himalayas and the *Saraswati* exists ethereally, invisible to the naked eye. But some later controversial discoveries of *Saraswati* while digging into the ground has provoked the long lost belief that the holy *Saraswati* flows under the ground from the point it disappears into a gorge in the *Vasudhara* Falls. Some others scientists suggest that it died a premature death about 5000 years ago and is flowing 60 metres below the ground and finally meets the *Ganga* and *Yamuna* from underneath the ground at the *Triveni Sangam.*'

Mubeen's mouth dropped open. 'Why do you know all that?'

'Passing interest. I've got some other facts for you too. Do you remember the line with the phrase, *father of the nation?* Well, Mahatma Gandhi's ashes were also washed away here. Another fun fact. This place holds the biggest human religious congregation on the entire planet every twelve years.'

'The Kumbh Mela.' Mubeen said, realization slowly dawning upon him.

'Exactly. This is the spot where our grandfather has placed our next clue. I've asked the doctor and he has said that I'll be up and about by morning day after tomorrow and then we will move out together. You and I. To Allahabad. How does that sound?'

'Awesome. But we will need to take some precautions. The ones who were after your grandfather's life are now after yours. You will need to tread with care.'

Aditya's face dropped. 'I know. But I wonder who would want to kill somebody like my grandfather who has done nothing but help other people? And then attempt to kill me! What on earth have I done to them?'

'That's what I'll try to find out. You follow your grandfather's clues and discover what he has in store for you while I will protect you. Don't worry.'

18

The bell sliced through the quiet cool morning ear and jolted the killer awake precisely at half past four. A moment later, he reached out and pressed the snooze button and sat up in his bed. He threw away the sheets, stood up on his feet and stretched.

Today was going to be another long day.

The killer slipped into his sweats and track pants and jogged to the gym located about a mile away from the house. The Tiwari family could have easily afforded a personal gym in the house but that would have defeated the purpose. The mile long jog to the gym warms up the body and facilitates the release of several hormones and other complicated stuff in the human organism that is required for real pumping. He had taken almost half a decade to perfect his routine and workout system for himself and he followed it religiously.

Two hours later, he was on his way back when his phone rang.

'Do you remember what job you have been assigned today?' a familiar voice asked.

'Yes, I do.'

'Good. Just checking in.'

'No problem.'

The killer hung up and slipped the phone into his pocket and resumed his jog back to the Tiwari mansion. A few minutes later, he reached and closed his room. He then took a quick bath, packed his stuff into a small backpack. He zipped them all up and shouldered it. He left his room and just as he was about to walk out of the door, Jaina asked, 'Where are you going?'

'Just a little bit of work,' the killer said, softly, 'I'll be back before anybody realizes I'm not here.'

'Take care.'

'Thank you, dear. I will. I always do.'

He left the mansion and got into his car. He started the engine and reversed out of the garage and gunned the engine and drove out and booted his GPS. It automatically began iterating a preset series of instructions. Everything was like clockwork; the plan was still in motion. He reached his destination, a small motel in the suburbs of Mumbai. He parked his and got out. He opened the boot and pulled out a pair of number plates from under a thick covering of cloth and cardboard. He quickly screwed out the first two and screwed in the two new ones. That done, he reached into his the car and inside a compartment under the dashboard, was a key. He retrieved it and walked into the motel. It was a rundown, dilapidated building, just suited for his purpose. He flashed his key at a surprised receptionist and went upstairs. He unlocked his door and got inside.

The place smelt largely of cigarette smoke along with other things he couldn't quite place. He opened the windows and switched on the fan and turned it to full strength. He then went into the bathroom, and relieved himself. He then quickly stripped down put on a new pair of jeans and a t-shirt along with a sweatshirt on top. The December chills were growing even chillier. He came back into the room. It was a lot fresher now. He closed the windows and turned down the fan a little bit. He then sat back on his sofa with his legs spread over the centre table and switched on the television. He flicked through the news and browsed through the movies. None were interesting enough so he decided to switch it off and go to sleep. His watch alarm would wake him up perfectly after three quarters of an hour when it would be time to move to the airport.

19

The next morning brought nothing new to relieve the ears. Mubeen adjusted a single sofa near the window in Aditya's bedroom and sat down, overlooking the huge palatial garden behind the Tiwari mansion. He lifted his legs up onto the sofa and took a deep breath in. The murder of the Mr. Harish Tiwari and attempted murder of Aditya Tiwari seemed unrelated from a detective point of view but something in his gut was telling him both were related. Someone wants to bring down the entire family and the business.

Wait. Was it the business? The immense wealth? Professional jealousy? He thought to himself. Professional jealousy doesn't usually go deep enough to murder the opponent in the business as well as his grandson. Then, could it be personal vengeance? Vengeance was the only thing that could force the human psyche to do pretty drastic things. Suddenly his phone rang. It was Aditya. He picked it up.

'Hey, the police just gave me the post mortem reports. Although everything looks gibberish here to me, maybe you might be able to make some sense out of it.'

'I'll be there in fifteen minutes.'

Mubeen reached the hospital under fifteen minutes and he smiled at him. Aditya seemed to have recovered a lot. There was a man standing next to him, engrossed in talking when he noticed Mubeen walk in.

'Mubeen! What a pleasure to meet you! You're now working for the Tiwari's?' said the coroner whom Mubeen had known for a long time. His name was Jayesh.

'Even you know him?' Aditya asked, dumbfounded.

'Yeah. But keep that under the hood for now okay? This shouldn't reach everybody. Now tell me, what do you have for me?'

'Okay. The killer was a really smart one. I cannot ascertain for sure the method used but I can tell you what I think has happened.'

'Go on.' Aditya said.

'Okay. I think you already know that your grandfather had a heart attack, or rather, a cardiac arrest. That cardiac arrest was an induced one, chemically. What was used here was a combination of potassium chloride and calcium gluconate. Potassium chloride is a very familiar ingredient in many prescription drugs. The molecules of this compound break down into potassium and chlorine, both of which are found in the human body. Now sodium, a naturally occurring element in the body combines with the free chlorine forming sodium chloride, or common table salt. Now if we happen to detect too much of potassium in the body, we could assume that the killer used only potassium chloride to poison the saline drip.

But after a quantitative analysis, the amount of potassium found from several samples were found to be slightly above average, now since this is a case of a murder, we take that into account but if it hadn't been one, it wouldn't have raised any alarms. And even the saline drip contains calculated amounts of potassium and chlorine so detecting anything from there is futile.

Now, when you add calcium gluconate into the mixture, which is what we believe, has happened, it becomes almost undetectable. The calcium replaces the chlorine thus creating an electrolytic imbalance in the system which interferes with the normal beat of the heart and thus creating what we call an *induced* cardiac arrest. Cardiac arrest requires immediate medical intervention and cardio-pulmonary-resuscitation or CPR must be immediately carried out in order to circulate fresh oxygenated blood into the system. If this is not done to the victim, death is assured.'

'But aren't these prescription drugs? Don't they need to have a doctor's prescription in order to purchase?' Mubeen asked.

'No. Potassium chloride is a common salt substitute found in any medical store. Also, calcium gluconate is available as a dietary supplement at any health store. These are raw materials any killer can procure. The only problem lies in the successful and undetectable administration of the substance. And in your case, the killer seemed to be prepared. He also seemed to know that late Mr. Tiwari was under medication and instead of injecting it directly into the body, he injected it into the saline bottle, which I must admit, was a smart move.'

Mubeen glanced at Aditya. His brow was burrowed in concentration.

'Thank you so much, Jayesh. Your insight was indeed helpful.'

'No problem. If you need anything else, just call.'

'I will.'

Jayesh left and immediately after Mubeen asked, 'So what do you have in mind?'

'Let us leave for *Triveni Sangam*, as soon as possible. Let me just get off this wretched bed.'

20

The killer woke up a few seconds before the alarm started ringing. He sat up, completely refreshed and picked up his stuff. He quietly closed the door behind him, so as to make as little noise as possible. He then quietly crept down the stairs and walked out of the reception area. Just as he was walking out, he gently placed the room key near the dozing receptionist with a wad of cash and went out. He placed his items in the car and drove out of the parking lot.

It was several hours after which the receptionist awoke, and befuddled by the presence of a key in front of her and the wad of cash. Seeing nobody around, he pocketed the amount and hung the key on the board behind him in its respective place.

And by this time, the killer had already boarded the plane bound for Hyderabad. He sat in his seat, sipping a piping hot cup of tea, looking out of the tiny window as the scenery swept by with increasing speed. Soon, the wheels left the tarmac of the runway and the killer could feel the pressure against him. About ten minutes later, the plane straightened its course and the feeling subsided.

He unlatched his seat belt and stretched. His next target was sitting in the exact plane he was, only in the business class and he was down in the economy class. But this target wasn't going to die yet. He had some beans to spill. They would dispose off him later.

Everything till now was going according to plan. His next target, another business tycoon from the media world was going down to Hyderabad for the release of some new channel from his production house. His name was Hiren Patel. The plan was to follow Patel through the airport customs till he reaches outside. He'll call for a taxi and a taxi, already paid to be positioned there opportunely crawls by. Patel gets in, the killer follows him inside. The driver of the car kicks the throttle and the pulls out of the airport parking lot as quickly as possible while the killer himself knocks out the man cold. They drive to a quiet suburb where they can contain the man and force information out of him. Clear and simple.

The killer got up from his seat and as if looking around for the washroom, he walked up the stairs. He was about to sneak upstairs when a hostess asked, 'Do you need something?'

'Uh... no. I was just looking for the washroom. Do you mind telling me where it is?'

'Oh, sure. It isn't that way. It's in the opposite direction. The sign there clearly states that.'

'Oh, yes. How stupid of me. Anyway, thank you so much.' The killer smiled at the lady and walked away in that direction.

21

Mubeen helped Aditya get up. A fresh set of clothes had already been neatly laid out in one corner of the room. Mubeen then walked out and Aditya dressed up. In the meantime, he examined the plastic packet the doctor had handed him the previous evening. It was a long one, smeared with blood. It was one of those untraceable bullets; there wasn't any slightest hint of a scratch.

'What's that?' Aditya asked.

'This was the bullet that was used in your attempted murder.'

'But why are you looking at it so keenly?

'To look for scratch marks.'

'Scratch marks?'

'Yes, scratch marks from rifling. Rifling consists of helical grooves in the barrel of a gun or any other firearm for that matter which imparts a spin to the bullet on its horizontal axis. This spin serves to gyroscopically stabilize the bullet thus improving its aerodynamic stability and accuracy. These grooves, as a result leave behind striations on the surface of the metal which can be used to uniquely identify which weapon was used for firing. But so far I can see barely anything. Professional criminologists might be able to say something about this. They look at it under a microscope and examine the fine lines made by the rifling of the barrel thus identifying the weapon used.'

'But what purpose would that serve?'

'If we identify the firearm used, we can narrow our search to a limited number of people who possess that weapon by cataloguing the number of these bought. Of course, if the weapon was smuggled in, that's something we cannot help. But if it wasn't, then tracking down a man becomes relatively simpler.' Mubeen ended.

Aditya nodded absentmindedly. 'Hunting down criminals is a tedious process, isn't it?'

'It sure is.'

About two hours later, both of them were on their way to the airport. Aditya seemed excited to be finally on his way to uncover his grandfather's clues. They were sitting in the airport lounge, sipping hot cappuccino waiting for their gate to open.

22

A little over seven hundred kilometres away, in the Rajiv Gandhi International Airport in Hyderabad, the killer picks up his bag, from the baggage conveyor belt just as his target does the same a few metres away from him and follows him closely. The killer pulled out his phone and called the taxi driver that had been placed.

'Are you ready?'

'Yes.'

'Come to the airport gate to pick him up. I'll follow a second later. Then we move out immediately. I want no alarms here, okay?'

'Understood.'

As the glass doors mechanically slid apart, a gust of warm equatorial wind greeted them, bearing a strange contrast to the cool air conditioned interiors of the airport. Patel stood at the edge of the road, looking about. Immediately a car slid in and from the corner of his eye, the killer noticed the driver nod at him specifically. Hiren got into the cab and the killer broke into a run and got in through the other side.

'Hey, what are you doing?" Hiren asked, dumbfounded.

'Oh, hey. I thought it was free.' The killer replied.

'Well, it's not. Do get out now. I am in a hurry.'

'Perhaps we could share?'

'How about no?' turning to the driver, Patel said, 'Hey can you pull over and we'll talk this through?'

Suddenly another man rose up from the front seat, a gun pointed straight at him.

'Uh... this is great.'

The killer smiled at him emphatically. The target had been acquired.

He pulled out his phone and called a familiar number.

'What is it?' asked a voice from the other side.

'Target had been acquired. He is now being transported to the safe-house for further questioning.'

'Make him spill all the beans.'

The person on the other side hung up. The killer pocketed the phone and gazed outside as the multitude of cars passed by and nobody gave a second glance. Also, the glass of the windows had been tinted so anybody sneaky enough to look in wouldn't be able to see much.

'What do you want from me? Just tell. If it is money you want, I have loads to share.' Hiren asked, his voice trembling.

'Don't tempt me with your money, you bloody harebrained fool! All I want you to do is answer a few simple questions of mine. Actually, just one.'

'What is it?'

'Tell me where the books are.'

An expression of horror and disbelief flew over Hiren's face.

'Ah... So you know exactly what I'm talking about, don't you? Yes, the books that you have safeguarded from the eyes of humanity. So spit it out. Don't worry; I won't let anything happen to you.'

Hiren stayed silent. His expression of horror had been replaced with dead seriousness. He could not let his secret fall into the wrong hands.

'Okay. It seems that I will need to convince you somehow. Have you ever heard of the name Mr. Harish Tiwari?' the killer asked.

The killer smiled as he noticed the wave of recognition pass of Patel's face as he said the name. It had the desired effect.

'Since you're not inclined to answer my question, I'll take that as a yes. This is obvious, if you come to think of it, really. Okay so, Mr. Tiwari was murdered in his bedroom day before yesterday. But you would know that... wouldn't you? Running a bunch of news channels, you need to keep up with the news yourself don't you? Anyway, you might know that he was murdered but did you know who murdered him? Or, how was he murdered? This piece of information could just make your channel the biggest in the country, I can assure you.'

Patel said nothing but the rhetorical questions were hitting home every time. His lower lip had started quivering with fear. But he still kept his mouth shut. He could not afford to speak anything. He would rather die, taking the secret with him.

'Okay. So, I killed him. Injecting his dribbling saline bottle with a potent undetectable combination that caused his heart behave wildly, interrupting the normal beat thus inducing a cardiac arrest. I could dispose of you in a similar fashion but I feel you are more useful and worthy to live than that old brat.'

'Y... you don't scare me.'

The killer pursed his lips and gazed outside his window. 'We'll see about that.'

23

About two hours and a little less than a thousand five hundred kilometres later, Mubeen and Aditya stood at the Bamrauli Airport looking here and there. Mubeen had flown to several places both in and out of the country but had never been to Allahabad. Similarly for Aditya. They exited through what seemed like the main exit and hailed a cab. The cabbie took them to a hotel which seemed pretty decent enough. The standards were a lot lower than what Aditya was used to but he reminded himself that he wasn't on a vacation, rather a mission, sort of.

They got onto their room and opened up a travel map they had collected at the airport. The map showed any and everything to be visited in Allahabad.

'Okay. Let's narrow down the search. Pick out the Goddess temples in and around the confluence of the three rivers. It has to be one of them.' Aditya said, brimming with excitement.

'Okay. There's the *Alopi Devi Mandir*. Then there's the *Lalita Devi Mandir* among the famous ones.'

'Now let's do a background research of the Goddess. Something has to match with the term "angry goddess" I guess.'

After twenty minutes of searching about on the internet, nothing popped up relating to any "angry goddess".

'I think we're missing some crucial aspect here. Let me see the poem again.' Mubeen said. Aditya fished into his bag and brought out the sheet of paper and handed it to Mubeen. He took it, and read it more carefully this time.

To a certain temple you need to go,

Where the angry goddess hath waited for days long,

Where the three waters converge unbound,

Where, like the goddess, the waters around are virgin,

Where, the father of a great nation such as this, rests,

At the foot of the eastern gate you shall find what you seek.

'Hey, have you noticed this? It says *"where like the goddess, the waters around are virgin"*. This description does not match anything here. The goddess is believed to be a chaste one, and she's really angry with something. Also she is waiting for something. Aditya, search *virgin waters*. Something related might pop up.'

Aditya did as he was told. Nothing significant turned up, at least nothing related to any goddess. 'Okay, try *virgin goddess*.'

'What sense does that make?'

'It says here, *"where like the goddess, the waters around are virgin"*.'

Aditya typed it out and several results popped up.

'THAT'S IT!' Aditya exclaimed.

'What?'

'The Kanyakumari Temple. *Kanya* means a young girl and *kumari* is a chaste young woman. We're at the wrong place!'

Suddenly it made so much more sense. This was locates at the southernmost tip of mainland Indian peninsula. That was the place where the three waters met, the Bay of Bengal, the Arabian Sea and the Indian Ocean.

'Here. I've got some more info on this. A demon king named *Banasura* had obtained a boon from Shiva that he could only be defeated by a virgin. Thus he wrecked havoc in the all the three worlds terrifying the gods in heaven. They approached goddess *Shakti* to rid the world of this menace. Answering their prayers, she promised that she would kill the demon at the right time and in the meantime, whilst as a human travelled to the place we now call Kanyakumari and did penance to marry Shiva. Her penance was so great that it attracted the attention of Shiva himself and he was so mesmerised by her beauty that he decided to marry her. While doing her penance, she had grown into a teenager, thus the name of the place.

Now, *Narada*, sees this and realizes that if she marries Shiva, her job to kill Banasura might slip out of their hands since it was preordained that he would die in the hands of a virgin. Therefore he had to find a way to scuttle the marriage. In short, what he did was that he set up the midnight hour as the auspicious time to marry. And when the auspicious time came by, Narada took the form of a cock and heralded the break of dawn thus fooling Shiva into believing that the auspicious time had passed and he left.

Back to the Devi, she sat waiting for her future husband to come, who never came and she continued her penance. Now, Banasura hears of this beauty asks her hand in marriage which is bluntly refused. Then he decided to take her hand by force which leads to a fierce battle between the two and ultimately *Banasura* is killed, thus fulfilling her destiny.' Aditya exhaled, smiling. 'We've been wrong this whole time. My grandfather's first clue was never here. It is in Kanyakumari Temple!'

24

'Now, Mr. Patel. I need you to ponder over your decision of not speaking up. Everything depends upon you. Everything you hold dear will be snatched away from you. I have seen working with loved ones works really well in cases like these. Your family? Gone. Imagine the face of your little girl drowning, the last gasps of air escaping through her mouth, water quickly replacing the remnants of air in her lungs. Imagine your wife, found dead in the middle of the road, mutilated beyond recognition, lying in a pool of her own blood. A highway maybe, it would look a lot more dramatic I feel. And all the time, you will be alive, watching their dead bodies on the television screen, bound to this very chair, regretting the very decision of not speaking up when you had that chance. You wouldn't really want that, would you?' the killer asked, sitting on the table in front of Patel.

Patel's body began shaking with fear. The killer smiled. He could imagine what kinds of thoughts were going on in his mind. What Patel needed was a little time alone. What the killer didn't have to spare was time.

'Mr. Patel. I'm going to give you some time to think over this. Say about half an hour? Would that be enough?'

Hiren made no reply. This was going to be more difficult that he'd thought. The killer continued, 'I'll take that as a yes, then.'

The killer stood up, dusted his pants and walked out of the little room in the safe-house and switched off the tiny light bulb which shone over Patel. Alone in the dark with nothing but your thoughts, time can draw out like a dagger, this was going to be the longest thirty minutes of his life. Just as he closed the door behind him, his phone rang.

'Hello?' he asked.

'Aditya and his so-called friend are now in Allahabad. They're onto something. I need to know what it is.'

'But I'm in Hyderabad with Patel. And how did you come to know that Aditya is in Allahabad?'

'I heard he was missing from his home. I called up a few friends at the airport who searched up flight directories for the day. His name turned right up.'

'Okay, I'll check it out. You don't need to do anything now, okay?'

'And what was the name of his friend?'

'Mubeen... Roy I think.'

The man on the other side hung up.

A minute later, his phone rang again. He picked it up.

'Your nephew-in-law lied to you. Mubeen Roy isn't his childhood friend. He is the city's top crime investigator and detective. Aditya has his suspicions. He doesn't trust anybody now, not even his own family.'

The killer's eyes widened in fear and shock. *Has Aditya really come to know about everything?* This was a new mess. The situation was careening out of control. He had to bring it under control now.

25

Aditya's cell phone rang, cutting through the night time serenity. He got up abruptly from his bed and picked up his phone. 'Hello? Aditya?' said a voice from the other side.

'Yes, uncle! What is it?'

'I saw that you didn't come home yesterday. I checked at the hospital and they said you were away. Where are you? I'm really worried about you.'

'Don't worry, uncle. I'm fine. I have my friend with me too.'

'Oh, no. But you need to come back home right now, wherever you are.'

'Why? I'm doing a little tour. I'll come back in a few days.'

'But where are you?'

'I'm in Allahabad and will be going on to Tamil Nadu. Why do you ask?'

'No. I was just worried about you. Nothing else.'

'Alright.' Aditya hung up. A few seconds later, the killer dialled another familiar number on his phone. The man on the other side picked up after two rings. 'Jay?' the killer asked his voice urgent.

'Yes?'

'Where are you now?'

'I'm in Delhi, overseeing some operations. Why?' Jay asked.

'Can you spare me a few days? I need you to track somebody for me and inform to me everything they do.'

The man on the other side of the line smiled. This was the moment he had been waiting for a long time. Finally somebody recognized his genius. 'Absolutely. Whom do I have to track down for you?'

'Aditya Tiwari. Only thing is that you don't have to track them down. I know where they are going to be. You just need to follow them around inconspicuously and inform me on every move they make. Understand?'

'Ah! The young charismatic Aditya Tiwari. I'll get right down to it. Where are they?'

'They are presently in Allahabad but they will be moving down to Tamil Nadu, I do not know where. You need to track them down there. I do not know anything more than this. You are going to be on your own there. Will you be able to do it?'

'Yes. Of course.'

'And you're going to send me updates every hour. I want to know everything they do as if I am the one following them and not you.'

'Consider it done.'

'Good.' The killer sighed as he hung up. He trusted this man. He would do the job for him.

26

Half an hour later, the killer walked into the darkened room. He switched on the brightest lights and saw Hiren squinting.

'Have you decided yet? I have people on standby near your home in Mumbai. You give us the answers we need and your family goes free, unhurt. If you don't, everybody dies. The choice is yours.'

'You're bluffing.'

'As I said, the choice is yours.'

'How do I know that you'll let my family go once I give you the answers you require? What guarantee do I have?'

'Ah. Dear Mr. Hiren Patel. I think you should know that you're in no position to do any sort of negotiation with me. So you will just have to take my word as my guarantee. And anyway, you are our enemy, neither your wife nor your daughter. You bunch of scoundrels have kept this secret away from mankind for more than two thousand years. You don't deserve to live. You deserve something worse than death. But not your family. They are ignorant of your misdeeds and they shouldn't pay for your crimes. But if you don't cooperate, you leave me no other choice.' the killer spoke silently but firmly, clearly depicting his seriousness.

'I will not tell you anything. Unlike you, I have sworn allegiance with my truest heart and I do not wish to break it. I wish to stand by the promise I made.'

'Ah. So you finally admit it. I was wondering when you would, if you had come to know of this earlier, you would have known how much we have infiltrated into your so-called secret community of scholars.'

It was a lie. A plain faced lie. But Hiren had no chance of knowing that. And his lie again had the desired effect. For the second time, Hiren lost his footing from stable favourable ground and had fallen into the murky waters of the killer's arena.

'So, what do you say?' the killer prompted.

Hiren bent his head down and shook it. There wasn't any way for him to escape the situation. There was no hope for him. But he had to let the other's know. A secret killer, who knew the identities of the Nine, was on the prowl.

27

Next morning, five and a half hours later and two thousand kilometres away, Aditya and Mubeen landed in Tamil Nadu. Wasting no time, they quickly hailed a cab and made their way to Kanyakumari Temple. Fortunately, their cabbie was an experienced one and he wove in and out of the heavy traffic skilfully, overtaking a car here or a cow there with utmost dexterity. They reached the temple under three hours.

Mubeen hired a local guide whose broken mix of English and Hindi and a little bit of Tamil here and there made it very difficult for either one of them to understand what he was trying to say. But they could make out the crux. But they weren't here on a vacation.

'So where is the eastern gate?' Mubeen asked.

'Right around the corner there, sir. But why that gate? That gate is always closed. You go in through northern gate.'

'Always closed? Why was it even made then?' Aditya asked.

'There is an old legend because of which the eastern gate is always closed. Our *Devi* wears a gem on her nose-ring which is sometimes referred to as the *Nagamani* or the gem of the cobra. It said to have been obtained from the hood of a cobra. It is sad that its brilliance is so great that many ships, while moving in the night see a shaft of light emanating from this gem and interpret it to be a lighthouse and they ultimately crash against the rocks and are shipwrecked. And the rock where they crashed is now called is the Vivekananda Rock which you see back there. Very few survive to tell the tale. So, to prevent such losses from happening anymore, the gate was closed. They are only opened during special occasions when the *Devi* is taken out for ceremonial baths.'

'That's interesting.' Mubeen said.

Aditya looked forlorn.

'Okay. Thank you for your time. You may go now.' Mubeen said, handing him a hundred rupee banknote. The man walked away happy. He had earned more than he usually earned every day. It was his good day.

'So, what do you think?'

'I don't know how we're going to search for whatever clue my grandfather has for me but I know for sure that were are in the right place.'

'How so?'

'Everything from the poem matches in this place. Even the *'father of the nation'* statement matches here. There's a Gandhi memorial here in Kanyakumari. I saw it on the travel map we took from the airport. All the pieces fit in. Except the location of the next clue.'

Unknown to either of them, one man took his position a hundred yards behind him. He put on a pair of shades, staring at the backs of the two targets he had in front of him.

28

The killer's phone rang just as he was about to deliver another futile threat to Hiren. Hiren was proving to be a difficult piece to handle. He picked up the phone.

'Hello?' he asked.

'I have acquired your targets and I have them in my sight now.'

'Good.'

It was about time. Evening had begun to fall as the sun began to dip over the horizon, casting an orange hue over the land. Hiren still hadn't given in. He went out of the room and dialled another number.

'Hello? It's me. Patel is refusing to tell anything. I threatened him with everything I have got but didn't get anything out of him.'

'Kill him and dispose of him such that it makes the news, okay? Let every one of the remaining eight realize that their turn is soon coming. And what about Aditya and Mubeen?'

'Okay. I have placed a man in their midst. He's going to report to me with everything he has. And I trust him. I'll be the first to know if anything happens fishy around there.'

'Don't forget to inform me. I need to know everything thing you do.'

'Yes.' He hung up. He picked up a small syringe from the table in front of him and pulled the plastic stem back and the vacuum created inside the tube sucked in the air. He burst into the room, the evil intent clear on his face. Hiren saw it too.

'Your time's up. I gave you more than ample opportunity to talk. Now you're going to die a pathetic painful death.'

Hiren began to hyperventilate. He began thrashing about and shouting when he saw the needle in his hand. The killer smiled. The more jumped about, the faster he would die. The killer brought down the syringe in a dramatic swing, making Hiren's heart beat over two hundred times a minute. That alone would have killed him if it continued. Blood pressure would have hit the ceiling. But just to make sure, the killer injected the tube of air into Hiren's bloodstream. Hiren stopped for a second as he saw what he was being injected with.

'What are you doing?'

'You'll see it soon enough.' The killer smiled.

Only minutes later, Hiren's eyes widened as his heart stopped beating with the air bubble reaching his heart. Then his body slumped down, his head almost falling over behind.

One down. Eight more to go.

29

The sun set over the horizon as Mubeen and Aditya silently made their way away from the temple towards their hotel room. The time was about seven in the evening.

'What is the closing time for the temple?' Mubeen asked, as they checked into the hotel an entered their room.

Aditya hunched down over his computer and a minute later, he said, '8pm. And it opens on 4:30am.'

'So, the temple closing hour is by 8pm and reopening time is half past four in the morning. If we were to break in, we need to give at least a three hour gap from the closing hour to ensure everyone from within the temple is out and also to ensure that whoever stays behind is sleeping tightly. We wouldn't want intruders during our search, do we? Also we must leave by four since they open up by four thirty they ought to be up and about by four. We must leave before that happens. So that leaves us a very thin time margin to do a comprehensive search of the eastern side of the temple, that too in the dark. So we go in and out and we have a time span of about three and a half to four hours. Will you be able to do it?'

'I'm not so sure myself. Will I be able to?' Aditya asked, meekly.

'You've got to. Your grandfather thought you were capable of it.'

Mubeen said, nonchalantly.

This seemed to spurn him up. He stood up from his from his seat, 'Let's do it.'

Mubeen smiled. He could see how much the young man loved his grandfather. Mubeen picked up the remote in front of him and switched on the TV. He flicked through the news channels and suddenly stopped on one.

Hyderabad residents are now horrified at the brutal killing of a well known personality, Mr. Hiren Patel. Mr. Patel was found dead in the middle of the road, his mouth open. Doctors on the scene claimed the death to be of a fatal heart attack but on further investigation by forensic experts revealed that indeed he had been murdered and there were rope impression on his arms and feet, suggesting that Mr. Patel had been held captive against his will. Finally a post mortem examination revealed that the man had suffered heart attack and wasn't strangulated. The heart attack had been induced, artificially. There were a few broken bones and several bruises all over his body indicating where all he had been tortured and mutilated by his kidnapper. The post mortem examination also revealed a needle puncture wound on Mr. Patel's things there he might have been injected with something. The doctors up to this point aren't able to say anything more.

To know more, stay tuned.

'What is happening in this country?' Mubeen exclaimed, exasperated.

'Do you think the murders are related?' Aditya asked.

'I simply have no idea. The only relation between them are that both happened by administration of something that caused an artificial heart attack. The detective side of me tells me that there is no possible way that these two murders can be related but my gut says otherwise. I'm inclined to go with my gut but I can't really say.' Mubeen shrugged.

Just in the room beside them, their secret tail was listening to every word that conspired between the two. He had already bugged Aditya with a tiny transmitter with a battery for five hours transmitting over high frequency FM in the crowd of the temple by appearing to bump against him and sticking the little chip on him.

The man smiled. It was one of the easiest jobs he had ever pulled. His employer was going to be really happy. He pulled out his phone and dialled the number. It rang thrice before it was picked up, 'Hello? Jay?'

'Yes. I have good news. They are going to attempt to get into Kanyakumari Temple tonight. I haven't been able to decipher the reason to do so but I am going to follow them inside and get to know the reason.'

'Have they spoken about anything else? Anything that might have seemed fishy to you? Anything out of place?'

'I have made a recording of their conversation which I overheard. If you'd like, I could e-mail it to you. You could listen for yourself.'

'Good thinking. E-mail that to me. And, be careful while you follow them in. The other person along with Aditya is a famous investigator and detective with an impressive track record. Be wary of him.'

'Don't worry.'

'If you get caught, which I believe is highly improbable yet I will iterate the fact just so you know, if they catch you sneaking up behind them, you don't know me. Mention my name and we never do business again. Is that understood?'

'Yes.'

'Good.'

30

Aditya and Mubeen set out at exactly half past ten in the night to reach the temple at eleven. They soon located the eastern gate and scrambled up to it. They flicked on two tiny flashlights and nodded to each other.

'You sure this is the right place?' Mubeen asked.

'It is pretty late to be asking that but I am one hundred percent sure this place is right. What place better to hide away a secret than that is less frequented by human encroachment? Also do you remember the line, 'where, *like the goddess, the waters around are virgin*' from the poem? Well, this exact line was supposedly said by Mahatma Gandhi himself and is written in stone here in Kanyakumari in the Gandhi memorial, quite literally. So, this has to be it.'

Mubeen nodded. 'But where do we start searching now? I mean, this place is immense!'

Aditya slipped out a folded piece of paper from his pocket and unfolded it. It was the poem.

To a certain temple you need to go,

Where the angry goddess hath waited for days long,

Where the three waters converge unbound,

Where, like the goddess, the waters around are virgin,

Where, the father of a great nation such as this, rests,

At the foot of the eastern gate you shall find what you seek.

'The poem says, *'at the foot of the eastern gate you shall find what you seek'*. This means we just have to search the region around the foot of the closed eastern gate. And hope we find our clue there.' Aditya said.

'Let's do this.'

Strong winds from the sea buffeted them as they looked about, carefully flashing their torches here and there and switching them off at the slightest sound. Mubeen suddenly heard the sound of a footfall behind him. He whipped around, switching off his flashlight. The bright light in the dark had taken most of his visibility but he pretty clearly seen the dark outline of a man which quickly slipped into hiding.

'What is it?' Aditya whispered.

'Someone's following us. You keep searching. I'll keep watch.' Mubeen said, placing his hand gently over the gun under his jacket in the shoulder holster.

'But that isn't possible. Nobody knows we're here!'

Mubeen said nothing. He kept his eyes peeled over the place he had last seen it. A minute later, he got back to searching.

Jay heaved a sigh of relief as the other person went back to searching. Something big was happening. But fortune ever seemed to desert him in times of need. Suddenly, his phone beeped with the incoming of a message. He cursed under his breath as he had forgotten to silence his phone.

This time, Mubeen was sure. Even Aditya had heard it; his face said it clearly in the dark. There was definitely someone out there, sneaking on them. Mubeen switched off his flashlight, pulled his gun out and slowly went down the steps to the place he had last seen it. He carefully peeked over and saw nobody. His eyes darted here and there, slowly getting accustomed to the darkness. He could hear the sound of the waves thrashing against the rocks, the wind whistling through the rocks, ruffling through his hair. In the midst of it all, he suddenly heard another clumsy foot fall behind him and he turned around rapidly and pushed the man behind him to the ground. With one strike to the jawbone with the butt of the gun, he knocked consciousness out of the man and stood up. He strode back to Aditya, holstering his gun back and was surprised to see an unusual smile on his face.

'I think I might have finally stumbled upon my grandfather's clue!' and saying thus, his fingers curled and went into an oddly shaped rock near the foot of the gate and he pulled something. Immediately after, a series of sounds emanated from the ground beneath them, like the turning of levers and gears which hadn't moved in a while and a moment afterwards the ground shifted beneath them and both of them slipped fell into a dark abyss.

When the man finally came to, he was surprised to find himself on the stairs in front of a temple. For a few minutes, he couldn't remember where he was. Finally, the bruise under the jawbone brought everything back. He was barely able to move his mouth. But the two were nowhere to be found. It was as if he had been out for over an hour but he had noticed the time on his phone when it had beeped and only fifteen minutes had transpired in the interim. He got up, dusted himself down, and massaged his jawbone as he fished out his phone from his pocket. He dialled his employer's number.

'I have bad news.'

'Don't tell me you've lost them.'

'Yes, I have. I was sneaking up on them when the other guy heard my phone's ringtone and came down to find me. I quickly hid myself in a different location and then tried to ambush him but damn he was quick. Within a second, he had me pinned down and knocked me out with a single punch.'

'He didn't talk to you? Say anything to you?'

'No. Just knocked me so hard I slipped out of consciousness for fifteen whole minutes. I hate to admit this to you, but whatever. Anyway, I'll be sending in the entire conversation transcript I have in some time.'

'Okay. But keep an eye out for them.'

31

Their drop into the abyss was a short one, cushioned by blanket of hay set up neatly just beneath them. There was a musty smell of oldness, as if this place hasn't been frequented by humans for a very, very long time. There was an air or eeriness too, as if someone might just creep up behind them.

Mubeen stood up and helped Aditya up. 'You know it was morally wrong to bring me into this mess. I shouldn't be here. Your grandfather wanted you to be here, alone. The secrets that are about to be revealed here are for you only, nobody else. I feel like disrupting some natural mechanism that is underway.' Mubeen said.

'Don't worry. Nothing will happen. I trust you.'

'Hey, what is that?' Mubeen asked, shining his light on a tiny object lying behind Aditya.

Aditya gingerly picked it up, eyeing it. 'I don't know.'

'It's a transmitting device, used to bug targets to be spied upon. I think the guy who had crept up on us had placed this thing upon you. This probably transmits audio data over a FM frequency. This means that the man had been eavesdropping on us this whole time. Here, let me destroy it.'

Aditya handed it to Mubeen who threw it under his shoe and crushed it. It squeaked quietly and then died away.

'There are some really resourceful people after you.' Mubeen said.

Aditya simply nodded, said nothing.

The entire place was shrouded in darkness save the light from their flashlights which barely managed to illuminate the surroundings. From their initial observations, they saw numerous intricate murals and paintings made on the wall around them. The frescos covered every inch of the wall available depicting some kind of a war scene. Soldiers in their royal regalia atop horses with various weapons in their hands were riding forward, killing enemies. As they walked forward, the scenes slowly shifted and the frescos showed dead bodies of soldiers littered over the battle field. The painter had been a very talented one. The gruesome scenes blood and gore of dying soldiers in a battlefield had been described vividly. At the very end of the passageway, the painting depicted the picture of a solitary king sitting on his knees, wiping tears from his eyes.

'I think I know what the entire wall is trying to depict.' Aditya said, his eyes, though physically looking at the mural, were somewhere else.

'What?'

'This is emperor Ashoka of the Maurya Dynasty, one of the greatest monarchs to have ever lived in the entire world. And the battle depicted here is the Kalinga War, the only major war he had fought eight years after his accession to the throne. It had been a bloody battle, a battle for pride since his ancestors had been repulsed in their earlier attempts to conquer the prosperous land of Kalinga. During Ashoka's reign, Kalinga had been the only kingdom out of the great Mauryan Empire and it was Ashoka's dream to complete the political unification of the Indian peninsula. It is one of the most

102

popular wars since no wars in the annals of human history had ever changed the heart of the victor from one of wanton cruelty to that of exemplary piety as this one. After the war, he had had a change of heart because of which he vowed never to take life ever again. So this fresco is probably an artist's depiction of the scene after Ashoka's army had defeated the Kalingan army.'

'Again, why do you know all that?' Mubeen asked, smiling.

'Passing interest.'

Cobwebs hung from the tall ceilings, a thick layer of dust covered the entire path. The path took a sudden swerve to the right which led to a flight of stairs down.

Aditya looked as Mubeen. 'Should we do this?'

'We've come this far. I don't think it would harm to investigate some more.'

They slowly walked down, cautiously taking each step, checking whether each stair would be able to take on their weight. The walls around the stairway closed in onto them, making both of them slightly claustrophobic. Soon the passageway widened opening out into a huge cavernous chamber. At the foot of the opening lay a little object which had no worldly significance in the place.

'A matchbox?' Aditya asked, surprised.

'Keeping in mind the assumption that everything is old in here, yes the matchbox does look a little out of place.' Mubeen said, picking it up. He patted the dust away and looked around the room with his flashlight. There was spherical and a pipe like hollow that passed right through the centre of the spherical wall and went up in circles to the top. Mubeen walked up to one end, struck a match and threw it into the hollow. Almost instantaneously, the substance inside caught fire and spread even faster than a wildfire through the hollow all over, spiralling up with in a fraction of a minute, illuminating the entire room, so much so that they had to squint their eyes for a few moments until the eyes got used to the sudden brightness. The brightness was so much that the flashlights in their hands looked like mere LED bulbs lit during the day.

'Wow!' both of them said in unison.

The room was extremely sparse; there was nothing inside the chamber except one single stone table rising up from the exact centre of the chamber. On it was another envelope. They walked up to the table and noticed small intricate writings etched all over the rock. On closer inspection, even the walls of the chamber were etched with the same writing. Definitely a lot of effort had gone into making this. The light also revealed a section of the wall that gaped out into darkness right opposite to the one they had entered through, probably an exit.

'Hey, I think I know what language this is.' Aditya said, letting his fingers feel the texture of the etchings over the wall beside him.

'Well, what is it? You seem to know quite a lot of things.'

'It is the ancient language of Pali! I remember my grandfather trying to teach me about world languages.' Aditya's eyes widened at a sudden revelation. 'It all makes sense! This place is probably a millennium old, probably built by Ashoka himself! Or maybe it was built by somebody else, much later. I cannot say. All I can say that it was built to have some link with Ashoka.'

'How can you say that?' Mubeen asked, quizzical.

'That is because Prakrit was the official language of the Mauryan court. And Pali is another name for Prakrit!'

It was a little difficult for Mubeen to wrap his head around this.

104

'Look, history was never my strong subject. Tell me what you want to say in clear and simple terms.'

'I cannot say anything for sure but what I can say is that whatever my grandfather left for me has something to do with Ashoka.'

Mubeen said nothing. Finally they approached the envelope in the stone table.

Mubeen motioned to Aditya and said, 'Go ahead. It's your legacy.'

Aditya rolled his eyes and gingerly picked up the envelope. An entire layer of dust fell off from the face of the envelope facing the top. Aditya slowly turned it around. A red imperial stamp fastened the edge of the flap to the back of the envelope. He tried to pry it open but the stamp came off easily as soon as he applied a little pressure.

'This has been opened by someone who had come here before me.' Aditya said, without looking up.

'Huh. Figured, that matchbox says a lot too.' Mubeen said, 'Now enough of your theatrics. Open it up and see what it says.'

Aditya opened it and pulled out a piece of paper from within and gently unfolded it.

32

The killer felt like throwing down his phone. Mubeen was turning out to be really smart, far smarter than he pleased. Suddenly the phone in his hand beeped with the incoming of an e-mail. It was the one containing the audio files attached. He instantly downloaded them, put on a pair of in-ear headphones and touched on the play icon.

The transcript began:

'What is the closing time for the temple?'

'8pm. And it opens on 4:30am.'

'So, the temple closing hour is by 8pm and reopening time is half past four in the morning. If we were to break in, we need to give at least a three hour gap from the closing hour to ensure everyone from within the temple is out and also to ensure that whoever stays behind is sleeping tightly. We wouldn't want intruders during our search, do we? Also we must leave by four since they open up by four thirty they ought to be up and about by four. We must leave before that happens. So that leaves us a very thin time margin to do a comprehensive search of the eastern side of the temple, that too in the dark. So we go in and out and we have a time span of about three and a half to four hours. Will you be able to do it?'

'I'm not so sure myself. Will I be able to?'

'You've got to. Your grandfather thought you were capable of it.'

'Let's do it.'

Then it was a recording of some news channel talking about some murder. It took a moment for him to realize it was about the murder he had committed. 'Oh, the irony!' he called out to nobody in particular. Then the conversation continued.

'What is happening in this country?'

'Do you think the murders are related?'

'I simply have no idea. The only relation between them are that both happened by administration of something that caused an artificial heart attack. The detective side of me tells me that there is no possible way that these two murders can be related but my gut says otherwise. I'm inclined to go with my gut but I can't really say.'

The killer smiled at the last line. There really was no possible way to pin anybody on this murder case. Unless, of course, if he goes and admits his crime publicly. Which obviously he wouldn't.

There was a long pause. He fast-forwarded through the transcript and finally, a few seconds later, words were being spoken again, this time in hushed tones.

'You sure this is the right place?'

'It is pretty late to be asking that but I am one hundred percent sure this place is right. What place better to hide away a secret than that is less frequented by human encroachment? This has to be it.'

'But where do we start searching now? I mean, this place is immense!'

'The poem says, 'at the foot of the eastern gate you shall find what you seek'. This means we just have to search the region around the foot of the closed eastern gate. And hope we find our clue there.'

'Let's do this.'

He didn't bother to listen to anymore of the conversation transcript. He didn't need to. The conversation revealed one solid unmistakable undeniable truth. The person whom he had killed had, through his actions, come back to life and was haunting him. He was leading his grandson to discover something by means of a string of clues that are revealed only to the worthy.

Aditya's presence in this race might prove to be disastrous. But not if he could turn that into his advantage.

And for that, he had to know about every step Aditya took.

Aditya himself would lead him there.

His only job was to follow him.

The killer smiled and dialled a number on his phone.

33

Jay kicked a small piece of rock as hard as he could to vent out his frustration. The rock went flying away, bounced on the flooring several times, making loud noises and finally struck the eastern gate of the temple. The hollow thud resounded through the night. He feared it might wake up somebody.

But where the hell did they disappear? Why didn't they tie me up and question me? Why just knock me out and then flee? True, it would have been difficult dragging an unconscious body back to the hotel room, even in the middle of the night. So fleeing was a more viable option.

By this time, his eyes had grown used to the darkness and he was surprised how much he was actually able to see in the pitch black. Suddenly he noticed a movement from the corner of his eye. He immediately crouched down, trying to appear inconspicuous. It was a man clad in a white dhoti looking about curiously, probably thinking what caused the sound. He looked about for a few more minutes and then went away, baffled.

He stood up and looked at the time. It was nearly four in the morning. He suddenly remembered what he had overheard and he quickly made his way outside the temple premises.

Aditya read through the entire contents, 'It's another poem.' He handed the sheet to Mubeen.

'Oh, come on! Couldn't your grandfather just made this any easier for you? Why couldn't he just say "here's the thing I want you to have, use it wisely."'

'It would probably defeat the purpose, I guess.'

Mubeen read through the poem.

To an old deserted city you need to go,

Where exquisite sandstone buildings rise from the sandy plains like golden desert citadels,

Where the Brahmins of Pali had resided and prospered,

Where the cursed land bewitches all those who venture in times unknown,

There, in the haunted temple shall you find what you seek.

'Oh, great! Now we have to go down to a haunted temple? I mean, what is this?' Mubeen exclaimed. Aditya simple stared at the letter.

'Okay. Here's the thing. We look for the clue in the day, okay? No night duty like today. Else I will not be following you.' Mubeen finished.

'You're scared of ghosts?' Aditya asked, finally breaking into a grin.

'I choose not to answer that question.'

The duo quickly exited from the other opening in front of them. There was a short flight of stairs that led them upward and opened out into a much wider hallway, much similar to the earlier one where they had seen the aftermath of the Kalinga war. Only this one didn't have any frescos to beautify the walls. Long dusty cobwebs hung from the curved ceiling, and a perpetual layer of dust ever seemed to cover everything. After about a couple of minutes of walking in the dark with nothing but their flashlights for illumination, they reached another flight of stairs that led upwards yet again.

At the end of the stairs, they reached a dead end.

'Now what?' Aditya asked, to no one in particular.

Mubeen looked around. He touched the wall beside him. It was moist. And soft. He dug his fingernails into the soft wall and pulled a handful out and examined it under his flashlight. Then he turned his flashlight to the hole in the wall. A few broken tree root nodules stuck out haphazardly. 'What are you doing?' Aditya asked again.

'We're in a trench. Well, not exactly a World War 1 trench but something similar. This is all mud around us, not stone anymore. And these are tree roots sticking out.'

'What do you mean?'

'Upwards is the way forwards. We have to climb up and that thing, whatever it is up there and get out. And hopefully that's not a tree up there.'

Aditya shook his head. Mubeen came up with a plan to do this. Both of them started digging small holes into the mud which would act as footholds while climbing. After about an hour, they had enough stable footholds for both of them. They climbed up precariously, holding on and balancing on each foothold. But at the top, a nasty surprise waited for them.

'Oh, come on! How on earth are we ever going to move this piece of rock?' Mubeen exclaimed, frustrated. 'Didn't your grandfather have any sense of leniency?'

Both of them pushed and heaved, and little by little the rock moved and then a gap opened up wide enough for both of them to squeeze through. They climbed up and lay down on the mud under a tree, gasping for their breaths. They could hear the waves of the sea lashing and frothing on the shore. They lay there, bathing in the quiet warmness of the crisp morning sun falling on their faces through the trees.

Mubeen was the first one to stand up. He dusted himself and helped Aditya up. Mubeen then pulled out a water bottle from his bag and drunk out of it like a camel and then handed the bottle to Aditya. Aditya finished the bottle and returned it.

'If anybody had seen us crawling up from the ground like that, probably imagined us to be bloodthirsty zombies crawling our way up from our graves a hundred years after our death. The very thought makes me laugh.' Mubeen said.

Aditya dusted himself off. He looked around and asked, 'Any idea where we are? Somewhere close to the temple, hopefully.'

'Let's follow the road down there along the shoreline. And yes, we shouldn't be that far from the temple.' Mubeen said, glanced at his wristwatch and said, 'It is already six in the morning.'

All of a sudden, Mubeen's phone ring cut through the serene morning air. He pulled it out of his pocket and picked up the call. 'Hello?'

'Mubeen? I have some news for you.'

34

'What is wrong with you? Why can't you understand Aditya is jeopardizing our mission? We must eliminate him right now while we still can or else everything will slip out of our hands, I'm telling you.'

The killer smiled contentedly and said, 'No. I'm not going to stop Aditya. Actually, I'm going to help him go on.'

The man on the other was stunned, his jaw dropping down. 'And why the hell are you going to do that? You know I'm resenting the very idea that I ever recruited you. I thought you would be committed to our cause but here you're supporting your devil nephew going on a wild goose chase across the country!'

This ticked the killer off. Even though the man on the other side of the phone was his superior, his words flowed out like a wildfire, 'Don't you ever dare to doubt my allegiance to the cause! Don't you speak those words ever again! Aditya is following the clues laid out by his grandfather that is going to lead to what we seek. The entire compilation of the knowledge for one and all is what we seek and I am pretty sure Aditya's grandfather is leading him there. I know it. And that is the reason why I am going to let him continue. He is going to lead us right to it! Don't you get it?'

'But why don't you get it? Even if he leads is to the secret, he too is going to learn about it. And then he would come to know about you, about us. Would you be able to face your nephew when he would come to know about all you do and know?'

'That is a risk I am willing to take for my allegiance. And I do not care what he thinks of me. All I know is how to remain true to our cause.'

'That sounds good but will you be able to face the situation when the time finally arrives? Think about it. Nobody should get to know about us.'

'I am prepared to face the consequences. But I'm telling you, if we follow him, he will lead us right to what we seek.'

The man on the other side sighed. There was no way to explain anything to him. But he was a precious asset. He was good at what he does. 'Do whatever you want to; I have nothing more to tell you. But be careful.'

'Thank you.' The killer hung up.

The man on the other side of the line called up one of the men standing near the door of his office. 'Avinash. Get your team together. I do not know how but I want you to track down Aditya and his friend Mubeen and finish them. Shoot to kill. No hostages, no traces to be left behind. I do not care how you do, just so that you do it. I do not want them pestering around anymore. Also I want you to keep tabs on Pravir and keep me updated with everything he does, everywhere he goes, everywhere he spends his money and whatever else you can think of. Report everything to me, however stupid it might sound to you.'

'With pleasure, sir.' Avinash said with a mischievous sparkle in his eyes.

35

'What is it?' Mubeen asked.

'Yeah, about the bullet you had given me. Well it's a 7.62x54 mmR or the man marker rounds, one of the deadliest sniper rifle rounds. From that, I could guess which rifle it originated from. Still, I examined the grooves over the surface and my guesses were proven true.'

'Okay, spit it out.'

'I believe it was fired from the Russian made Dragunov sniper rifle, probably the SVDS variant, one of the best and the most versatile in its class. Don't ask me the full form of the acronym, the Russians make it so difficult to pronounce.'

'Thank you so much. Also, can you get me a comprehensive list of the buyers of this weapon in India? I need everything, name, occupation – everything.'

'Sure, no problem. But, one thing has been pestering me for a while.'

'And what's that?'

'Where the hell did *you* get the bullet?' emphasising on the word.

'Ever heard of the Tiwari family? Well, the grandson got shot with this. I was lucky enough to obtain the bullet before it reached the hands of the police.'

'Oh my god! Aditya Tiwari was shot with this? How is he? Did he survive?'

'Yes, he is alive and well. Fortunately.'

'Okay. Call me if you need anything else.'

'Sure. Thanks.' Mubeen hung up.

'Who was that?' Aditya asked.

'A friend who specializes in bullet identification, in the forensic department. We now know which weapon was used to shoot you.'

'Don't bother telling me what it was. I don't even care. Anyway, let's get going. We have another clue to decipher.'

They walked down the path, following the shoreline, enjoying the crisp cool air washing into them from the ocean, energizing and invigorating them after the hours spent under the ground. The clean cool air refreshed them. On the road, they met a coconut seller whom they asked for directions and also had a coconut each. After an hour of searching, asking and redirecting themselves every time they met somebody on the desolate road, they finally reached their hotel and flopped down on their beds.

It had been a long night. It was a well deserved rest.

But they had no idea what lay in wait for them.

In the room beside theirs, the killer's spy picked up his phone and dialled a number. A moment later, it was picked up. 'I've got them back under my radar!'

'That is the best piece of news you've given me the whole day. Now never let them out of your sights for even one moment, understand?'

'Yes, sir.'

36

Avinash gleefully walked into his assigned into the room where his team had already assembled.

'Okay. Here's the thing. We have to track down and eliminate two targets. Target 1: Aditya Tiwari. Target 2: Mubeen Roy. We do it in the quickest possible manner. We locate them; track them for some time to know their moves. Then we go in and out, killing both of them. No traces or evidences to be left behind. This operation shouldn't be too difficult for us, would it?'

'NO!' all of the people assembled spoke in unison.

'Good. I need you to track down their credit cards, their debit cards or whatever forms of money they use. I want to know whenever they withdraw or deposit money. I want to where they deal with their accounts. If possible, hack into their accounts and monitor each and every transaction that takes place. Red-flag their phone numbers. I want to when they call, whom they call, and what is the purpose of the call. Hack into their e-mail accounts, Facebook, Twitter and every other social media they have their presence on. Hack into online shopping accounts. Hack into security systems wherever they stay and follow them. I want to know every step they take. Hack into government secured sites and extract their date of birth, place of birth, passport stamps, everything thing you can salvage out of the digital world. Dig into the internet and extract everything you can get your hands on – backgrounds, history, achievements, places they've been to and anything and everything else you find should be on my table every four hours. Survey, analyse, formulate and then attack. That's my motto. Understood?'

'YES!' all of them shouted in unison once again.

'We have to work very quickly for this operation. The time gap is extremely thin and we have got to move very fast on this one.'

All the operatives quickly scrambled to their terminals.

37

Several hours later, almost during mid afternoon, Mubeen and Aditya woke up. They freshened up quickly, put on a fresh set of clothes and after a sumptuous lunch comprising of the daily South Indian cuisine four different kinds of rice preparations topped with delicious *sambar* and summing up the meal with a little bowl of nice thick sour curd, they headed back to their room to study the next clue they had in front of them.

To an old deserted village you need to go,

Where exquisite sandstone buildings rise from the sandy plains like golden desert citadels,

Where the Brahmins of Pali had resided and prospered,

Where the cursed land bewitches all those who venture in times unknown,

There, in the haunted temple shall you find what you seek.

'Now let's look through this carefully. *Old deserted village*. That would mean that the village is uninhabited. Nobody lives there anymore.' Aditya said.

'Isn't that obvious?'

Ignoring the comment, Aditya continued his examination. *'Exquisite sandstone buildings rise from sandy plains like desert citadels.* Sandy plains would probably mean a desert. Also the last two words suggest that our next location is in a desert. That much is clear. From the third line, it begins to get interesting.'

'Huh.' Mubeen murmured, almost nodding off again.

'Where the Brahmins of Pali had resided and prospered. Here, Pali probably suggests the name of a place. But, isn't that a language?' Aditya murmured to himself, a moment later, he continued, *'where the cursed land bewitches all those who venture in times unknown.'*

'So witches live there? Oh, I'm beginning to regret coming along with you. How about I sit it out this time while you go find your grandfather's clue?' Mubeen asked, pinching the bridge of his nose.

'Oh, come on Mubeen! Witches don't exist. At least no more. Did you know women by the hundreds and thousands had been burned alive at the stake in the seventeen and eighteen centuries for being convicted as witches practicing black magic? In India, around two thousand suspected witches, mostly women, were murdered in the past decade itself! That being true, I'm pretty sure that race is quite extinct. Don't you think? No chances of them being here.'

'Again, why do you know that?' Mubeen asked.

Aditya again ignored the question. 'The last line seems pretty clear. We have to find our clue in a haunted temple in the deserted village. The only thing remaining is to figure out which village the poem is talking about.'

'Correction: *you* have to find *your* clue in a haunted temple in the deserted village.' Mubeen said.

'You're still afraid of witches and haunted houses and temples? Come on!'

'I again choose not to answer that question.' Mubeen said, staring outside the window, gazing at the sun setting over the horizon.

'Anyway, let's analyse the poem. *Exquisite sandstone buildings rise from the sandy plains like golden desert citadels.* I think that probably means somewhere in Rajasthan since that is the only state with a desert in it. Also, *golden* could also suggest the Golden City of Jaisalmer. There are hundreds of sandstone buildings all over the city of Jaisalmer, which is probably why the name *golden* is suggested. That is the only line that is clear to me. Nowhere in India would you find so numerous sandstone structures as in Jaisalmer. It is one of the most beautiful places to visit in India, of course, if you could bear the oppressive heat and the smell of spices.

'Let's get going, then. But are you a hundred percent sure? We cannot risk going off in a wrong direction yet again. There are several powerful people after you and probably after what you seek.'

'I cannot see any other viable option apart from this. This part is pretty obvious.'

'Let's go then. You book the tickets online while I get my necessary papers straight to travel with my weapons.'

About a thousand miles away, one of the computers pinged in recognition of an activity on Aditya's credit card. The man who was almost on the verge of dozing off woke up in frenzy and pulled his phone out and dialled a number, 'Sir? I think I've got some activity here!'

38

Avinash jolted awake at the call. He picked up the ringing phone from his desk, 'Hello?'

'This is from Centre 1. I have detected activity on Aditya Tiwari's credit card.'

Avinash smiled. He hadn't expected the breakthrough to happen so soon. 'I'll be down there in a moment.'

Avinash hung up, quickly grabbed his car keys and dashed out of the room. He pulled out of the parking area and sped through the bustling roads and reached the office ten minutes later after breaking God knew how many traffic rules along the way.

'What have you got?'

One of the people sitting at their computer terminals spoke up, 'Credit card used online to buy two plane tickets. Probably one for himself and the other one for Mubeen.'

'Where?'

'Tamil Nadu to Jaisalmer Airport, Rajasthan. Today evening. They're in quite some hurry it seems. '

Another guy spoke up, 'He just now got an e-mail confirmation for his flight booking. He got an SMS too. Both are confirmed tickets, business class. This man has a rich taste.'

'He is the grandson of a man worth tens of millions. Get me a flight out of here for me to Jaisalmer right now. Also tag their phones numbers. Record each and every of their conversations and also locate where they are, live.'

'Okay.'

Avinash nodded and dialled a number on his phone. It was picked up after two rings. 'I need you to assemble a track team by today evening in Jaisalmer. I want at least four men on them, watching their every move, following them wherever they go and I want to be updated after every hour. I want to know where they will be staying for the night too. I also want two more men who would be on standby, waiting for final instructions from me. Understood?'

'Yes.'

'Do you have any questions?'

'What are we to do if one of them turns hostile?'

'Shoot to kill. But try not to let that happen, okay?'

'Yes, sir.'

'I'll be coming down to Jaisalmer myself to oversee the operations. You better be prepared by the time I come down.'

39

Aditya and Mubeen quickly packed up in fifteen minutes. Their flight was in about three hours. They checked out of the hotel, hailed a cab and reached the airport. There they waited for about an hour and a half until the gates opened and let the passengers in.

'You booked business class tickets?' Mubeen asked while looking at his ticket, surprised by such generosity.

'All the economy class tickets were full. Four business class seats remained. So I booked those. Why, is there a problem?' Aditya asked.

'Problem? Ha, no. Just saying.' Mubeen said. It was just one of those several moments that he had being having recently when he realized how poor he was, looking at the plush and high class living standards of the elite.

Soon, the plane taxied onto the main runway, quickly picking up speed and took off. A minute later, he took off his seatbelt as a hostess came by serving food and beverages. Mubeen enjoyed the luxuries of the business class while he still could. The seven hours flight time is going to be one of the best he would probably ever have. He had several glasses of that savoury wine, until a point he realized he would get a little too tipsy. The food was great too.

Outside the window, Mubeen could see the glorious sun slowly and gently dipping below the horizon of the white puffy clouds shading the sky in a garish yellow. The white puffs of clouds reflected off the few remnant rays giving the effect of golden hued waves, frothing up onto the shoreline.

'Have you figured out the rest of the poem yet?' he asked.

'No. But some more parts of it have become a little clearer. *The Brahmin's of Pali* would probably mean the *Paliwal Brahmins* who resided in the kingdom of Pali, somewhere in the northern parts of Rajasthan. A bunch of them must have migrated to the village referred here and must have prospered. You, something really funny just occurred to me.'

'What is that?'

'The underground location of the first clue, the language on the walls down there, the ancient scripts, and now this, about the *Brahmins of Pali* everything point to one common word. Pali. Pali was the official language during that time in his court.'

'Might be a coincidence, don't you think?'

'I know, the evidence aren't enough to put two and two together but still, if you were to look at it, it seems pretty obvious, doesn't it?'

'I don't know.'

Several hours later, the plane touched down with a jerk, waking Mubeen out of his fitful slumber. He glanced beside him and was surprised to find Aditya sitting upright in his seat, fully alert and awake.

'You didn't catch a little nap?' Mubeen asked.

'No. I've been thinking. And yours was far more than little.' Aditya replied.

'All this while, all you've been doing is thinking?'

'Yes. I was trying to figure out the poem. Jaisalmer is a pretty big city, don't you think? It is like finding a microscopic needle in a cosmic haystack. Hell, we don't even know where to look!'

'That's what the rest of the poem is about isn't it? You've deciphered only a part of it, there's a major that we haven't yet been able to solve. That part should tell us more about it.'

Aditya just nodded without saying anything more.

The plane gradually slowed down, taxied out of the runway, parked near a gate and about two minutes later, all the passengers of the plane were making their way out. Aditya and Mubeen walked out quickly, picking up their baggage from the conveyor belt and quickly exited the airport.

Just a few metres behind them, a man folded the newspaper in his hands, picked up his sunglasses, put them on and followed them closely. His job was simple. His job was just to identify and locate the targets and signify to the remaining team which person to kill. The man adjusted the little object in his ear and then spoke into his handheld mic, 'Targets are in position. They have exited the airport and are now waiting for a cab.'

'Roger that.'

40

Mubeen and Aditya stood under the hot sun, breathing in the heated air waiting for a cab.

Suddenly, out of the corner of his eye, Mubeen noticed man stand a few metres to their right. It was the way in which he stood that caught the eye of Mubeen. The man folded his arms and looked straight ahead into the sky. Something about him said that he wasn't waiting for a cab. Suddenly, a black sedan zoomed out of the parking lot and came to a hasty halt in front of them. A moment later, one of the automatic windows rolled down and from within a gun came out, with a silencer attached in front.

Mubeen now acted out of pure instinct. Everything seemed to be stuck in a time warp, everything happened in slow motion. He threw the bags in his hands towards the window while at the same time shouldering Aditya to the ground with all the might he could muster up. Just as they hit the ground, Mubeen heard one of the bullets whiz by his ears and ricochet off the concrete just above him along with a muffled groan that escaped Aditya's throat as the weight of both of them fell on his wounded arm. Tiny fragments sprayed all over them, some even puncturing his skin.

A fraction of a second later, all hell broke loose. Everybody in the vicinity heard the shots even with the silencer on. Pandemonium coursed through the crowd, resulting in shrieks and cries of fear and anguish. Everybody started running here and there. Out of the corner of his eye, he noticed the man who had been standing metres away from them was nowhere to be seen. He stood up cautiously and turned around to watch the car speedily pull out of the place. Mubeen pulled out his gun from the shoulder holster and fired a few shots, blowing off the rear lights of the car and also shattering the windshield on the back of the car.

Suddenly, Mubeen had an idea. The road in front had a sharp turn to the right. Mubeen took a precise aim and waited. Seconds later, the car with the assailants took the turn a little too fast and the car was on the edge of losing the balance of the momentum. Mubeen took advantage of that and shot at one of the rear tyres of the sedan. The tyres, already under a lot of pressure from the speeding and the heat burst violently as the bullet struck its surface, causing the car to lose the balance and it overturned onto the side and skidded to a stop a few metres away.

Mubeen heard the wail of the police siren as he began approaching the vehicle. He quickly strode forward, kicked open a door and roughly pulled one of the men out, the one who had taken the shot at Aditya. All the others were motionless, probably dead, probably not. This one's head was bleeding from several places, shattered pieces of glass sticking out of some of the wounds.

'TELL ME WHO YOU'RE WORKING FOR!' Mubeen shouted, as he landed a punch on the man's face. The man spit out blood from within his mouth and smiled menacingly, baring his bloody teeth.

'TELL ME!' Mubeen shouted.

The man shook his head, implying a no. Frustrated, Mubeen kicked him as hard as he could in his guts. The man coughed, gurgled up some more blood, coughed but said nothing. He tried getting up. Mubeen landed another kick in the guts. He then grabbed the man by his hair and pulled his head up and said to him, 'You're going to tell me who you're working for or you'll get hurt even more. If you want to avoid that then speak up.'

'You can hurt me however the hell you want to but all response you'll get is my smile. That is the problem with you people. You don't have enough freedom to see to it that justice is provided. All you can do is this.' The man raised his crimson blood smeared hands, where some of the fingers were bent in odd unnatural angles.

Soon, the police vehicles careened into the scene; cordoning off the area with yellow tapes with 'DO NOT ENTER' emblems printed all over. Mubeen produced his necessary papers. Thereafter Mubeen withdrew from the crowd along with Aditya and made their way to their pre-booked hotel in the suburbs.

'Aditya, I am going to ask you a very important question. Do you know anybody who might be after you? Who might have intentions to hurt you in any way? I am asking because the ones who attacked you were highly trained mercenaries and I mean highly trained. Their mode of operation, their quickness, everything clearly showed expertise. You need to think about the question I am asking you, okay?'

'I have no idea whatsoever. I mean, what have I ever done to hurt anybody else?'

'Family business? Elimination of opponent in competition? That might be a reason for them to kill both your grandfather and you, the only major proprietors of the business.'

'My uncle is handling the business, not me! Then why try to kill me?'

Mubeen pursed his lips, looked out of the window and said nothing.

41

Avinash kicked the chair in front of him to vent out his frustration. The chair slid a good three metres before coming to a stop striking the office wall.

'All of you couldn't perform a simple task of shooting straight? Both of them were standing in the open, no protections from anywhere yet you were the ones hurt and wounded?' he shouted, 'Do you have any idea how many strings I had to pull just to have you guys get out?'

All the three of them who had been assigned to the job stood, holding their bruises and broken bones. Most of the wounds had been patched up so the bleeding had stopped. 'And that Mubeen tackled all of you at once, without even a mere scratch on his skin.'

'Sir, we underestimated him. We'll take him on the next time.'

'Well, you know what? There isn't going to be any next time. Especially for you.' Avinash pulled out is Beretta 9mm and fired three rounds at each of them.

42

Jay alighted from his employer's chartered helicopter in one corner of the Jaisalmer Airport. Suddenly his phone rang. He picked it up.

'Are you positive about the location?' the killer asked.

'Yes, I am. I even know the hotel they're staying in.' Jay replied.

'Then get right to it. Do not lose them even for a moment. Understood?'

'What are you going to do when you get them?'

'I have other businesses to attend to while you take care of this. If you can perform this operation as per my expectations, the rewards will be monumental, I can assure you that much.'

'I have one question. Aditya seems pretty harmless to me. Why are you doing this?'

'None of your business, Jay. Your job is just to track them, follow them, see where he leads us and report directly to me. The only thing I can tell you at the moment is what we're doing is big. It's bigger than all of us. It is going to change the rest of the world as we know it.'

Just as the killer hung up, the phone began ringing again. It was the Corporation.

'Are you aware of your next assignment?'

'Yes, I am. I need not be reminded twice.'

43

'Let's get back to the task at hand. The faster we figure out the poem, the faster we get towards our goal.' Aditya said.

Mubeen was too lost in thoughts to answer.

Aditya produced the piece of paper from his pocket and stared at the poem again.

To an old deserted village you need to go,

Where exquisite sandstone buildings rise from the sandy plains like golden desert citadels,

Where the Brahmins of Pali had resided and prospered,

Where the cursed land bewitches all those who venture in times unknown,

There, in the haunted temple shall you find what you seek.

'So, here we are in Jaisalmer, where *exquisite sandstone buildings rise from the sandy plains like golden desert citadels*, but Jaisalmer is anything but deserted and neither is it a village. It is a full-fledged city, bustling with both national and international tourism and culture. That leads us to another question. Which village are we talking about?'

'What do the last two lines want to say? Does it have a straightforward meaning or some underlying meaning that we don't realize as of yet?' Mubeen asked, snapping out of his contemplation.

'I think it means what it means. It's pretty clear that the place is haunted, or at the least, believed to be haunted. There can't be any other possible meaning. What bother me are the second and the third lines.'

Aditya switched on his laptop, and searched *Brahmins of Pali* on Google. He browsed through a couple of the top links related to the three search terms and then finally something struck him.

'That's it! *Brahmins of Pali* literally is another name for *Paliwal Brahmins* or the Brahmins of the kingdom of Pali!'

Mubeen seemed unsure, 'So how does that help us? Do you know where the clue might be now?'

'No, not really. But this clears up the mess a lot. It just needs a little more research. But we're several steps closer to finding out the clue.'

Aditya typed away at his laptop, clicking relevant links. About fifteen minutes later, he pushed his laptop away, a resplendent triumphant smile on his face.

'I've found it. All the points mentioned in the poem match perfectly with this place. That one thing about the Brahmins was literally the key to the entire poem!'

'Care to share?'

'Our next clue lies in a city named Kuldhara, fifteen kilometres away from Jaisalmer, in western Rajasthan. It is said that the city was built by the *Brahmins of Pali* or the *Paliwal Brahmins* who had fled from their home country of Pali, ruled by a tyrant king and had found solace in this place. They built their city from ground zero, approximated to be in the year 1291 AD. Kuldhara is or was the name of the largest village in a community of 84 villages in the region. They grew prosperous because of some mysterious technique that applied to harvest bumper crops in a seemingly dry remorseless and arid desert and their business acumen was renowned. But suddenly overnight, approximated to be somewhere in the year1825 AD, they disappeared. Why did the villagers leave such a developed and planned settlement after having lived there for seven centuries is a question that still remains unanswered to most scholars.'

'Also, everything structure built there was made out of golden desert sandstone but the place is completely desolate. Nobody lives close by, let alone in the city. And that,' Aditya said with a mischievous smile, 'is a perfect place to cook up some horror stories. What better a place for a bunch of ghosts to live and prosper than a highly developed yet desolate city in the middle of the desert with nobody to interfere in their activities?'

Mubeen rolled his eyes and asked, 'So we have to find our next clue in the so-called haunted temple in this haunted village named Kuldhara? Doesn't all this sound a little too fictitious? I mean what if at the end of this all we find that it was one big practical joke? No offense.'

'My grandfather wouldn't undergo so much trouble to lay such intricate clues, put up such expensive props and highlights just to crack a practical joke.'

'Right.' Mubeen said, nodding to himself.

44

Avinash's phone loud ringing cut through the post murder scene serenity, shaking everybody out of their stupor. He pulled it out of his pocket and picked up the call.

'Sir, I just got a good piece of news. I know where they're staying,' a man said from the other side of the line, 'from Aditya's latest credit card transaction.'

'Thank you. Good job.'

Avinash hung up.

'I need a two man surveillance team to keep tabs on our two targets in fifteen minutes. I want to know where they are going, what they are going to do – everything.'

About few miles away from where Avinash had set up his base, Mubeen and Aditya packed up their stuff into small backpacks and set out. They went to a local car rental shop to get a car for their road trip to Kuldhara.

'So, how would you like to pay, sir?' a gangly old man asked. They had selected a rundown car rental shop to hire their car so that tracking them down would become slightly more difficult for their pursuers.

Aditya was about to give his card when Mubeen clutched his arm. 'Cash.'

'Why?' Aditya asked, in hushed tones.

'Credit card transactions can be tracked, didn't you know? I believe that's how they have been able to track us till now.' Mubeen said.

Aditya paid in cash. Aditya took the driver seat and Mubeen took a seat next to him. He pulled out the pocket map from the aforesaid location and took to guiding Aditya.

'Sir! They're on the move! They have moved out of their hotel, fully packed and then headed to a car rental. Do we intercept them right now?' one of the spies reported.

'No! Follow them. Do nothing to let them know that you're following them.' Avinash replied.

'They just rented a dusty old sedan from the rundown car rental shop. They're employing standard tail evasion techniques, cash payment and relatively difficult to be traced resources. With this, we can assume that they still have no idea that they have a tail.'

'Good. Try to keep it that way. And get your vehicle and follow them inconspicuously. We'll follow you right behind. Make sure you have your tracer on so that we can track you down.'

Five minutes later, Avinash and his team were on their way. The team comprised of five hardy ex-army mercenaries locking and loading their weapons into place for the mission ahead. They looked like they were going to take on an enemy army rather than two men completely oblivious of their oncoming doom.

The sun was setting over the horizon as Aditya dropped away from the main road onto the way towards Kuldhara. Fifteen kilometres shouldn't take too much time to traverse, unless something pops up.

Unknown to them, another car broke away from the main road, just like theirs, following them.

'So, do you think they're still onto us?'

'I don't know. Neither can I say. From what I have seen of the past incidents till now, they have seemingly unlimited resources and the men are highly trained. So I can hazard a guess that they aren't too far behind us right now.'

Mubeen had no idea how right he was.

45

'Sir, they have rented out a car from a local car shop,' Jay said into his phone, 'and I have their vehicle number.'

The man on the other side of the line said, 'Good. I want you to track down their phone numbers and keep tabs. Get a car and follow them. All your expenses will be paid by me to your secure offshore account.' Jay nodded and hung up.

Jay paid the money, jumped into his car, and kicked it to life. He slid out of the parking lot of the car rental and sped out. He pulled out the small handheld GPS from his pocket which was giving live location of Aditya's phone. The device showed that he was about a kilometre from his target. Jay wove in and out of the traffic following the GPS feed wherever it went. The traffic was so dense, he almost bumped into another car at an intersection crossing even with the red light signal and the hundreds of horns blaring everywhere, he made it out and he finally come into direct view of the vehicle Aditya and Mubeen were in. He kept a safe distance of about four hundred metres from their vehicle.

Several minutes later, they broke away from the main road.

Quite unknown to him, two more vehicles followed them down the road towards a similar destination, one in front of him between him and Aditya's car and the other behind him.

46

Several hours later, the plane landed smoothly onto the runway in Genève Aèroport, Switzerland. The killer walked out following the queue. He picked up his bag from the conveyor belt and walked towards the exit after passing through the customs. He tried to look as inconspicuous as he could as he exited the airport.

Just as he walked out of the controlled environment of the airport, the arctic cold hit him like a pincushion on his open face. He pulled his coat tightly over his body and slipped on a pair of gloves. Snow was falling all around him; the sky was completely overcast creating a gloomy atmosphere in the entire region.

He hailed a cab and got into it.

'Where would you like to go?' the cabbie asked, his voice thick with his peculiar accent.

The killer pulled out a piece of paper from his pocket and read out loud from it, 'CERN headquarters, 385 Route de Meyrin.'

Teddy Kapoor, Director General at the CERN was lumbering through the incandescent hallway of the building towards his personal room. He was greeted several times along the way by his subordinates and by some of the most brilliant and intelligent minds on the planet clad in whites lab coats. He nodded his acknowledgement to everyone of them.

Just around a corner, he reached his room, opened the door, went inside and closed the door behind him. All the lights inside were switched off. *Funny, I thought I never switched off my lights.* Shrugging, he went inside and just as he was about to place his hands on the switches the television monitor in his room suddenly came to life. Teddy blinked in the flash but a moment later, he eyes grew accustomed to the light and he paid attention to the channel being shown. It was a news channel broadcasting news about two famous people who have been murdered in a span of a week in India.

Teddy, otherwise would have dismissed such news and was about to do so when he noticed the two faces being flashed on the screen.

His eyes widened as he recognized both of them.

'Ah, so you recognize these two men, don't you? Don't bother lying to me; I can see the look on your face.'

Teddy's heart began beating at a rate much faster than what was good for his old body. He looked about frantically for the source of the voice in the darkness. He suddenly heard a click behind him as the door to his room was locked and the lights switched on, illuminating the entire room. Teddy felt a presence behind him. He turned around to face the killer.

The killer spoke again. 'I wanted to start off by saying I killed both of them. And I would not hesitate to do the same to you if you don't give me what I need.' The killer said, putting on a pair of latex gloves.

'What do you want?' Teddy asked, his entire body shaking.

The killed walked around the room and brought around two chairs

Teddy's desk. He sat down on one and offered the other to Teddy who sat down shakily, perspiration already lining his entire forehead in the perfectly air conditioned room. The killer smiled. This one was going to be fun.

The killer leaned forward on his seat and whispered near Teddy's face, 'What I need are a few answers from you.'

47

Sun had begun to fall over the horizon as Aditya drove his car through the rustic road.

'Do you think it's the right time to be visiting a haunted place? I mean, this place has been deserted for almost three hundred years and has barely seen human existence in that interim.' Mubeen asked.

'Are you still afraid of ghosts? You're a battle hardened soldier, a private investigator handling corpses every other day and here you're scared of ghosts?' Aditya asked, shaking his head and then continued, 'This might calm you down. During the flight, I had read up a few articles I had found about this place and several paranormal activists had visited this place and have found no evidences of any such activity.' Aditya laughed.

Mubeen looked out of his window. Out of the corner of his eye, on the side mirror, he noticed three more vehicles hotly in their pursuit. Two were simple sedans and one was a minivan.

'Do you see the three vehicles behind us?' Mubeen asked.

'Yeah, I had noticed them long back but I didn't pay much attention then. Why?'

'No, just asking. Normal things don't remain normal with you around anymore, you know? So, just letting you know.'

Mubeen kept glancing at the mirror from time to time, keeping a watch. Suddenly a shot rang out and the mirror he was looking through was no longer there.

'Damn!' Mubeen exclaimed, pulling out his own gun.

Aditya lost his cool and turned the driving wheel suddenly to the right, swerving the car to the right and righting it just in time, a fraction of an inch before it was to hit the rocky outcropping beside the road.

Suddenly, a head popped out from one of the windows of the sedans right followed by a pair of hands clutching an assault rifle. He took aim and pressed the trigger.

'DUCK!' Mubeen shouted as he bent down. Aditya barely managed to keep the car on the road from his crouched position. Bullets shredded the back windshield of their vehicle, ripping through the leather seats. The fusillade continued till the man ran out of bullets in the clip.

Mubeen realized that and knew he had to take advantage of that. He rose up and started firing wildly at the car behind. His volley of bullets shattered the windshield and had successfully forced the man to protect himself from the glass shards rather replacing his empty clip of his assault rifle. Mubeen quickly changed his own empty clip just as the other man did and before he could start firing, Mubeen had already fired two rounds at the man. The bullets pierced the chest instantly killing him.

Mubeen then looked towards the driver. He could see fear in his eyes. The driver pulled out his own revolver and started firing. Mubeen had no choice but to duck.

Just behind this vehicle, Jay drove on, wide eyed. A complete mayhem had suddenly been unleashed in the scene. Someone wanted Mubeen and Aditya dead really bad. He looked through his rear view mirror at the vehicle behind. He could only imagine what the minivan carried.

He fumbled around for his phone and finally found it. He dialled his employer's number. It was picked up after two rings.

'Update. There's a road rage going down here in the middle of the road. Actually it's more like a scene out of the movie *Death Race*.'

'Tell me clearly. What is happening down there?'

'Can't you hear it? A bunch of heavily armed hooligans are hell bent of killing Mubeen and Aditya. Their car is taking on heavy automatic and submachine gun fire from these guys and I don't see how long they're going to survive this onslaught. As far as I can see, Mubeen is okay since he's firing back and Aditya too is okay since he's the one driving the car but I can't see him so I cannot say for sure. I don't know how the hell he is driving a car like that.'

Several thousand kilometres away, the killer shouted into his phone, 'Damn it!'

He felt like throwing away him phone but he couldn't do that yet. Keeping an eye on Teddy seated in front of him he kept his phone to his ear, listening to everything he could.

Suddenly he heard Jay shout a curse and a fraction of a second later he heard a loud bang and a crunch of steel crushing into steel and a moment after that, an explosion.

During the same time, Mubeen had rose up from his ducked position and tried to take an aim at the driver of the vehicle behind him. Aditya's nerves were completely frayed and he just couldn't cope up with the situation and keep the wheel straight.

'Come on Aditya! Keep the car straight on the road! I can't take a proper aim because of this kind of driving that you're doing.'

'I can't! Something is wrong with the car!'

Mubeen shook his head and took a precise aim and fired emptying his clip in the direction of the driver. *At least one would find its way home* he thought. In the end, two of the bullets found their target and killed the driver instantly. The vehicle suddenly went out of control and the limp hands moved the steering wheel in to the left swerving the car in the same direction and crashing into rocks and came to a halt a precious few seconds later. The car behind this one, containing Jay, hadn't thought of this and hit the first in a head-on collision.

Somewhere within this mess, a few drops of petrol ignited from the several sparks and that led up to the fuel tank of Jay's car which, a moment later, imploded into a thousand parts and pieces along with burnt human remains. The entire place reeked of burning tyres and sulphurous odour combined with pitch black smoke from the wreck.

The minivan behind came to a screeching halt, safely away from the crash site.

48

'Jay?' the killer asked. Silence was the only reply he got after the explosion. He stamped his foot as hard as he could on the ground. 'Damn it!' he said as he cut the line. He then turned his attention to the man in front of him. He took a deep breath in and exhaled slowly.

'So, will you answer my questions? I have travelled a long way just to meet you and I wouldn't like you to mess my day, it is already messed up as it is. And you know the consequences of not answering my questions properly too. So it shouldn't really be a lot of problem.'

'What do you want from me?' Teddy shouted.

'Ooh, calm down. You don't need to shout in here, okay? It's a closed room, nobody will interfere us here. Coming back to my first question. This question is a little unnecessary but still I would like to make things clear. You are a member of the Council of the Nine. Am I right?'

The man said nothing but his eyes widened as heard the name. His brain was going into overdrive, cooking up a million unanswerable questions.

'I do not know what you're talking about.' Teddy replied.

The killer pulled the gloves back to remove all the air pockets. The then clenched his fingers into a fist and landed a punch on Teddy face.

The killer leaned back against his chair and said slowly, 'As I've already said, don't lie to me.'

Teddy knew there was no use pretending. The stranger in front of him knew it. He decided to keep his lips tightly sealed. He couldn't afford saying anything. Two others had died before saying anything to this man. He couldn't betray any information.

'I'll take your silence as a yes, alright? My second and last question. Tell me,' the killer said slowly, 'where are the books?'

'Get me a map! Quickly! I need to know where they are going. We lost two men and we wouldn't want them to die in vain, do we?' Avinash barked.

Somebody in the car produced a piece of paper out of their pocket and handed it to Avinash. He took it and unfolded it. 'Where are we right now?' he asked switching on the light.

'We are somewhere around here on this road.' Another said, comparing the map with a reading from his phone.

'So, if we follow this road,' Avinash said, moving his finger over the line, 'it leads us to... nowhere. It goes to some place in the middle of the desert. It says the name of the place is Kuldhara or something. Ring any bells, anybody?'

'No. Not really.'

'Does the road branch out anywhere?

'Minor roads, they don't look so important. But we don't know, they might be headed anywhere in the desert for a picnic for all we know.'

'Get me more information on Kuldhara. Now! I am guessing that's where they're headed. Nothing apart from that amounts to anything significant in the area.'

Up ahead, Mubeen and Aditya were speeding up the dusty roads in their bullet shredded car. Hundreds of bullet holes beautified the hull of the car serving as a proof of the hard time it had been through recently. The sun had now set completely into the horizon, casting an eerie silent darkness over the desert road. They drove on silently over the moonlit road. Mubeen glanced out of his broken glass window at the billions of colourful stars illuminating the cloud free and pollution free skies of the desert. He could feel the relatively cold night air ruffling through his hair.

'Hey, Mubeen,' Aditya said, 'I have a question in my mind.'

'What is it?'

'Why the hell did I ever decide to take on this quest?' Aditya began laughing, a laugh of relief and reprieve coursing through him.

'I have on damn clue.'

Not very far behind them, a minivan made its way towards them slowly but surely. They had accumulated everything online hit they could find over the internet about the location and were on their way.

49

'I have no idea what you're talking about.'

'What did I tell you? You don't need to lie to me. Just give me the answers that I seek and you're free to go. It's that simple.'

This time he changed his tack.

'I cannot simply take your word for it. I need a guarantee that you'll let me go after I tell you about the location. For all I know when I tell you the secret, you will kill me, once your purpose is served.'

The killer thought for a moment. Half of his question had already been answered. There was a location where all this knowledge is being kept and protected. He pursed his lips, thinking over it and then said, 'You are in no position to negotiate, Teddy. You will have to take my word for it.'

Aditya's car came to a screeching halt as they noticed a huge sandstone structure in front of them. Both of them got out with their flashlights and pointed it towards the structure in front of them and visually explored it under the light.

'I think it is a gate to enter into the city.' Aditya said.

'You think?'

'I'm quite sure. See the rounded structure as it goes up from either side and then meets up at the centre up top?'

'Let's go in. Some more of those pursuers wouldn't be too far behind us. Let us get to it as quickly as we can.' Mubeen said.

They walked in through the gate, their flashlights sweeping over all the contours of the desolate golden city. They walked up the cobbled steps, passing through broken, rundown, ramshackle houses down the road. Some were almost intact, in their natural condition with a few bricks missing here and there but most didn't survive the test of time. Sandstone bricks lay strewn apart imparting the region an eerie atmosphere.

Broken steps led up in several houses, among which some were missing. There wasn't a sound in the night except their footsteps and the occasional banter.

'I see why people were spooked at night here. These dilapidated buildings, cobbled steps do give off that kind of aura. Hey is that the temple?' Mubeen asked, pointing his light at a building in front of them.

The building looked much better preserved than the others around it. Its walls were up and sturdy. It had some ventilation holes up on their ceilings and conical designs the top resembled a lot like a Hindu temple. Intricate designs rose up to the rounded bowl like tips. In short, it looked everything like a Hindu temple from several centuries back.

At the gate of the city, a minivan comes to a stop beside Aditya's rented car.

'Our guess was correct. They are indeed here.' Avinash exclaimed, 'And now that they're out of their car, it will be far easier to kill them. Put on your NVGs. We have a hand above them with those. They won't be able to see in the dark. Also I want every one of you to search every nook and cranny of this place. They can be anywhere. Chances are that they have realized we have turned up and they have switched off their flashlights else they would have no way to navigate in the dark.'

'Did you hear that?' Mubeen asked, his ears perked up, trying to pick up any sound that might signify trouble.

'Hear what?' Aditya asked.

'Tyres crunching on the gravel outside the city gate. I heard the same sound when we reached this place. We have company, Aditya. You have some really persistent pursuers who also happen to be extremely talented and very resourceful.'

'Thank you Mubeen.'

'It wasn't supposed to be a compliment. Now run inside the temple! Hopefully they don't know we are going to be there. Maybe they do but all I can do is hope for the best. Switch off the flashlights. We don't want them to spot us so easily.'

They lightened their steps as they walked towards the temple. As their eyes became accustomed to the darkness they began to move faster through the rubble of the desolate city.

'Hey, did you notice something?' Aditya asked.

'What?'

'Why isn't there any flashlight beams dancing around? If they're looking for somebody in the darkness that is a necessity isn't it?'

Mubeen thought for a second. 'No. Not if they have NVGs. You're pursuers are beginning to irk me a lot. They have everything from high tech gadgets to talented manpower. And we're just two people.'

Mubeen didn't know how wrong he was this time.

50

Aditya and Mubeen explored the inside of the temple with the help of their flashlights but partially cupping the palms on the face so as to prevent too much light to leak out of the place. They shone their partially obscured flashlights over the walls, scrutinizing every corner.

'This temple has no idol.' Mubeen said, quizzically looking around.

'Yeah. I had read about that. Maybe the *Paliwal Brahmins* were too fond of their idols that they decided to flee the place with those. I do wonder how they did it.'

'Maybe the temple was under construction and the idol hadn't been created or erected upon this place when they fled. Who knows?'

'What do you expect to find anyway? I mean, do you have any idea what you're looking for in here. If we're just sightseeing, well it is just not the right time to barge in upon a place and also we have a bunch of goons, probably heavily armed ones, behind us. So I think it is a really bad time to be doing that.'

'I'm looking for something that looks really out of place, you know, something that just isn't supposed to be here.'

'Like a witch sitting in the corner cooking something up?'

'Maybe.' Aditya said, giggling.

'Wait. I think I found something. Aditya, come here quickly!' Mubeen exclaimed under his breath.

'Sir, I found them. I think that's the temple. I can see a few flashes of light there. I'm quite sure there's some activity going down there.'

Avinash peeked through his NVG and then glanced with his naked eye. He nodded to himself. 'Let's go. We've found them.'

Six of them, armed with heavy artillery advanced quickly towards the unwary duo.

'What is it?' Aditya asked.

'Look at that symbol on the floor. Doesn't that look familiar?' Mubeen asked, smiling.

'The Ashoka Chakra!' both of them said together.

Both of them crouched down and fingered the symbol. 'That certainly looks out of place. The Mauryan Empire existed and died away long before the village of Kuldhara was even born. This is certainly it. And especially so since everything we have found till now pertains to something related to Ashoka or anything related to that. But the question is, now what?' Aditya said.

'Shush!' Mubeen whispered, pulling out his gun. A moment later Aditya heard them too. The crunch of boots of the rocks and rubble and the clicking of metal objects against each other, probably weapons.

They could hear their own hearts beating in their chests faster than normal. What would they do now?

Mubeen regained his cool faster and whispered urgently to Aditya, 'Do exactly as I say now. Take my flashlight and be ready to light them completely when I say you to do so. Alright? I'm just going to hold them back just enough to buy us some time while you figure out what to be done with that symbol, okay? And stay here, do not move. And try not to get killed in the firing, okay?'

Aditya nodded nervously, gripping the two flashlights in his hands. Mubeen stood up, his gun in tightly in his hands and pointed it towards the open doorway of the temple. He focused all the cells in his eyes towards the doorway.

The sounds of footsteps began to come closer and closer as they waited inside in the pitch darkness waiting for the inevitable to happen.

Outside, Avinash and his team slowly crept up to the temple doorway. They silently undid the safeties on their weapons. They stopped a few feet away from the doorway as Avinash motioned to them to stop. It was a part of their plan. They would suddenly burst into the place, pull out their targets from the confined place and kill them in the open and dispose off their bodies in the desert and nobody would even notice.

Avinash took a deep breath in, exhilarating the inevitable victory he was about to achieve. He exhaled heavily and then motioned for them to move in quickly.

51

'TELL ME!' the killer shouted.

Suddenly there was a knock on the door that resounded around the room. The killer whispered, 'Tell them that everything is okay and you were talking on the phone with an old friend.'

'Is everything alright, Dr. Kapoor? Do you need anything?' came a voice from the outside.

Teddy was about to cry out for help but then noticed the killer two feet away, looking at him menacingly.

'Dr. Kapoor?' the voice asked again, 'Are you alright?'

'No, everything is alright. Just talking with an old friend of mine, don't worry.' Teddy replied.

'Okay.'

After the killer was sure that person on the other side had went away he asked, 'Now. I want you to know something. I don't want to deal with anymore of your pathetic, reticent scumbags living in the shadows, hiding knowledge from humankind, keeping it privy to some people who believe they are more enlightened to know something. You cannot hide and lock away the basic necessity of advanced knowledge from a man and keep it in the circle of a few!'

'But knowledge in the wrong hands can mean total devastation of this very same humankind and we serve to prevent that from happening.'

'You haven't been very good at doing that have you? Let us see, World War 1? Or maybe the World War 2? The atom bombs? Hydrogen bombs? Those didn't turn out too good, did they?'

Teddy kept his mouth shut. He couldn't answer that.

'No answer, just as I had expected. Now spit it out and tell me where you have hidden it!' the killer screamed, his look vicious.

'It might here. It might there. It might not be anywhere! It may be everywhere!'

'Stop speaking in riddles you old fool! Give me my answer.'

'It's not like the treasures of the ancient times, hidden under a rock here, or in a sunken ship several thousand feet under the Pacific Ocean! You may not be able grasp your mind around this. Knowledge cannot be held in the palms of your hands. Neither can it be stored away in a dungeon in some remote corner of the world, away from all eyes, maybe except a few. It is out there in the air and yet nobody can see.' Teddy said, suddenly smiling, 'It is everywhere and yet it is nowhere you can get to.'

The killer stood up in a quick motion, grasped Teddy's face in his hands and gave it a twist in a direction it should never be twisted in and left the head. Teddy's face lolled down in an unnatural direction.

The killer opened the door and seeing no one around walked out silently. He then pulled off his latex gloves from his hands and stuffed them into his pocket and walked towards the exit of the immense CERN building.

52

'NOW!' Mubeen shouted to Aditya, cocking his gun towards the entering intruders and fired a few rounds at the walls.

NVGs work in the principle of picking up any and every ambient light in the vicinity and focusing them in the darkness enabling the wearer to practically see in the dark. But, if too much light goes into it, the amount of light focused becomes too much for the human eye to handle and may cause serious problems or at the very least temporary blindness if taken off quickly. So, the men shrieked, both from the blinding light in their NVGs piercing into their eyes because of the combined brightness of the two flashlights and the deafening noise of the bullets in the confined space. They dropped their weapons and pulled off the devices from their faces and threw them down, desperately rubbing their eyes in order to get rid the light still burning in them. They had ducked down in a desperate effort to blindly evade the bullets.

'Aditya, find it quickly. I can hold them off for only so long!' Mubeen said, as he went forward, kicking their weapons away from their easy access.

Aditya frantically began rubbing the area, to find some crevice or cranny that might hold a secret meant just for them. He blew sand away from the corners and suddenly something struck him. He was looking everywhere around the symbol of the Ashoka Chakra. What he hadn't noticed as of yet was that the symbol itself was etched upon a little circular area and a distinct line gap going around it, looking too much like a button of sorts.

'They're getting up, Aditya. Whatever it is you're doing, do it fast. They might not have their weapons but they're five and we're just two.' Mubeen said, firing a round just above the heads of the men on the floor. The bullet flattened itself just above the head on the wall and ricocheted off.

Aditya nodded at Mubeen and looked back at the symbol. He placed his finger on it and tried pressing it down. It didn't even budge. 'Damn it!' Aditya whispered. He rubbed some more dirt and sand out of the area, trying to find something to help him clue this thing up. He found nothing.

He could feel frustration rising up his stomach as more and more of his efforts to press it down failed. He could feel time slipping out through his fingers as the button didn't budge downwards. His heart began beating faster as the anticipation of death began overwhelming him. Out of the corner of his eye, he could see the men rising up, their eyes finally getting accustomed to the darkness.

Am I missing something? Aditya thought. *Am I doing something wrong? Is the thing stuck?* Suddenly one of his flashlights slipped from his grip and fell from his hands onto the ground at an angle and he noticed a wedge on the side. He finally realized it. The button was meant to be pulled out, not pushed in. A little wedge at the side had been made specifically to lever out the button to reveal the secrets underneath. In his pocket was a pocket knife for which he thanked his stars for remembering to carry it along. He pulled it out, wedged it into the hole and gave a hard push.

Avinash couldn't believe his pathetic luck. He hadn't imagined that he would be outsmarted in such a spectacular fashion by some petty investigator. With a pair of flashlights, Mubeen had downed all of six trained battle hardy men without any application of force. He still couldn't rub the light out of his eyes, it almost seemed as if somebody had torched their eyes and they were writhing as a result.

He knew he was in no position to fight back right now. They could barely see, and it would take a lot of time to adjust to the darkness. Their enemies not only had the advantage of having light but also clear vision which would be able to react faster than theirs.

One of the men tried standing up. Just as he put one leg up a bullet hit the wall beside him, sending pieces of sandstone all around. 'Stay down! I won't miss my target the next time.' Mubeen shouted. His stern voice boomed through the closed area.

Avinash felt like punching himself to death. This was a dishonourable way to be defeated. He couldn't believe he had gotten himself and his team into a situation like this. He had to get out of this somehow.

Aditya couldn't believe what was in front of his eyes. The button had come up and now he could now pull it up. He grasped it with his other hand and pulled it out of the ground. It was a solid cylindrical piece of sandstone, somewhat like a fat cigar. He pointed his flashlight inside and tried to peer into the little opening in the ground at the same time.

'What is it, Aditya? Did you find anything?'

Aditya felt crestfallen. 'No. There's nothing inside.'

Mubeen stayed silent for a moment, looking back at his captives.

They were still trying to get the light out of their eyes.

'Hey. Try the object itself. The thing that you pulled out from the ground, maybe it has something on the inside.'

Aditya's eyes widened in realization as he turned the cylinder in his palms, 'Why hadn't I thought about this?' he said, looking at the other side of the object. He closely inspected it and towards the inward side he noticed a thin line that went all around the square body. He dusted off the sand, held that end of the object and pulled. Like a cap, it came off smoothly revealing another secret compartment inside, and this time it wasn't empty. Aditya smiled and nodded to Mubeen who looked ahead and was surprised to find a gun pointed four feet away from his face.

53

The killer sat at the airport terminal in Geneva, contemplating the turn of events. His flow of plans was going haywire. Everything in his plan was getting derailed because of the presence of Aditya. They were right about Aditya being an obstruction in their objective of releasing all the knowledge of the Nine to the public. Nobody had any right to keep such information a secret, privy to a select few.

But what he had heard from Teddy had shaken him. It wasn't anything close to what he expected to hear.

It's not like the treasures of the ancient times, hidden under a rock here, or in a sunken ship several thousand feet under the Pacific Ocean! You may not be able grasp your mind around this. Knowledge cannot be held in the palms of your hands. Neither can it be stored away in a dungeon in some remote corner of the world, away from all eyes, maybe except a few. It is out there in the air and yet nobody can see. It is everywhere and yet it is nowhere you can get to.

The killer couldn't help but thinking, w*hat on earth did he mean by that? That made no sense whatsoever!*

The second most predominant thought in his mind had was the people who were trying to kill Aditya. He couldn't let that happen. He couldn't let Aditya suffer and pay because of the mistakes of his dead grandfather who was also leading him on a similar path. That just couldn't happen. Aditya was his only object of love and he couldn't afford to lose it. He might ultimately have to sacrifice his own life for the cause but he couldn't have Aditya messed up.

He picked up his phone and dialled the familiar number. It rang thrice before it was picked up. 'Hello?' was the voice from the other side.

'Why are you trying to kill Aditya? Why do you have men after him? What has he done?' the killer asked.

'If you were to look at it like that, he himself hasn't done anything. But he just happens to be at the wrong time in the wrong place. I told you to put a leash on him but you didn't do anything. Now I have to take the matter into my own hands. I just cannot trust you with this job.'

'You can't trust me? After all that I have done for our cause, you don't trust me? Why don't you understand? If we follow him, he will lead us right to what we seek! It is as simple as that.'

'But that would expose us. I don't like to repeat myself again and again but I cannot let that happen. It will jeopardize us and our very existence. If they catch a whiff of our presence, the Nine won't stop at any length to obliterate us from the very face of the earth. It has happened several times over the past, the most recent one being the destruction of our headquarters in Chernobyl in the city of Pirpyat of Ukraine in the year 1986. They had somehow gotten in, tripped off and destroyed all the systems in the Chernobyl nuclear power plant leading to an explosion of the core leading to the death of over five hundred thousand people in the area.

History recounts it as one of the biggest disasters in the world but I remember it as the biggest mass human murder by one organisation. I cannot let that happen again. I cannot let history repeat itself and I want to liberate knowledge.' The man on the other side seemed convincing. It was as if he was retelling the tale of his life. 'I had lost my son because of that incident. I curse myself everyday from that day on for not being there and dying along with my son but I had been away doing some work. By the time I was back, they had cordoned off the area and from what I could gather, my son was dead. I couldn't even go in and see my son because if I did, I would die of ulcers all over. His body was probably disposed off somewhere, wrapped in a lead lined bag to keep off the radiation. Imagine my pain, my anguish. There wasn't anything that I could do for him. The helplessness I felt was unbearable. The unbelievable amount of pain and anguish I went through during that time.'

The man on the other side hung up. The killer pocketed his phone and pondered over his future course of plans. Aditya was the one that mattered to him the most. He couldn't afford losing him. He was like a son, but not his son. He never had been able to father a child, and Aditya was the son he never had. He couldn't afford to lose him. He couldn't hurt him anymore.

This was it.

On the other side of the line, the man smiled mischievously. Things were getting pretty interesting. The scene was changing and he had to change along with it. He picked up his phone again and dialled Avinash's number.

There was a change in plans.

And he just hoped Avinash hadn't succeeded in what he had been assigned to do.

54

'Surprise!' Avinash smiled gleefully, his gun four feet away from Mubeen's face. 'Any last words before you die?'

'What do you want?' Mubeen asked; his brow furrowed tightly, still holding his gun pointed straight at Avinash. Both men stood for a moment, each of their guns facing the other. By this time, all the others had stood up and collected their weapons and the muzzles were pointed directly at him.

'Me? Nothing. Well, maybe your dead body along with his. Don't take it personally, okay? I have no grudge against you. I don't have a score to settle with you. I just do this for the money. Nothing else. We've been trying to track you down for quite some time. You credit card usages, you phone calls. Everything. My client surely wants you dead really bad.'

'And who might that be?' Aditya asked, his teeth clenched with fury.

'Well, I respect my client's privacy. I do clean business. So I won't tell you who wants you dead, even if I want to.' Avinash said, enjoying the moment. All he could think about was the substantial raise that was about to magically appear in his offshore account once this deed was done.

'So you won't let us go?' Mubeen asked, stalling the man in front of him to think of some idea.

'What kind of a question is that?' Avinash asked, snapping out of his dream.

Just a moment later, Avinash's phone rang. Mubeen couldn't do anything as such. The moment his finger would press on the trigger, five more would press down one their respective weapons all of them pointed towards him. The only way to hold this situation in balance was to maintain his position, pointing the gun at the man in front of him.

Avinash pulled out his phone and recognized the familiar number of his employer. He picked the call up and exclaimed, 'You have called right on time!'

'You have called right on time!' Avinash said on the other side, 'Or else you might have missed it. We had some difficulty tracking down these targets for you but we finally have them now and were about to kill them.'

'I'm glad you haven't killed them yet' the man said.

There was a pause on the other side but then Avinash asked, 'Why?'

'There has been a change in plans. I want you to take them alive and bring them to me here. In a few hours, my private plane will be waiting for you in Jaisalmer Airport to bring them to me here. The payment for the job will be made on delivery.'

Avinash hung up from the call. He looked up and said, 'Orders from above. You both are lucky men. Today is not your day to die.'

'So we're free to go?' Mubeen asked, uncertainly.

'No,' Avinash smiled, 'you're coming with us.'

Mubeen's eyes flicked about here and there, looking for a safe exit point. He had to do something. He couldn't just walk into their open arms, probably walking into their nasty trap. They had just got their lives back; none of the men would actually shoot to kill. It was a situation he had to take advantage of.

Just as Avinash was pocketing his phone, Mubeen moved with lightening speed. With a quick kick, he knocked the gun out of his hands and then grabbed his neck in his arms, his gun's barrel against Avinash's temple. Before the other men could blink thrice, Avinash was in Mubeen's strong arms in a locked position unable to move an inch.

'Move and he dies!' Mubeen shouted to the other men.

The men looked stunned.

'Drop your weapons and slowly kick them away!' Mubeen shouted.

The men hesitated for a moment. Mubeen pressed the barrel into his temple.

'DO IT!' Avinash shouted to his men.

The men dropped their weapons yet once again that night. Then they gently kicked the weapons out of their reach. Mubeen shifted his

169

weight and moved towards the doorway of the temple. Aditya followed numbly behind. Both of them slowly moved out, and started walking towards the parked minivan at the gate of the deserted village of Kuldhara. Fifteen minutes of strenuous trudging in the dark, they reached the vehicle, the men following closely behind, and the weapons in their hands.

Mubeen didn't mind that. They wouldn't dare do anything. He was in control of the situation now. Aditya sat in the driver's seat, strapped his seatbelt on and ignited the engine. The minivan groaned to life.

Mubeen, freed Avinash's neck and quickly pulled out his phone from the pocket and threw it towards Aditya. Mubeen then struck hard behind Avinash's head with the butt of his gun and quickly climbed into the minivan. Aditya pulled out of the place and just at the turn Avinash's men started firing wildly at them but by that time, they were too far in the dark to actually get a right shot.

55

'Why did you take his phone?' Aditya asked.

'Simple. We know he last talked with his employer on the phone. I am assuming that the employer was the same person who was involved in your grandfather's murder. Based on that assumption, we can use the last used number on the phone and track it down.'

'So, you're going to turn to the authorities for help?'

'After all this?' Mubeen smiled, 'Never. I know just the man who can do this really well and whom I can trust to keep his mouth shut. Anyway, did you find what we undertook so much risk for?'

Aditya produced the thin cylindrical object from within the pocket while balancing the wheel at the same time. Mubeen took it and examined it between his fingers. He spotted the thin line going across the cylindrical surface and uncapped it slowly. The cap came of easily and inside was the prize. Aditya switched on the little bulb near the rear view mirror to have a look at the thing too.

'Hopefully this is not another poem.' Mubeen said, inverting the case and a rolled piece of paper dropped out. He gently pulled the remnant out and opened it out and flattened it against the dashboard.

'And it is yet another poem.' Aditya said, smiling.

Neither of them could make out much of the poem in the low light in the middle of the night. Mubeen carefully refolded the piece of paper and inserted it back into the tube and recapped it. He also remembered to pull out the battery of the phone they had pulled out from Avinash's pocket which would temporarily deactivate any tracking devices in the device.

They reached the city of Jaisalmer a little after midnight and checked into a hotel, this time paying in cash. They offloaded their stuff in the hotel and decided to check out the poem the next morning. They were just too dead beat and called it a night.

Meanwhile, Avinash and his team stood fuming at the gate of the village of Kuldhara beside the rough worn out wreck of a car which Mubeen and Aditya had used to reach the place. When he checked it out, it was running low on fuel; sometime during the shootout, somehow a stray rock from the road had struck the fuel tank of the vehicle and it had been leaking out its precious contents ever since and by the time Avinash tried starting the car up, it coughed and started for a moment and then the old engine died away a few moments later.

He stamped his foot on the ground futilely, as if doing that would magically produce a car out of thin air.

56

The man at the head of the Corporation kicked the desk in front of him, stubbing his toe in the process. Avinash had failed miserably. He hadn't even been able to capture them, let alone kill. Avinash attributed the failure to the underestimation of the one named Mubeen Roy who seemed pretty innovative in serious situations and tactics of evading their spying capabilities.

Things had seemed to be falling into place but were now slipping out of his hands through his prone fingers. Both Mubeen and Aditya had escaped unscathed and he had nothing, literally nothing with which he could lure the killer back into what he was doing, hunting down the Possessors. If he were to obtain the knowledge of the Nine, he first had to take out the main Nine Possessors, each a leader in their own subjects.

But the main question that pestered him was that what on earth was Aditya doing? The Community of the Nine had existed since the day that twisted Mauryan king named Ashoka had created it after the great battle to acquire Kalinga after which he had supposedly undergone a change in heart and had adopted the path of Buddhism. That was what the history textbooks said. What had actually happened was that after the battle of Kalinga, Ashoka had realized that military strength wasn't enough to rule in the world. He realized that the pen was indeed mightier than the sword.

So, he created a secret community of nine people to undertake research in nine of what he thought were dangerous in the hands of others apart from him. Legend has it that he had entrusted each of them nine books in a secret assembly soon after the Kalinga War and all of the Nine Possessors had been indoctrinated into their respective fields. He sought to acquire those nine books or rather the storehouses of knowledge. The community grew in size and in numbers on a global scale but their main focus has remained unaltered.

While he did all this, on the outside he had to show what he proclaimed himself to be, a follower of Buddhism and undertook several measures to actually make people believe that. And he had been successful in doing that. People know him more as the great Emperor Ashoka rather than the hideous scheming and selfish little man. History books called him Ashoka the Great. He had gone to the extent of sending his son and daughter to the place now called Sri Lanka to preach his so-called Buddhism. Was there some ulterior motive for doing so, he couldn't say.

What he knew was that he had to get his hands on the knowledge. Who knew what kind of advanced technologies lay buried under the tarps. It would certainly make him the most powerful man in the world. And he would not let anything come in the way of him realizing that dream.

If the pawns of his game played out their roles properly, nothing could stop him in his endeavours. Not even God himself could do anything.

His train of thoughts stopped for a moment. Yet this Mubeen had turned out to be far smarter than he had imagined. And Aditya was surely on the trail of something else he wouldn't be wandering off on a tour to seemingly random and unconnected places.

But unfortunately, everyone had a weakness. The only job was to find out what it is. And he had found one. He remembered the conversation he had had with his pet killer before his first assignment. His job had been to kill Harish Tiwari and to make sure that he was the only one at home so that nobody is there to witness anything if anything goes awry. The other family members had supposedly gone to a business party in the city and the grandson was out on a date.

A date.

The team at Avinash's disposal were versatile enough to get the name out of the internet. Everybody literally had their entire lives written into the fabric of the internet. In a world where social structure and relationships was everything, this was it.

It was time to put bait in the water to trap the fishes and hit two birds with one stone.

It was time to finish unfinished business. He picked up his phone and touched on the last number that had a few minutes back. It rang twice before it was picked up, 'Give me Avinash on the line.'

On the other side of the line, there was a ruffling noise as the phone exchanged hands. Finally Avinash spoke up, 'Yes, sir.'

'I have another job for you now. I am hoping this is going to be a lot easier than capturing Mubeen and Aditya.'

Avinash's pride was hanging on the balance. He was ready to do anything to get back at those two who had escaped his through fingers, making him look foolish. 'Just give me the orders, sir.'

'Get your tech team ready.'

57

Avinash smiled as he hung up on the call. This was really going to be a lot easier. And far more effective. You can escape from the Corporation once. Never again. He dialled another number on the phone. His head of tech operations picked up on the other side of the line. 'I need you and your team to track down somebody for me. Forget about Mubeen and Aditya for now. Understood?'

'Now?' the man on the other side asked, 'at this time of the night?' probably looking down at his watch and wondering what the hell he was doing there.

'Yes. Right now.'

'Well, whom do I have to find.'

'I don't have a name. But I have a relationship. Wouldn't that be enough for someone like you to pull out something?'

'I thought you hired me to be a hacker and a computer geek. Not a petty social network stalker and find out who's dating whom! What are you doing anyway?'

'Just do as you're told to do, okay? Don't ask too many questions. You get paid to do what I tell you to do. So do it.'

'Okay. And by the way, your phone has gone out of service

suddenly. I cannot trace it anymore.'

Avinash exhaled heavily. Mubeen was indeed smart. 'Mubeen stole my phone, intending to do something with it and he is smart enough to pull out the batteries to prevent detection. I'm starting to like this man.' Saying thus, Avinash hung up.

Then turning to the others behind him, he said, 'I am going to take this vehicle out and when I reach, I'll have another guy drive down for the rest of you. Until then, stay put and don't show up with your weapons unless absolutely necessary. I am going to take one of you with me and all of you will stay here for each other's company. Huddle up men, this is the desert. It is going to get colder as the night passes on. Understood?'

'Yes, sir!' they said in unison.

Avinash smiled, acknowledged them and said, 'Good.'

The men stood in the dark, dumbfound with assault rifles in their hands as Avinash stepped into the dilapidated thing of a car. Fortunately, the tires were intact. He could at least get somewhere before finding another soul on the desert road to steal another car. He motioned for one of his men to follow him into the car in the front seat. The back seats were too damaged to be used for sitting.

58

The morning sun crept up the eastern horizon, illuminating the golden sandy expanses of the state of Rajasthan, the light slowly creeping up through the streets and houses, casting long shadows in the opposite direction.

Suddenly the bell rang, instantly waking the two of them. Mubeen was up, holding his gun pointing it towards the door. Aditya slowly walked up to the door and gingerly grabbed the doorknob. Just as he was about to twist it open, a thick white envelope slid in from under the gap of the door. Aditya peeked through the peephole, trying to find who it was. He couldn't see anybody outside. He turned the doorknob and glanced outside with the same result. Puzzled, he closed the door behind him and picked up the letter and walked back into the room.

'That's strange. It has nothing written on the top. That probably means that this was hand delivered just for you. You've got any ideas?' Mubeen asked, looking over his shoulder.

'None whatsoever. Probably another note from my dead grandfather. Now I am really beginning to doubt whether my grandfather is really dead or not and this is just one big setup to tell me something. But why take so much effort to do such a simple thing?' Aditya replied, flipping the envelope over.

'It might not be as simple as you think. Go ahead, open it up. See what it contains.'

'Hey, it has a seal. Like the ancient times,' Aditya said 'to secure the package within.'

'Yes. Any tampering with the seal leaves a very recognizable mark on the paper. By the way, did you notice something peculiar with that seal?' Mubeen asked.

'What is it?'

'The seal is an almost identical replica of the one we had found on the letter back in the secret alcove under the Kanyakumari Temple! From the looks of it, I say the impression was made by the same stamp. I hadn't paid attention to it that day but now the symbol looks really familiar.' Mubeen exclaimed gleefully, looking up at Adiya.

By this time, Aditya too had noticed the familiarity of the symbol etched on the red seal. 'It all makes sense now. We had seen this very symbol on the paper which my grandfather had left for me in that box!' Aditya said, exhilarated by the sudden series of revelations, 'Guess where it is found. It is a really popular symbol.'

Mubeen thought for a long moment. Then he said, 'I am afraid I am from the army. This means I have a lot of things and knowledge I can be proud of. But knowledge of ancient symbols? Not one of them.'

'Well, this is the inverted lotus symbol under the famous Ashoka Pillar in Sarnath. Well, most Ashoka Pillars across the country has this but the one in Sarnath is the most popular since almost the entire thing was found with little destruction with the passage of time.'

'So that's the reason why it all makes sense. Everything somehow boils down to the name of Ashoka. What is his significance in your quest?'

'Well that's the part I haven't figured out as of yet.'

Aditya gently tore the paper along the along the seal, careful not to destroy the contents in the process. He then pulled out the contents. A piece of paper came out along with a credit card. Mubeen eye brows rose up as he carefully gazed at it. Aditya opened up the letter and read through the contents.

'Dear Mr. Tiwari.' Aditya began, 'We trust this will fill your needs. The pin code and other information are provided below.' At the very end of the page was the same symbol engraved deeply as on the seal.

'Did you win a lottery?' Mubeen asked.

Aditya didn't answer. His mind was somewhere else. Mubeen gave Aditya a few minutes and then said, 'I hate to break into your stream of thoughts but you have another clue to uncover, remember? Take this a blessing and thank your stars for this. This is a platinum card so the usage limit is going to be pretty high. Whoever our secret benefactor is, he surely knows what kind of a situation we're in. Now let's get that clue open and solve the riddle and be off. I am beginning to become wary of all this.'

'Benefactors. It's plural.' Aditya said, almost in a haze.

'What do you mean?'

Aditya looked towards him and said, 'It says here '*we trust this will fill your needs*'. So we have a couple of people and not one.'

Mubeen thought for a moment and then said, 'So? Does it matter?'

'I don't know. It might.' In fact it did. Something had suddenly struck Aditya. It was a story his grandfather had once told him when he was a little kid. He couldn't recall everything of that conversation; bits and pieces were all he did remember.

Something was forming in his mind. He was involved in something really big. He just wasn't sure yet whether his assumptions were realistic enough. What he did remember was the stuff of legends, of myths – nothing that bore significance to the reality. But suddenly things happening around him didn't seem very real. It was something right out of a Tom Cruise action movie.

'Let's thank our *benefactors* and you take a look at that riddle, now. We do not have a lot of time. If these *benefactors* can track us down to our hotel location, I don't think our pursuers are too far behind us again. They always manage to have some trick up their sleeve. So get to it.' Mubeen said, stressing on the word.

59

The killer walked through the air conditioned passages of the airport in Jaisalmer towards the exit with nothing but a bag in his hands and a strong determination on his mind. The Corporation had enough of its ways. It was time to change now. Aditya was not going to be harmed in any way.

Just then he remembered to switch on his phone. A minute later, it beeped with an incoming e-mail message.

```
I am pleased with your job. Here's your
next assignment. Soon our dream will be
realized we will set the balance right.
Too much power has been yielded to the
wrong people for far too long a time.
```

And an encrypted, password protected zipped file was attached to the e-mail down below.

The killer smiled, shaking his head and downloaded the attachment. It was the standard protection scheme that the Corporation always used for its employees for jobs like these. He opened it up. As was the standard procedure, the screen went blank and a dialogue box popped up in the centre of his phone with the message –

Identifying recipient phone signal, please wait....

This stayed open for some time after which it again beeped in recognition of the phone identity and asked for a fingerprint check. The killer placed his index finger on the biometric scanner of the phone which instantly beeped and the device began identifying the myriad of lines and ridges along the surface of the skin of the index finger. A moment later, it pinged again in recognition.

The file opened up but asked for another password which every employee had been provided with at the onset. Nobody except the employees would be able to access anything from the device. Except for picking up a call, every operation requires an authorized finger to be used. The file finally opened up and in it was the name of his next target from among the Nine.

The killer himself saw no purpose following those orders. There was a time when he would have blindly adhered, but now there was a better way and the head of the Corporation seemed hell bent of destroying it. Aditya was going to lead them right up to what they seek, clue after clue. But they were targeting Aditya's life maintain their secrecy, to rub off their footsteps from the sands of time. But that wasn't going to be possible. Their effort was meant to leave behind an indelible mark in the pages of history.

The killer was resolute. He was not going to rest until he saw to it that Aditya was appropriately protected and the knowledge of the whereabouts of the nine books of knowledge. He was drifting away from the Corporation. But it was for the greater benefit of achieving the end without Aditya's life hanging on the line.

60

Mubeen and Aditya finally sat down on chairs with a table in between them. Mubeen pulled out the laptop booted it up while Aditya opened up the little cylindrical object and pulled out the prize of their search from within. He placed the rolled piece of paper on the table and gently unrolled it and placed two weights on either side to flatten it out completely against the table.

'So, here it is.' Aditya said, looking into it properly for the very first time.

An ancient monument is what you need to find,

Where the mounds and piles of bricks bury,

The ashes of enlightened one in repose,

When the sun reaches its closest zenith for the day, that which you seek rests

Beneath the shade of the torana of the Vidishas

'Okay. Ancient monuments and ancient temples. That is always what we get. Couldn't it be something more modern, more accessible?' Mubeen asked to nobody in particular.

'*Ashes of the enlightened one* would certainly mean the Buddha, more so even in the context of Ashoka adopting Buddhism later in his life after the Kalinga War. Legends say that after his death, the ashes of the Buddha had been divided and spread all over the country in different places and monuments were built upon them to commemorate the memory his existence which still serves as the holy shrines for the people following Buddhism all over the world. And there are hundreds of such structures and nobody knows which ones contain the ashes of the *enlightened one*. But which one does the poem mean?' Aditya said.

'The fourth line is easy. The sun reaching its closest zenith for the day would probably mean the time of noon or the middle of the night when the other side of the planet is experiencing noon, when astronomically and technically the sun is the closest to the earth, when the planet goes around the sun in its elliptical orbit. For us, it must be the noon else there wouldn't be a *shade* under which our prize is resting.'

'Good one. That makes sense. So we have to visit our location at a particular time of the say, that being noon. But what does a *torana of the Vidishas* mean?'

'*Vidishas* would probably be a name of someone or some place. I've got no idea about the *torana* part though. Alright, you keep pondering over this while I'll go out and fetch the two of us a new pair of SIM cards for our phones. I don't want them dropping in every time we make a call.'

'Alright. I'll stay put right here, pondering over this. And see what I can yield from the internet.'

'Okay.'

61

The killer would almost give anything for a short nap that afternoon after the long flight from France. He looked almost ready to drop into the seat of the cab he was in and go to sleep. But he couldn't do that. He had to find Aditya before the hired thugs of Corporation did. But what else could he do right now? The killer didn't even know whether Aditya was still in Jaisalmer or no. And he certainly couldn't call and find out.

And even Jay was dead. He could have been so useful right now. Suddenly his phone rang. He picked it up, it was the Corporation. 'I see you're back in India! Everything fine down there?'

'Why don't you tell me? One of my most loyal men died a little less than twenty four hours back. Do I even deserve an explanation from you?'

The man on the other side stayed silent for a while. Avinash had reported the exploding up of a civilian vehicle along with one of theirs with two of Avinash's men in it in their road rage battle against Mubeen. It wasn't completely a civilian either. It was the killer's spy tagging behind Aditya and Mubeen. This was fantastic news for him. Avinash had unknowingly and unwittingly done what was needed to be done. He could barely contain his excitement. He brought his voice down to a serious tone and said, 'I don't really know what you're talking about.'

'Oh, I've had enough of your insolent lies. Stop trying to kill Aditya and follow him! He will lead us right to what we seek.' The killer almost pleaded. 'We will have the knowledge of the Nine in the palms of our hands and we can spread it among everybody.'

The man on the other side of the line smiled ruefully at how naïve the killer was in his workings. Who'd want to give it all away when you can have it all just for yourself? 'But you know what? Both of them have slipped out from under me. I don't know where they are anymore. But,' he said with a pause, 'I have a plan to reel them both in.'

'You will not do anything to bring harm to Aditya. If I come to know that you, at the very least, lay a hand on him to hurt him, I will search every corner of the earth and I will find you and I will kill you. And you know that the truth and I can very well do it. Do you understand?'

The smirk was wiped off the face on the man. He knew that too well. But it was a bargain he was prepared to take. 'Don't dare threaten me. I know what I'm doing. And no, I wasn't going to hurt them, at least not yet.'

'You are not going to come anywhere near them and neither are your thugs,' the killer said, 'namely Avinash and his goons are to be found near Aditya.'

The killer hung up, frustrated. He wondered what the head of the Corporation had in his mind. Something in his gut told him it wasn't going to be pretty. The cab wove through the dusty roads towards the hotel he had booked a few hours back over the internet. He looked out of his window. He had no idea where Aditya was in the huge city, and along with a guy like Mubeen who supposedly had a lot of field experience, tracking him down would be a lot tougher.

The killer had one idea though, but it involved involving the Corporation. He picked up his phone to make another call.

The man at the head of the Corporation picked up his phone for the second time in the past five minutes. It was his killer. 'I have an idea.'

The man smiled. The killer was so easy susceptible to emotional provoking. 'What is it?'

'I'll call Aditya while your team tracks down his phone signal. That's the only last option we have, considering the assumption that Mubeen still hasn't changed the SIM cards of their phones.'

'Do you think we haven't already tried that yet?'

'Aditya will pick up my call.'

'Alright, I'll get my team ready in five minutes while you prepare yourself. Have something useful to say else he might become suspicious, provided he hasn't already. I will give you a call when everything here is set up.'

The man at the head of the Corporation hung up. Things were turning out even better than he had expected them to. The killer turning to him with ideas. Even he knew any plan was better than a plan involving Avinash. Avinash was a smart and a ruthless fellow who would stop at nothing to have his goals achieved.

Several miles away from the killer, Mubeen stood at a local electronic supply store who sold SIM cards too. He bought two of them, both of them prepaid. It was going to take at least a day for those to get activated. There wasn't anything they could do, except wait under complete electronic silence.

Just as he was walking back, he remembered the phone in his pocket that he had pulled out from the pocket of the one he had been holding on to as a human shield. He stopped in his tracks on the pathway beside the main road, pulled out the phone and tried starting it. He pressed on the power button but nothing happened. 'What the hell?' Mubeen exclaimed under his breath, 'what kind of a phone is this?'

He then held on to the power button of the phone, remembering that he had pulled out the battery to switch it off to avoid risking detection and then placing it back in. Suddenly, a moment later, the screen blinked to life and displayed the company logo. Several precious seconds passed by as the phone finally switched on. He fiddled with it and found that it was password protected. Just for the fun, he tried a few random numbers and characters he could conjure up but, as he had expected, nothing matched. He gave up and went back into the store.

'Hey, can you unlock a phone? I had set up a password on it but I think I have forgotten it because none of my attempts seem to be working.' Mubeen asked the man, smiling as genuinely as he could, handing the phone over to the man.

'I cannot guarantee success but I can give it a try. Would you like me to do that?'

'Sure. Go ahead. But do it quickly, I don't have a lot of time.'

The man tried one of his own hotchpotch wild card guess on the password and just as both of them had expected, it didn't work. The man then opened up the back of the phone and examined it. He then saw something and then pulled put the battery while the phone was still on. Mubeen leaned over the glass table to have a look. It was a little microchip attached to the phone under the battery and a thin wire going into the phone. 'Bingo.'

His eyes widened as he realized what the chip was meant for. It was something he knew very well and so did the man working on the phone.

'Can you pull it off?' Mubeen asked.

'I can, but it will completely wipe out all the data the phone contains and then when you switch it back on, everything will be as clean as new. It is a very sophisticated piece of technology. And if this phone belongs to you, some really powerful people are after you and they probably have been hearing everything you have every said on this phone.'

'How did you come to know about this?'

'I had read about this somewhere. It is surprising what you can find out when you let your fingers do the walking through the internet.'

'Is it active right now? If the phone is kept like this, will they be able to track me?'

'No. But they will be the moment you switch it back on. This is because the microchip is powered by the phone battery and it has no backup power of its own.' The man placed the battery back into the phone, slid the back cover into place and handed it back to Mubeen and said, 'You'd better keep this thing switched off and use the new SIM cards you just bought.'

Back in Avinash's headquarters in Mumbai, one of the men huddled in front of a computer jumped up and exclaimed, 'Hey,

Avinash's phone had been stolen and switched off, right?'

'Yes,' someone answered, 'but why do you ask?'

'Avinash's phone is back on the grid! I have no idea how. I can see it. It is still in Jaisalmer, that's for sure. My computer is scanning to pinpoint and hone in on a location.' Several tense seconds later, the blip on the computer screen went away as suddenly as it had popped up. 'Damn it!' he exclaimed. He hit a few keys and commands on the keyboards but all of his attempts were futile. Nothing happened. The phone had been switched off yet again, for reasons unknown.

'What happened?' someone asked.

'It's gone. My guess Mubeen has come to know about this. But at least we know he's still in Jaisalmer. And we also have a general location where. We should inform Avinash about right away.'

'Go ahead; inform the tech head about this.'

Just as Mubeen turned around a corner on the street he was walking on, he took off in a sprint towards the hotel they were staying in, hitting and bumping against several. But he didn't care. For all he knew, Aditya might have already been taken hostage by their pursuers.

Avinash pulled out the new phone he had bought for the time being in Jaisalmer. Fortunately he almost had all the numbers in his mind so was able to connect up pretty quickly. Suddenly, it began ringing. It was from the offices in Mumbai.

'Yes.' Avinash said into the phone, 'What is it?'

'We have news. Mubeen is still in Jaisalmer. We can also give you a local region in which he might be in but I couldn't pinpoint his exact location, he switched of the phone before the computer could receive complete precise data.'

This was gold! 'Tell me more'

62

Several metres horizontally away on the main road, the killer glimpsed a man running like a madman though the street in the opposite direction. But unfortunately, his mind was too preoccupied with something else to actually notice Mubeen sprint past, bumping into several others. If he had paid a little more attention, he might just have recognized him.

Just then, a call shook him out of his stupor. It was from the Corporation. They were ready to start tracking. He picked up his phone and dialled Aditya's old number, hoping that he hadn't already changed it yet.

Mubeen cursed himself for choosing to come so far away from the hotel they were staying in. He had done it in a safety precaution so that even if he was caught, Aditya would remain out of harm's way. But that effort had lead to him being at least one and a half kilometres away. He thought of catching a cab but it was peak morning time, waiting for a cab was a futile waste of time. And he didn't know what else his pursuers had rigged up to track them down and so he couldn't risk calling Aditya via his old number. Even a public telephone booth might expose Aditya's position, if not his own.

Wiping beads of sweat from his brow, he resumed his jog towards the hotel. He could see the building slowly looming up in the distance. Invigorated, he picked up speed.

The harsh ringtone of a phone broke through the serenity of the room in which Aditya was in, browsing through the hotel's free Wi-Fi service, looking to find something that might crack the jackpot for him and decode the poem. As he picked up the call, he wondered where Mubeen was at the moment. He was taking a long time to come.

'Hello?' he asked.

'Hello? Aditya?' asked a voice from the other side.

'Is that you, uncle?' Aditya asked, his brain deconstructing the voice and picking out the nuances of his uncle's voice.

'Yes. Where are you? People are so worried here in Mumbai! Why didn't you even bother to call us once?'

'Sorry. See I wanted to but I was a little busy.'

Mubeen ran up to the door, slid his key into the slot turned it and opened the door. He was horrified to see Aditya chattering away on his phone. 'Aditya! Drop the phone right now!' he shouted.

Aditya jumped up as he turned around to face. 'It's my uncle here!' he spoke, cupping the phone in his palms.

'Your pursuers won't care about that. They have our SIM cards on their grids and are probably on their way here. Switch that off before they actually get a lock in on your position!' Mubeen exclaimed, horrified that Aditya still hadn't realized.

The killer punched the seat in his cab in frustration. Mubeen always had to intervene at the wrong time at the wrong place. Aditya cut the phone after a hasty apology and then probably switched the phone off. But he had a decent corner of his heart for that man. After all, he was the one who had kept Aditya alive in quite a few situations.

He then picked up the phone and called the Corporation tech team leader. 'Did you get him?'

'Yes. Our men are already on their way.'

The killer was appalled. They're going kill him. 'Tell me where he is.'

'No, sir. I cannot. I'm sorry.'

'Come on! You can't be doing that. You have to tell me.'

'I've been given specific instructions not to give away that information to you. I am sorry about that but I am just following orders. Trust me, it's nothing personal.'

The killer hung up and threw down his phone on the seat. It bounced off the cushion and struck the fortunately closed window on the other side and fell back onto the seat and it lay there. The killer could barely believe himself. He felt stupid; he himself had suggested the idea of calling up Aditya. But he hadn't envisaged the problem of Mubeen jumping into the scene and the man took full advantage of the sudden opportunity fortune had offered him so gracefully. He had walked like a donkey right into that man's trap. And now he was in a cab, with nothing to leverage himself against that man who had, with such an elaborate sham, trapped him.

63

Aditya quickly packed up both of their stuff as Mubeen kept watch from the window. Fortunately for them, the room had been a road facing one. The figures on the thermometer were rising as the morning wore on into the noon. The roads were clear up till a point, all there was the general traffic, seemingly unsuspicious crowd walking through the pavement.

Suddenly, it seemed as if the cars appeared out of nowhere. Four black SUV's roared and stopped right in front of the hotel. Men in black uniforms with weapons in their hands poured out of the vehicles and marched quickly into the hotel. One more sedan came to a halt behind the SUV's and a man stepped out, who seemed to be the one in charge. He folded his hands and stood leaning against the vehicle.

'Quickly!' Mubeen exclaimed, 'We've got to leave NOW! They're here, damn it!' Mubeen walked up to the television set and switched it on to a random channel.

'What is the purpose of doing that?'

'I'm buying us a few seconds to flee because frankly, I don't think we can escape too far before these guys catch up to us. We have to utilise every resource we have in our hands to buy ourselves more time.'

Aditya shouldered his own backpack and handed Mubeen his. Both of them exited the room. 'Follow me wherever I go.' Mubeen whispered.

Mubeen led Aditya through a maze of corridors which led up to a stairway. Mubeen pushed it open and went it, 'Fire escape. Good thing I had checked it out in the morning. Hopefully they haven't covered up this exit, else we're screwed.'

They quickly ran down the stairs, making as little noise they could.

Avinash stood up in anticipation from his leaned position as one of his men walked up to him to give a status update.

'Sir, they're not in their rooms. We broke in and found traces of a hasty retreat – open windows, crumpled bed sheets and a television running.'

'They're probably aren't too far away! Maybe they haven't even left the hotel premises. Come on, let's go! Spread out; check out for all the back doors, emergency exits, fire exits. Everything thing you can find. I don't want them to escape from my fingers now.' Avinash said, as he jumped into his car and kicked the accelerator and sped out to move around to the other side of the hotel.

Aditya and Mubeen calmly started walking after exiting from the emergency fire exit. 'Running would do more harm than good; it would attract a lot of attention to us.' Mubeen said, shouldering his bag.

Just as they were about to turn around a corner, the black sedan skid onto the side road and sped towards them. Mubeen looked back, recognized the car and started running, Aditya following closely behind. Mubeen took a swerve into a narrow alleyway where no car would ever fit. He went inside and waited for Aditya. Seconds later, he made it in and so did the car halt just outside the alleyway. A man jumped out from the car and began running towards them.

'RUN!' Mubeen shouted, pulling out his gun and pointing it towards the man who came to a stop several feet away from him, 'Don't move! You might not survive your next step.' Mubeen said to the man, unhooking the safety of the gun.

Avinash smiled Mubeen pointed the gun towards him. He stopped and gazed into his eye. 'I am honoured to finally meet the great Mubeen Roy! I have to say, you've been pestering us for quite a while.'

'Good. That means I have been doing my work pretty well.'

Avinash laughed. 'You have no idea. I'm impressed. In fact I'm so impressed I'll make you a promising deal. I am prepared to forgive you for the way you insulted and escaped from me back in Kuldhara and also I'll let you live, provided you return my phone and give up Aditya.'

'Yeah, that surely is an enticing offer but I guess it has to be a no. I'm already involved in this and I cannot sacrifice my client. That's my rule.'

'Well well, well! A man lives by his rules; you're truly a man beside my heart. But you know what? Rules are meant to be broken, aren't they?'

'In my world, no.' Mubeen said as he fired a round near the man's leg. To his surprise, the man didn't even flinch. He just stood there, smiling as if he knew Mubeen wouldn't actually shoot an unarmed man.

Mubeen then decided to take a rash step. He had to break his rules. He aimed at the man's left leg and fired. But the gun just clicked. It was empty. He was out on bullets, the remaining cartridges were in his bag and now he had to improvise. But the man in front of him taking advantage of the moment of distraction and lunged at Mubeen, felling him to the ground.

Mubeen went completely still for a moment as realization of the quick turn of events dawned upon him. The man's hands were at his throat, choking the life out of him. Soon, Mubeen could feel his vision slither out of his grasp, sensations dying away. The image of his killer became more and more obscure.

Suddenly, something happened and he felt the pressure over his throat loosen up. He drew in deep breath, filling his oxygen depleted lungs to the brim. He exhaled through his mouth, feeling the air and freshness course back into his body as he tried standing up. At his first attempt, he fell back down feeling woozy behind his head. His vision began to clear in the seconds that passed and he saw what had happened. Somehow Aditya had decided to run back to his rescue and knocked the consciousness out of the man in front of him and from the looks of it a kick under the jaw might have done it.

'Why did you come back? You should have run away from here to a safe place!' Mubeen croaked.

'I couldn't have your death and my incapability to help you in your time of need to prick my consciousness whenever I think of you. Also, I couldn't let this stupid oaf choke the life out of you.' Aditya said, smiling.

'I think you might have killed him. He's just there, still as a rock.' Mubeen said, laughing and kneeling down to check the man's pulse. It was still there.

'What is it?' Aditya asked fearfully kneeling down beside Mubeen, 'Is he still alive?' He surely didn't like to have a murder on his consciousness, even if it was someone who was trying to kill him. He had practically left the job of killing to Mubeen, if the need arose.

'I'm afraid he is.' Mubeen said, checking the man's pockets. He found a wallet with a business card with the name Avinash Murthy written in capitals. He found little else. Both of them stood up, dusted themselves off and went off in the opposite direction, caught a cab and went off to the airport.

Avinash's new phone began ringing and vibrating in his pocket, slowly and gently nudging him awake. He sat up, looked around and tried to remember where he was. A moment later, everything came back to him. He then fumbled with the phone and picked it up.

'Have you captured them yet?' the man on the other side asked, his voice impatient.

'No. Yet another unfortunate turn of events, I had chased them down alone with my team back at the hotel and I almost had choked the life out of Mubeen's body but suddenly out of nowhere, Aditya emerged and knocked me out.'

'Damn it! We have to go back to plan A immediately. Bring in the bait and wait for the fishes to come by themselves. In the meantime, check out the local airport. That is probably the only viable option they have to evade us.'

'Okay, sir.'

64

The killer sat in his hotel room and flicked through the local news channels, looking for something that might give him information about Aditya's survival. Finally he found one that piqued his interest. It was showing the CCTV footage of a hotel security camera, showing four black SUV's, undoubtedly belonging to the Corporation, parked in front a hotel and armed men dressed in black entering the hotel, coming out within a matter of minutes, probably a reconnaissance. The entire place was deserted except of the four SUV's and a sedan at the back. He couldn't make out the faces but he was pretty sure who came out of the sedan. It was Avinash.

A minute later, Avinash jumped back into his car and sped off to God knows where. But it was good news nonetheless. It probably meant that Aditya and Mubeen had escaped from the hotel somehow. He couldn't say anything more on the report, but the news also said that the sedan had been seen about half a kilometre away from the scene in front of the hotel, parked haphazardly in the middle of the road. This dampened his spirits. So Avinash had spotted them. But surely two men could easily overcome one.

But again, there was no knowing Avinash. For all he knew, Avinash had killed them. The news channel had nothing further to report for the evening and he switched off the TV. He picked up his phone and decided to know it once and for all. He called the head of the Corporation.

'Did you get them?'

'Unfortunately no. But we had a backup plan in place. And now we're going by that. And surely you won't be a part of that. You have your mission to accomplish. Do that.'

'You cannot keep me away anymore. I've done enough of your killing and I am not going to do it anymore. I'm coming for you. You'd better beware.'

'You're threatening me?'

'Do you feel threatened? Well then, that is indeed a good sign.'

'You don't know what kind of a mistake you're doing. You're threatening our entire existence with your stupidity and valuing of the life of one mere man which would lead us to the most precious thing ever kept a secret from humanity. And we probably wouldn't ever get as good a change at this than this.'

The man on the other side smiled as silence ensured on the line. He knew just when to poke the coal and it would flare up and when and how to pour water to stop the flames. It was time to reveal the secret to the killer. It would completely shatter him.

The next call was also going to be his last.

65

'Why did your uncle call you?' Mubeen asked under his breath

'I don't know. Before he could say something he wanted to say, you barged in and asked me to hang up on the call.'

Mubeen nodded and looked here and there, scanning the area for any suspicious activity. 'What do *you* think he might have called you for?'

'No idea whatsoever. We last talked at my grandfather's funeral before I was shot. And after that when we were in Allahabad. He had then asked me about where I was then, and I had told him and I had also told him where we were going next. I felt he had the right to know.'

'From now on, if you get any call, from anybody apart from me, do not pick it up. Okay?'

'But my family has a right to know what I am doing and where I am, don't they?'

'Yes, they do. But your life hangs on the balance here and nothing is more important that. If you have to surf the internet, use the cafes. Forget using any and all media of online information and data transfer like e-mails and chats. Also avoid social media. They can track you down very easily. Understood?'

'Yes.'

'Anyway, have you figured out the poem yet?'

'No, one part still remains a mystery to me. And that part, I feel is the key to the entire poem.' Aditya said, pulling out a piece of paper he had written down and made a copy of the poem on.

An ancient monument is what you need to find,

Where the mounds and piles of bricks bury,

The ashes of enlightened one in repose,

When the sun reaches its closest zenith for the day, that which you seek rests

Beneath the shade of the torana of the Vidishas

'Which part?'

'The significance of the last two lines. *When the sun reaches the closest zenith for the day*, as you said, means noon but what does that signify? What does a time of the day have to do with the next clue which we are looking for? It doesn't make sense.'

'Maybe figuring out the last line might help. Don't look at me; I don't know anything about history.'

'*Beneath the shade of the torana of the Vidishas.*' Aditya said to himself again and again. 'Where have I heard a similar word? Why does it sound so familiar?' Aditya racked his memory to pin point a time in history when he had heard that, maybe read about that. It seemed to close to his grasp yet still out of his outstretched arms. He punched the seat next to him as frustration and desperation began to take control of his psyche.

'Calm down, Aditya and think it over coolly. We have a little time. But you have to get us a location, at least the state. Then I can book the tickets for our flight.'

Aditya nodded absentmindedly as his mental rungs turned and turned. Suddenly an old couple sat in the space on the seat just beside Aditya. Looking at his expression, the old lady asked, 'Where are you boys going?'

'Ah, that is difficult. We do not know where we are going to go, yet.'

'Why? And what is this?' the woman asked, looking at the piece of paper in Aditya's hand. She leaned forward and pulled out the paper from his hands and began reading. He was about to rudely pull the paper away from the lady when Mubeen subtly restrained him.

'It's a game a bunch of us friends are playing. We had created a list of clues for each other and whoever discovers the other team's final location wins.' Mubeen said, improvising on the spot. 'This is our current clue and we don't know where to go.'

The old husband chortled under his breath. 'Look at these boys. Roaming around the country like hooligans spending money like water even before they can earn some decent savings for themselves. I wish you luck for your future boys.'

'Shut up, old man!' the woman said, 'Just because we didn't enjoy ourselves doesn't mean our younger generation wouldn't either. We are now stuck up in our houses with arthritis in both our knees, unable to walk properly dreaming about our young days. Don't stop these young men from doing what they want!'

Turning to them, the woman kindly smiled and said, 'I'm sorry child but this poem makes no sense to my old brain anymore.'

'Let me take a look, you old woman' the man said, pulled the paper away from her, 'your memory began failing to serve you even before you married me half a century ago. Gladly I still have my own resources at my disposal.' The old man put on a pair of heavy spectacles and looked at the piece of studied the writing.

Aditya looked questioningly at Mubeen who just nodded – asking him to let the situation work itself out.

'Son, this is really simple! Couldn't you boys make up something difficult?'

Mubeen and Aditya sat up glancing at each other, their eyes wide in anticipation.

'Could you tell us where this poem is telling us to go?' Mubeen asked, almost falling from his seat.

66

The lead technician back in Mumbai picked up his phone and dialled Avinash's number. It rang one before it was picked up.

'What is it?'

'I have a name. Though I am not really sure of its accuracy, okay?'

'Just give me the name and get to work on finding out where the person lives.'

'The name is Rivannah. Rivannah Shah. And finding out the location is going to take some time. Though her Facebook account says that she lives somewhere in Mumbai, pin pointing her location is going to take time. When she logs into her account, if she ever does, I can track down the IP address of her internet connection, hack into the system of the service provider and get her current location. But as I said, it is going to take time. Once I get her IP address, it won't be that hard.'

'Okay. Good job.'

Avinash on the other side hung up rather abruptly. The man shrugged carelessly, ignorant of the full consequences of his discovery.

Avinash excitedly dialled another number. The man leading the Corporation picked up.

'Sir, I have news. We have the name. My team is working to track down her location and my team back in Mumbai can handle it.'

'How much time will it take?'

'We cannot say for sure yet. It depends upon her.'

'Alright. Where are you now?'

'On the way to the airport, just like you instructed.'

'I'm asking because your little incident at the hotel has hit the news and you're in TV. Someone snooped up the CCTV footage of the hotel and sold it off to the media channels and that was it. It is everywhere now.'

'Oh.'

'But rest assured, your face is barely visible in the footage. So nobody will be able to hone in on you just yet. You can still move about freely for now.'

'Okay.'

Several miles away, the killer hopped into a cab with his bags and stuff and ordered the cabbie to take him to the airport. It was the only logical place they could flee to. Evening was setting in and the traffic began to increase and the cabbie had to halt every now and then.

But the airport would be under the maximum amount of scrutiny by the Corporation too. Probably Avinash was on his way there too.

Perhaps he was already there. He couldn't think of any more of these horrible thoughts. He tried to push these out of his mind and he tried as hard as he might but couldn't do it. Those questions still crept back into the void to tickle his imagination cooking up horrible scenes, listing out the ways in which things could go seriously wrong.

He looked out of the window, his face on his palms, his feet continuously tapping away impatiently. He picked up his phone and dialled the number he almost had by heart.

'Hello?' was the question from the other side.

'Yes,' the killer replied, 'this is me.'

'What do you want now?' the man on the other side asked.

'I presume your venture of capturing them was unsuccessful, yet again. If I were you, I would have kicked that incompetent little prick Avinash out of the job long ago. He's incapable of doing anything substantial.' It felt good to the killer. This was his form of outrage.

'What do you want?' the man on the other side repeated.

'Same as you. Only to be distributed among others.'

'You are a fool. Did you really ever think I was going to give it all away? All that information, all that knowledge is of no use if distributed. Where's the fun in that?'

It was now the killer's turn to be stunned. 'What? I thought we both had the same mission, just different ways. What are you talking about?'

'What I'm saying is I'm a businessman. Whenever I see any object, any commodity, I see an asset or I see a liability in it. So you see, the vast storehouse of knowledge that the community had for all of two millennia is serving no purpose except rotting in some corner. When I see the knowledge, the amount of technological advancements that are lying hidden from our view, I see an asset. A gold nugget. If I get hold of that, I can use it to invest and generate income, multiply my net worth several times over.

Coming to you, even you are, or rather were an asset. A really valuable and useful one too at that, to begin with. The only thing about you is that you're a human. Humans change. Things and objects do not. And neither does money. When this is all over, I'll probably be sitting in a coop in some corner of the world in my own private island with my own private army and you,' the man paused for a dramatic effect, 'won't be able to touch me.'

'You lying scum! You thieving bastard!' the killer was in a short of words and curses to hurl at the man on the other side of the line.

'Curse me all you want but this is the reality. You can't become a Robin Hood now. Accept the fact and live through it.'

'YOU USED ME!' the killer shouted, frightening the cab driver.

'Yes, I did. And I feel this is the right time to tell you because our mission is about to end. What I have in my mind is surely going to succeed and mind you,' he said, 'you are not a part of the plan this time.'

Hot tears began to pour down from the sleep deprived eyes of the killer. He could barely believe himself and the situation he was in. All those lives, all those innocent lives that he had taken were probably laughing at him now from the skies above, at the futility of his being. He could curse and blame everybody around but in reality there was only one whom he should blame. Himself.

'But, why me?' he asked, almost sobbing.

'As I said, then you were an asset. Now you're a liability, you're of no service to me anymore. Avinash serves me better now. He does what I tell him to, unlike you with opinions of your own.'

The man on the other side smiled once again. It was done. The killer was officially out of business.

67

'Son, are you sure you haven't been able to solve this clue?' the old man asked genially.

'No, sir. We couldn't.' Mubeen said.

'I mean, if an old man like me could solve this, why couldn't young lads like you do the same? Literally, I've played a lot of games and quizzes in my long life, but none as easy as this one here.' The old man was quite literally beaming in pride.

'Where is it that we have to go now?'

'Ah, taste the suspense, my boy while I taste my glorious victory.' The old fellow was surely insane. Perhaps he wasn't, he didn't know what situation Aditya and Mubeen were in.

'Is it something related to Ashoka?' Aditya asked, testing the theory that was forming in his mind.

'Well, yes it is. It is something made during his rule. I assume you know the answer by the now.'

'That I don't know. The Ashoka question was a hunch that I had. Please tell us what the location is.'

The old woman was now the one becoming irritated. 'Come on,

old man! Spit it out already! We don't have all day for this, you know.'

'Okay, so here it is. Let me explain.'

An ancient monument is what you need to find,

Where the mounds and piles of bricks bury,

The ashes of enlightened one in repose,

When the sun reaches its closest zenith for the day, that which you seek rests

Beneath the shade of the torana of the Vidishas

'The first two lines are easy enough but without much meaning until you know the actual answer. The third line, *the ashes of the enlightened one in repose* would mean Buddha but I know for a fact that Buddha's ashes weren't stored there. Parts of the ashes of his initial disciples and their articles were found here. I don't know if Buddha's ashes ever survived the test of time.'

Aditya's eyes began to widen in slow realization.

'And the purpose of last line, *beneath the shade of the torana of the Vidishas* is hazy but what it means is clear. The *Vidisha's* were ivory carvers approximately during the first century before Christ. They had made the *toranas*, or gate like structures for the current king around an ancient structure called the –'

'Sanchi Stupa!' Aditya exclaimed excitedly. Turning to Mubeen, he said, 'We have to go to Madhya Pradesh. Now.'

68

Avinash halted his car near the airport and switched off the GPS that had led him there. He parked the car in the lot, stepped outside and began striding towards the entrance of the airport. He walked through the customs and looked around for the familiar faces of his targets. Hundreds of people were milling about in the airport and honing down on two people was going to be difficult even with a dedicated team with him.

But it wasn't really necessary to make all this fuss. Once they had Rivannah in their hands, Aditya would come to them like a lamb to the slaughter house and surely Mubeen would come along. He waited for a few more minutes in the airport, looking around casually and then motioned to his team to move out.

If he had been a little more careful, he might have noticed Aditya and Mubeen come up and stand in a line to book their tickets directly to his right a few feet away from him. But fate isn't so cruel and neither is she so quick. She strikes when the time is conducive enough to her.

Both of them stood as if they didn't know each other. Aditya reached the counter of Air India first and booked his ticket to Raja Bhoj Airport in Bhopal. They had looked it up and found that it was the closest airport to Sanchi. He subtly handed the new card to Mubeen after his transaction was over for him to buy his ticket. It took Mubeen some time to go through the legalities and procedures to show his licence and other certification papers for his to carry a firearm and cartridges onboard the plane.

The next flight to Bhopal was due in two hours, so they had a lot of time to kill. They more time they stayed there, the more dangerous it became for them. They went back to sit with the old couple they had met some time back, their flight was also due in about two hours and a half hours so they would have each other for company.

The killer stood in a queue about three feet away from which Aditya and Mubeen bought their ticket. He had no way of knowing where they were going. He had to know about it and there was no outright way he could do it. He couldn't call – it would certainly raise some eyebrows.

All he could do was go as close to them as he could and eavesdrop on them. But the airport was so packed, there was barely enough place to sit, let alone get a seat he wanted. He put on a cap that covered most of his head and shaded his face and began walking towards the duo talking animatedly with an old couple. He pulled up his collars and placed his palm on his mouth as if wiping it, obscuring his face even more. He knew there was a slight possibility of Aditya not being able to spot him but Mubeen wouldn't be so careless. With all his things in place, he began his walk towards them.

'I finally know why the word *torana* was ringing a bell in my mind trying to tell me something but I wasn't able to come to any concrete conclusion. It is interesting to note that similar gate like structures are also made in Japan, popularly called as *tors*, bearing a striking resemblance to the beginning of *torana*. Those *tors* gates also bear striking resemblance in structure in our Indian version *toranas* around the Sanchi Stupa, which probably suggests exchange of ideas and trade among the two places in those ancient times.' Aditya said, beaming.

'Again, why do you know that?' Mubeen asked.

'My grandfather used to tell me about these weird facts almost all the time.'

Suddenly, Aditya sat up straight his eyes wide as something struck him in his mind. He became motionless and his mind went through the pages of history of his childhood, the nights his grandfather had spent with him telling stories, which were both unique and intriguing. He regained his composure a few moments later and looked about.

'What is it dear? Why do you look so distraught?' the old lady asked.

'Oh, no. It's nothing. I just happened to remember something from my childhood, about my grandfather who passed away recently.'

'I'm sorry, dear. I didn't mean to intrude there.'

'It's okay. No worries.' Aditya said, putting on a smile.

The killer sped off from the place. He had heard all that he needed to. *Sanchi Stupa*, he thought to himself, *if I have heard it right, they're going to Madhya Pradesh*. He went straight to the brochure counter and located the brochure for Madhya Pradesh, places to see. One of the most famous one would be the Sanchi Stupa. He read through the article in the brochure concerning the Stupa. Finally he found what he needed. The closest airport was in Bhopal, Raja Bhoj Airport to be precise and Sanchi was an hour's drive from there with easily available car rentals from that airport.

He quickly booked his own ticket and sat down in a safe corner, maintaining quite some distance away from Aditya, to wait for his flight.

69

Back in Mumbai, the tech lead sat up after having spent almost an hour hunched down on his computer terminal and rubbed his hands in satisfaction. He had successfully located Rivannah, poked and sifted through all the files and now, probably he knew more about her than what she knew about herself. He now knew, apart from her home, starting from the hotels frequented and preferred, her best friends her favourite dishes, her favourite bands and musicians right to what colour she liked and which zodiac she belonged to, everything the internet had to offer.

It is surprising to actually know how much information the internet has and it is really interesting for those who know how to tap into it and sift through all the digital mess. It is a really time consuming process to clear all such digital mess and bring out all the web had about one single person among the several billion who are active and persistent users of the awesome technology. This was one of those few man made things that had gotten so intertwined in the human lives, that a world without it would now seem impossible and fictional.

He cracked his knuckles in satisfaction and e-mailed the entire document containing every pertinent detail he had found out about the girl to Avinash. He then picked up his phone and dialled Avinash's number. Avinash picked it after a several rings.

'I have sent you all the details of the girl named Rivannah Shah. You will know almost everything about her in the document. I trust that will fill your needs.'

'Very good. I will check into it shortly. Thank you for help, I really appreciate it.'

This was better than the last time. The tech lead smiled and hung up. Suddenly one of his juniors came up to him and said, 'Sir, I have some activity on Pravir's credit card.'

Avinash opened up the e-mail and went through the document he had been sent. Nothing was actually relevant to him except for the location of the girl named Rivannah Shah. That was all he needed. He found it on the second page of the document, copied it to his phone clipboard and sent that specific location and a picture of the girl to his team already set on standby in Mumbai. The team had been instructed to arrive at the location, do a reconnaissance of the area and kidnap the woman in the picture.

This was a quick in and out operation with nothing that could possibly go wrong with this plan.

70

Mubeen and Aditya sat down in their fortunately consecutive seats on the plane and latched on their seat belts and waited for the plane to leave the ground. A hostess come up to them and asked if they would like some drinks. Both of them politely refused, just asking for some juice. Soon, two of the hostess began motioning the instructions for the flight as the speakers rattled them off. The plane lurched a little and started moving towards its runway as directed by the air traffic control centre. It went through a series of turns and finally stopped in front of one. Several minutes later, the captain began addressing them as the plane began to pick up speed. Everything began to vibrate and the aircraft tore through the atmospheric hindrance and slowly losing the grip of gravity as its nose began to tilt upwards. Another tense minutes passed by and finally the plane corrected its course, set itself straight and smoothened out for the flight.

They unbuckled their seat belts and sat back for another long waiting period.

Several seats behind the duo sat the killer, hunched up on his seat, pretending to be asleep. He was going to follow them and he was going to make sure the Corporation doesn't come near enough to touch Aditya and also find what he sought.

'What happened to you while we were talking to the old couple? You seemed stunned, almost shocked.' Mubeen asked.

'I had a revelation. Not the spiritual kind but a revelation. I think I know what we're heading into. But I'm not sure if I should say it to you.'

'Why?'

'It's a kind of 'if I tell you I'd have to kill you' kind of thing, you know. A secret, sort of, that my grandfather had once told me about. Then, I had thought it was the stuff of imagination. But I'm having my doubts now. It seems all too real now.'

'You can tell me. What is it?'

'My grandfather had told me about a council of nine scholarly people that King Ashoka had made during his reign.'

'I know something, even though my knowledge of history is sketchy. Akbar made the council of Navratnas in his court not Ashoka. I know that much at least.'

'Yes. But what I am telling you is something you will never find in history textbooks. History textbooks say that Ashoka after his brutal massacre of the army of Kalinga, he was so distraught that he had adopted Buddhism and had given up all dreams of military conquests. But what has now become a sort of conspiracy theory for fanatics is that he created a council of Nine scholarly people. Their job was to research and accumulate all of the world's dangerous knowledge that might threaten the existence of humanity and store it somewhere safe away from human eyes to avoid the threat of extinction.'

'But, in my opinion, if there really is something out there, it hasn't been particularly responsible in its self-assumed role of protecting humanity from extinction. Even since 1942, countries are continuously spending more and more on defence budgets and stockpiling hundreds and thousands of nuclear armaments, a mere handful of which is actually required to wipe out life from the entire planet.'

'As I said, it is just a legend. I do not know about the presence of such an organisation. It is just a story that my grandfather had told me when I was a kid. Remember that letter that came along with the credit card?' Aditya asked, 'It said, *we trust this will fill your needs*. That set me thinking. And this time, I don't think I am too far off the point.'

'You're right about that, I guess. Nobody in their sane mind would write "*we*" instead of "*I*" to express the meaning unless it was meant to be so.'

'And also, every clue we have uncovered yet, right down to the one we're following now involves the presence of Ashoka somehow. The first one had a painting of the Kalinga war, a clear depiction. The second one in Kuldhara with the Paliwal Brahmins – significance of the name with the language and also the symbol of the inverted lotus. Everything thing links up to Ashoka. And now this, the Sanchi Stupa's initial version was made by Ashoka himself.'

Aditya suddenly looked towards Mubeen, his eyes wide with yet another revelation.

'What is happening to you? You're having your *Eureka* moments more frequently than hiccups today!'

'Well, I just realized something right now.'

'So did Archimedes, just a really long time back, mad enough to run naked through the streets to tell his king of the revelation he just had. Anyway, what is it?'

'Sanchi Stupa's initial version was made by Ashoka himself but it not anywhere close to what we see now. What looms before us now is actually the addition and stone veneering made during the Sanga rule which extended soon after the Mauryas.'

'Okay. So?' Mubeen asked, not entirely sure what that meant.

'So whoever put the clues didn't put them in while Ashoka or the Mauryan Empire was still up and about. It was done probably centuries later, maybe a millennium later, who knows? I'm beginning to feel that legends aren't always just legends. There might be some truth that probably exist even today right here amongst us. Who knows?'

'I don't know.' Mubeen said, abruptly ending the conversation. He finished up the remaining juice that the hostess had provided, made himself comfortable in the seat and dozed off as the evening sunset didn't provide for anything to look out to.

Only time would reveal what it has in store for them.

71

Just as Avinash finished instructing his team back in Mumbai about capturing the girl, another call came in. It was from his tech team leader.

'What is it again?'

'We have found some activity on Pravir's credit card.'

Avinash sat up. 'Go ahead.'

'A plane ticket was booked from Jaisalmer to Bhopal, Raja Bhoj Airport. I tracked down the ticket details and from the information I have, the plane is probably already in the air bound for Bhopal.'

'Damn it!' Avinash stamped his foot. If he had paid a little more attention in the airport, he might have downed all three of them at once. 'Get me a seat to the same location in the next flight that leaves from here right now!'

'Yes sir.'

Avinash hung up from the call and dialled another number. 'Sir, we have another lead.'

'What's that?'

'Pravir is travelling to Bhopal, Madhya Pradesh. Which I am inclined to believe in pursuit of Aditya and Mubeen. So, they're going there too. What should I do now? I am hopping onto the next flight that leaves out of here for Bhopal but what should I do once I reach there?'

'Do nothing. If you can track them down, simply follow them. Do not make any move to attract any attention, okay? They need to be at peace before we play our final card and turn the tables around, understood? You just keep them in your line of sight if you can, though it isn't a necessity.'

'Perfectly.'

'Good.'

Two hours later and a thousand kilometres away, Mubeen and Aditya got off their flight. Both of them had slept off during the flight and were now refreshed. They immediately booked a cabbie for their hour long drive to Sanchi. Evening had set in, slowly shading towards the night. They had grabbed quite a few snacks and drinks from the airport lounge with their seemingly unlimited credit limit.

They hopped into their cab and began devouring the stuff they had bought, garlic breads with extra cheese dips, slices of pizza and to top it all off with several doughnuts and two cans each of Mountain Dew.

Their hour long drive to Sanchi was going to be busy.

72

About three hours later, Avinash was fastening his seatbelt on the plane. The plane would reach in about two hours so that would leave him no time in the day for tracking them. It had to happen the next day.

He sat back, enjoying the cool conditioned air from the vents caress his face as he began thinking. Back in Mumbai, his team was going to break in and kidnap Rivannah about the same time he was to reach Madhya Pradesh. The attack had to happen in perfect coordination. While Rivannah stays in their custody, Aditya would throw up and spill his secrets all over and Mubeen wouldn't be able to do one damn thing about that.

An hour later, the duo reached Sanchi. They asked the driver to take them to a hotel close to the main tourist attraction site of the Stupa. The driver left them off and they checked into it, and sat down to wait till the next morning.

'Are you sure about this clue?'

'One hundred percent. There can be no mistake. Everything ties up perfectly.'

Mubeen opened up the piece of paper with the poem in it and laid it out flat on the table. 'Now to figure out one last part.'

An ancient monument is what you need to find,

Where the mounds and piles of bricks bury,

The ashes of enlightened one in repose,

When the sun reaches its closest zenith for the day, that which you seek rests

Beneath the shade of the torana of the Vidishas

'You said there are four gates around the Sanchi Stupa and the remaining space covered by a tall balustrade. Which one is this poem referring to?' Mubeen asked.

'Things become really sketchy here. I was planning to check out the area and find out under which gate our next clue lies.'

'But why?'

'Because most places say that the ruler had employed the ivory carvers of *Vidisha* to carve and sculpt the gateways. But there's also an inscription on the southern gateway that specifically says that only the northern gateway was built by them. It does not mention anything else about the others. So my guess would be the northern *torana*. But where is our clue going to be? We would look suspicious if we were to squat down and start digging the entire area around the *torana*.'

'I guess, since it is the time of noon, the sun will be right above us meaning that the shadow would almost be right under the *torana*.'

227

'You have a point.' Aditya said, nodding.

The killer's cab came to a halt in front of another hotel, but not the one Aditya and Mubeen and put up for the night. Whatever the option, he didn't care. There was only one place Aditya would go on the next day and he knew where.

He suddenly remembered the day he had killed the old man as he was unpacking. Even after his death, he had been leading his grandson more and more into the deadly maze evading the killer's grasp every single time. He had to admire that about the man. Even death couldn't stop him from keeping his legacy alive. But this time would be the last. He was going to end this once and for all. He would not let Aditya fall into his pitch black abyss of the Council of Nine. Aditya couldn't mingle in the dirty business of his lineage, of his descent.

Knowledge was something that every man and woman deserved and has every right to attain and assimilate. And nobody, not even God had the right to withhold knowledge from man, let alone some puny men scurrying through mortality believing something that is wrong and dying for that cause.

The killer knew something about Aditya that only he had known apart from late Mr. Harish Tiwari. And that secret would die along with him.

73

Rivannah was driving back from her grandfather's house, after having spent the entire evening with them. It had been one of her weekly routines; she came up to meet her grandfather and grandmother once every week. Suddenly her phone began ringing. Keeping her eyes on the road, she fished the phone out of her pocket and picked up the call.

'Hello?' she asked. In her answer to her utter dismay, some old item song began playing. It was a stupid advertisement call. Frustrated she hung up and threw the phone on the seat beside her. Just as the phone landed, a shot rang out and she felt one of her car's rear tyres burst. Her home was just around the corner of the street and her tyre had to burst at this time. She slowly brought the car to a halt.

Shaking her head, she unbuckled her seatbelt and stepped outside to assess the damage dealt. Modern tubeless tyres weren't supposed to cause a problem such as this. Her rear right tyre had gone completely flat, much to her surprise. The street lights were enough to tell her that this wasn't just some waylaid pin in the middle of the road but something far stronger, more potent.

Suddenly two flashlights switched on behind her, suddenly illumination up the scene in front of her. She turned around and the light instantly blinded her. He placed her hands over her eyes and said, 'Hey! Switch off that light.'

There was no response. The two flashlights remained there, their state unaltered. She tried moving forward and the lights suddenly switched off, plunging her into darkness yet again and again she was blind, this time in the dark. Now she began to feel frightened. *What is happening?* Rivannah thought to herself. She just stood, fixated in her place. Finally, when her pupils adjusted to the darkness, she saw something in front of her, right in front of her eyes, about a foot away.

It was a circular rusted thing with little symmetric perforations going all around and it had a tangy smell, the smell of gunpowder. To her horror, she finally realized it was a nozzle of a weapon. She shrieked and took a few steps back only for her to feel another cold metal nozzle press against the back of her neck. She turned around, horrified.

'What do you want?' she shouted, trying to get some attention of some passerby if her luck favoured her.

She saw two more men walk down the pathway on her right apart from the three around her. She shouted for help, frantically waving towards them. To her astonishment, they kept walking in their slow pace but right towards her. Realisation finally dawned upon her that they were not the usual passerby's. Rivannah tried to run in the opposite direction but just as she was about to do so, a cold hard hand gripped her shoulder. The strength was so great she wasn't even able to move under the grasp.

Finally, one of the men walked up to her and said calmly, 'Please, Miss Shah. We are not here to hurt you. Cooperate with us and you'll walk away from this mess without a scratch. I promise you. There's no hope for you to escape us if you try running, I can assure you that much.'

'What do you want?' she screamed.

'We want you.'

With that statement, something rose up within her. It was as if she had tapped into a store of all her womanly powers and she tore away from the grip that was restraining her and kicked him hard on the shins. The man didn't even wince. Unfazed, she landed another punch on the face which did seem to have some effect. The man took a step back from the impact but instantly regained his poise but didn't do anything to hurt her.

The man spoke up again, 'Miss Rivannah, these men are under strict orders not to hurt you. But if you provoke them into breaking their orders, nothing can stop me from disobeying those orders.'

'What do you want with me?'

'I'm not at liberty to answer that question, Miss Rivannah. You will have to come along with us to know.'

'What is this about? I'm not going along with you unless you tell me that.'

Brave girl, the man mused. He grunted and motioned to his men. Two of them stepped up and gripped her hands and the third brought out a black cloth and tied it around her mouth to prevent her from screaming. Then they pulled her down the road towards a small minivan that was waiting for them just around the corner. They pushed her inside and locked up the door behind her with three others inside along with her in the back. The two others climbed up into the front and they drove off.

Meanwhile all this, hearing the ruckus a nearby resident had called in the police. Several minutes later two Mahindra Scorpios drove into the scene. The landlady of the property facing the road came down as the police vehicles reach the location. Superintendent Ravi Tandon came up and asked the woman, 'What did you see here?'

'The thing that first struck me odd was a loud sound, like a shot ringing out. Naturally, I went to the window to investigate. I saw the young girl come out of her vehicle and looking down at the rear right tyre, so I presumed that her tyre had burst.'

'And that isn't entirely too far from the fact. Tyre bursts do sound something like that. Go on.'

'Yes. But then from this vantage point, I could see three men come up on her. And as far as I knew, the girl didn't notice them coming up until the last moment when two of them suddenly switched on their flashlights, probably to blind her, which they were successful in doing. I couldn't hear anything but her scream of protests. All of them had weapons in their hands and I cannot tell what kind but they seemed fearful. Two more men had come up from round that corner,' she said pointing towards the road, 'and started talking to her. I couldn't make out anything they said.'

'Anything else that you noticed seemed a little odd?'

'Everything seemed wrong. That's why I called the police.'

Ravi nodded and thanked curtly, before turning and walking towards the vehicle. It was a standard Audi 320d with one of its tyres completely flat. He squatted down and touched the rough fabric of the tyre, brushing his fingers over the little metal wires that were awkwardly sticking out from within. Suddenly he realized something. *This is a tubeless tyre; it isn't supposed to burst like this. These are built to last and hold out against a puncture.* This meant that either something like a bullet had struck the tyre or the tyre had been continuously used even after a puncture, a product of negligence.

Superintendent Ravi wasn't prepared to place his bets on the latter option. The lady had said that the men had weapons so a shot had been fired and a bullet or a casing might be found if the location is searched thoroughly.

Ravi stood up and called one of his deputies. 'Get me a profile on the number plate of the car. I want to know who the car belongs to. Also, search for a driver's license in the car. That would quicken up the search procedures.'

'Yes, sir.'

Several minutes later, his deputy came up to him and said, 'Sir. I have an ID. The driver's license has the name Rivannah Shah.'

'Get me everything you can find about her.'

74

Back in Sanchi, most of Mubeen's night had been spent cataloguing all his previous contacts and sending alerts to all he could trust about his new contact. And the remaining part of the night had been spent pondering over the turn of events.

He had been able to hold out against this unseen foe for this long but how much longer would he actually be able to? Their onslaughts were becoming more and more desperate and craftier than the last. Who knew what they were going to do next. Aditya's remaining family was there but they were well protected by the Mumbai police force, which comes in as perks of having a direct relative with lot of money and fame, naturally.

Several hours later, his phone with the new SIM card rang. That was puzzling. He had just sent out his contacts and who'd be desperate enough to call so quickly? He picked it up and the name on the screen was Ravi Tandon. Mubeen remembered after a moment, Superintendent Ravi Tandon, the one with whom he had solved his last case two months back involving the murderers, giving him so much popularity and fame. And Ravi was one of those few people who knew about his mission with Aditya. Trusting the right people always came to help in the right moments. Ravi Tandon was one of those kinds of people whom you could bank your trust upon blindly.

He picked it up and said, 'Hello? Ravi?'

'Yes, Mubeen. It is me. I know you're busy but I have a new case on my hands. Bother to listen? Your helpful suggestions could just make my day.' Ravi said from the other side.

'Sure, go ahead. I can't sleep anyway.'

'Well, a few hours back, at about in the night, a girl has been kidnapped in the most surprising manner. An old woman, the landlady of the property facing the road had called us up but we reached the scene a little late. There was a white Audi 320d in the middle of the road, and it was being driven by a twenty one year old girl named Rivannah Shah. We checked in with the parents and confirmed it. Every week, on this day she went to meet her grandfather and came back in the night.'

'Okay. Interesting.'

'Then we had a conversation with the lady who had witnessed it all. There were a total of five men that had approached the girl and talked to her. All the woman had been able to hear were the shrieks and shouts of the girl as she tried to flee. We checked in at the surrounding homes and several people reported hearing similar things. No male voice had been heard by anyone and they had weapons so nobody had dared approach the scene.

The lady explained to me in detail everything that happened. Three men first approached Rivannah and accosted her. Until then, she was unaware of their presence until suddenly they switched on their flashlights, probably to temporarily blind her, which they did. Then they switched off the lights, again to derange her from her position, and shrouded her in complete darkness. She was yet again blind just as her eyes were beginning to get accustomed to the light. She tried moving but they poked her with their guns.'

'I guess that was a scare tactic and so was the light show. Scare tactics like these tend to mentally scare people into doing the things they're not supposed to do in those situations, and also to force people into doing things they wouldn't usually do in their normal state of mind.' Mubeen said.

'Yes, I thought about that too. Any normal person would have their nerves frayed with a weapon pointed right at their faces. Then she began screaming out. I talked with the lady at depth later and she told me what she heard. Rivannah shouted out things like *what do want with me*. This case is looking really weird. No kidnapper would linger around any longer than what they should. But these people seem something else altogether.

The thing that struck me as odd was that the rear right tyre of the vehicle was punctured, the cause to which was unknown but it was the reason Rivannah had gotten out of the car to inspect the damage. The lady we talked to reported hearing a shot ring out and on seeing the girl inspecting the burst tyre, she assumed it was of a tyre burst, which I believe was a safe presumption.

But when I investigated it closely, I realized something obvious. The tyres were tubeless tyres, built to last and hold out for sometime before completely running out of air making it impossible to drive using those. But this tyre looked as if it had been shot at. We haven't found any casings from the location or the bullet but we're going to do a residue test as a last measure to my theory. What do you have to say?'

'Whoever did this executed the plan with flawless perfection, they left no traces behind. And as far as you've explained to me, if I'd be in your place, I would be waiting with a team of experts with the Rivannah's parents for the next call from the kidnapper for a ransom. I see no other way out of this.'

75

The night passed by uneventfully enough for Mubeen. They were safe enough, for now. Their pursuers had no idea of their present location. Soon, Mubeen dozed off for the last remaining hours till dawn.

He had no idea how wrong he was, yet again. Their pursuers were close, but not enough. They were safe, but not safe enough.

The killer sat up in his bed, sweat pouring out of every pore in his body. He had begun to have nightmares. All the people he had killed, those were taking their toll on him. Killing a person is not really an easy job. Pulling a trigger of a gun is easy, but when you come to terms with the fact that the consequence of pulling that trigger might instantly kill somebody is a pressure that is really difficult to handle. And then when you see the mutilated corpse in front of you, totally limp, probably bent at an unnatural angle, it can literally scare everything out of you.

But he had endured it all. The only thing he couldn't endure was the fact that Aditya was under imminent threat from two directions, the Corporation and his blind quest for the Council of the Nine. He had to stop Aditya. But what could he say? That he had murdered his beloved grandfather in cold blood? That would be the worst kind of punishment Aditya could suffer.

The killer had thought of suicide as an option but it didn't solve the problem. There was only one thing that solved the problem. He had to get the clues laid down by Aditya's grandfather at all costs before Aditya himself would get to those. That way, neither Aditya would get any portion of it nor would the Corporation. It would be returned to the where it belonged. To the people. And the internet made things a lot easier.

And, he thought, *if it came to such a point. I'm ready to divulge all my dark secrets just to save Aditya from that horrible world.*

The killer had made up his mind. He would silently follow Aditya and Mubeen into their next clue and somehow snatch the next clue away from them. That way, Aditya would be forced to resign back to his home, oblivious of the reality and he would achieve his objective and prevent it from getting into the hands of the Corporation. He just couldn't let that happen.

He couldn't think of a plan to do what he intended to do. But he was fine with that however. This time, he was prepared to go with the flow and act as the situation presents itself in front of him.

76

The morning sun rose up from the horizon, washing onto the bustling landscape of the region. Mubeen awoke early after a fitful sleep followed by Aditya. The ordered breakfast to their room and began munching down meaty delicacies after a long while.

While eating, Aditya asked with his mouth full of food, 'Whom were you talking to last night?'

'Superintendent Ravi Tandon, an old friend of mine. He just had a new case of kidnapping of a girl in Mumbai and he can't make any head or tail of the case. So he called me up.'

'Oh, okay. Who's kidnapped, by the way?'

'Some girl named Rivannah Shah.' Mubeen said, concentrating on his food. Suddenly he heard a loud clang as the fork struck the bone china plates. Mubeen looked up to find the horrified face of Aditya, his eyes wide, his mouth open.

'You know her?' Mubeen asked concerned, setting his own plate aside. 'Are you alright Aditya? If you know something, you need to tell me now.'

'It's them!' Aditya said hoarsely.

'What do you mean Aditya?' Mubeen said.

'It's them, those people who are trying to get to us and kill us.'

'Aditya tell me, what relationship do you have with Rivannah?'

Aditya turned to face the window, his face forlorn. 'She's the love of my life and now they have her. What are they going to do to her?'

Mubeen was shocked. Their pursuers had crossed every reasonable line there was in order to catch them. This was way beyond their league. This had to stop, now.

Mubeen jumped up from his sofa and grabbed his back. He opened it up and pulled out the phone he had snatched out of that man's pocket back in Kuldhara. A plan was already forming in his mind. He held the phone in his hand and pondered over the consequences of his plan, the things that could go wrong. They had thrown away their old numbers so there was no way for their pursuers to contact or track them down. The only way that was possible was to switch on the phone. But that involved a risk of letting them know of their current location. It was a risk that had to be taken.

Rivannah's life was in danger; it wasn't just a kidnapping for ransom money. It was bait designed to taunt and weaken Aditya and make him do their bidding. But he couldn't let that happen. Aditya had to finish the mission his grandfather had set him on and along with that Rivannah's life had to be saved. Things were getting more and more twisted as time progressed. God knew what else their pursuers had up their sleeves.

First things first, he picked up his own phone and dialled Superintendent Ravi's phone. It rang twice before it was picked up. 'Hello? Mubeen?'

'Yes, this is me. I have some news. Disastrous news. Rivannah is

Aditya's girlfriend.'

'Aditya? Aditya Tiwari?'

'Yes.'

'So? This isn't a Bollywood scene where the lover leaves behind the police investigation and goes on to hunt the kidnapped woman, kill the kidnapper and ending with a flowery romantic scene. This is reality.'

'I know. But reality is even worse than you think. You don't yet know the entire story of Aditya.'

'What do you mean?'

And Mubeen told him the entire story, of how Aditya receives a clue from his dead grandfather which throws him into a treacherous clue hunt jumping about in the country followed by trained mercenaries whose orders probably were to shoot to kill. He told him how he had been able to hold them off till now and now this.

'This is not a ransom money kidnapping.' Mubeen said, ending his story. 'This is a purposeful and deliberate attempt to use Rivannah as leverage to influence Aditya and coerce him into doing the things they want him to do.'

'But who's *they* you're talking about? I don't get it.'

'That's the part even we don't get. We still don't know who our pursuers are and what they want to achieve. The only thing I do know is that they want to kill him, their efforts have demonstrated that much pretty clearly till now.'

'So what do you propose we do right now?' Ravi asked.

77

Avinash bolted up in his bed as his phone began ringing. He picked it up and looked at the number. It was from his team in Mumbai. In anticipation and excitement, he got off his bed and picked up the call, enjoying the morning sun. 'Hello?'

'Mission successful, sir. Miss Rivannah Shah is in our custody.'

'Treat her well, alright? Give her food to eat, water, anything she asks for except her freedom.'

'She is demanding the reason why we've kidnapped her.'

'Brave girl.' Avinash said. 'Don't tell her anything.'

'Okay.'

Avinash hung up and instantly dialled another number. He had to inform him about this. 'Hello?' he said into the phone.

The head of the Corporation just said, 'Yes, Avinash.'

'We have her.'

'Good.'

'But the question is, how do we get this news to them? My tech team has been tracing and following their phone but for some time, they haven't even popped up on our radar. Our best guess is that they've bought new SIM cards to replace the old ones. There's no way of knowing their new numbers now. Unless they decide to call us directly and that is a highly unlikely option.'

'Why do you need phone numbers when you have news channels? The media will do the job of telling them of the news. You stay put for now. And they know how to contact you.'

'How's that?'

'They have your phone. They might not be able to operate it but I reckon Mubeen is smart enough to have realized by now what kind of a phone that is so the moment he switches it on, your tech team can handle it from there. They can easily track your phone's location. I believe you team is already there, right?'

'En route.'

'Okay. They'll get the news soon and as soon as they try to communicate through your phone, get a location on them and get a hold of them. Then once you have them, you can dispose of Mubeen the way you see fit. We need Aditya only. There should not be a scratch on him otherwise we wouldn't be able to squeeze a word out of him. Understood?'

'Yes sir.'

78

'That's the part I'm unsure about.' Mubeen said. 'Here I have Aditya who's already out of his wits and without which he cannot complete the hunt his grandfather had entrusted him to do.'

'Why's that so important?' Ravi asked.

'Even I don't know. I just know that it has a huge significance because Aditya's pursuers are becoming more and more desperate to end the chase and kidnapping Rivannah had been one of their boldest steps. A part of your force is protecting the Tiwari family so they couldn't touch any of his family members. So they picked up the next option they had.'

'His girlfriend.'

'Yes. I have a plan to contact our pursuers but I have no idea what I'm going to talk about with those killers. They cannot contact us because I have dumped our old SIM cards and replaced them with new ones which only a few of you know and I trust you won't share it with anybody.'

'You have my promise. But what if they track you down? They would naturally expect you to contact them.'

'I have a plan that takes care of that. But the question is how do I free Rivannah and at the same time have Aditya me to complete his grandfather's last wish before dying. Or rather, his last wish *after* dying.'

Suddenly Mubeen felt a hand on his shoulder. He turned around to see the tear streaked face of Aditya, his eyes bloodshot. 'I'll talk to you later, Ravi.' Mubeen said, hanging up.

'I'm going to give myself up, Mubeen. Thank you for all you've done for me but I cannot let Rivannah get hurt just because me. I cannot let that happen. I know just thank you are two really simple little words with little effect but that is all I have now.'

'Even I won't let anything happen to Rivannah, but you can't turn yourself in to them. We can think of something to free her. Trust me.'

'I'm tired of this, Mubeen. I've had enough. I'll tell them whatever they require of me. I don't care about my grandfather's last wish. All I care is that I do not want others whom I love to get hurt because of me.'

Mubeen firmly gripped Aditya shoulders and shook him. 'Aditya! Snap out of your delusions! Do you think they're going to let her go even if you turn yourself in? Probably they'll kill both of you. Would you like that?'

Aditya's head dropped down and he walked away. This was going to be really difficult for him.

'Aditya! We have to visit that Stupa now. We need the next clue in our hands.'

Aditya whipped around, the expression in his eyes ferocious. 'You think I'm going to go hunting for a stupid clue now after all this? Rivannah is their hostage and you want me to find another petty riddle buried ten feet under the ground?'

'That is the thing that might save her, Aditya. You need forgo your emotions and think clearly. I know the decision is tough but it is the only leverage we have against whoever has kidnapped Rivannah. You need to understand that.'

'The only thing I understand and see it now is that Rivannah is their hostage and the only one option I have to save her is to give myself up and tell them everything they require of me. I will not watch her suffer because of me knowing the fact that I could have prevented that.'

'Trust me they don't have the audacity to do that. If the police got its hands on some definitive proof that Rivannah had been hurt somehow, they won't survive. And it wouldn't serve their purpose if they were to hurt her. Their only purpose is to capture you and make you a puppet in their hands and we yet don't know the consequences of that happening. So you need to calm down a little bit and think over your decisions one more time.'

'What help would that do? God knows how many more clues my grandfather has scattered all over the country and by then, who knows what will happen to Rivannah.'

'You just cannot do that, Aditya. You had appointed me for this job two weeks back and I intend to see you through it safe and sound. I cannot let anything happen to you and you know that very well.'

Aditya said nothing and walked away. This was becoming really difficult for him. Things were turning out well.

Several minutes later, Aditya walked up to Mubeen and asked quietly, 'What do you plan to do next?'

Mubeen sat up, 'We find this clue and we call them.'

'Can't they track us down like that? I mean, using that phone is a big risk.'

'I have a plan to handle that situation. Now first let's get ourselves to the monument and get whatever petty thing is waiting for us buried ten feet beneath the ground.'

'What about Rivannah?'

'They can't reach us in any way. I took care of that. So they'll now probably expect us to hear the news from somewhere and try to contact them ourselves, which is a big risk but we have no other option now, do we?'

'Right.'

79

The killer walked about near the monument, pretending to look at the impressive structure of ancient India but actually looking out for two faces amongst the dense crowd. It was still late in the morning yet the swarm of humanity was unending. He had come here long back, just as the authorities had throws open the area for visitors, fearing Mubeen and Aditya might try to do something early. Till now, his search had been futile. He kept his cool instead of being frustrated for losing them yet again and kept searching.

It went on almost up to the afternoon when he began to finally acknowledge his frustration of having lost them, yet again. He couldn't help but think, *why aren't they showing up?* After having done several reconnaissance tours of the entire park consisting of several temples and Stupas, he finally positioned himself neat the entry, to catch them when they entered.

Finally his hard work paid off as he noticed Mubeen paying his entry fee at the gate. But he was surprised to find that he was alone. Aditya was not along with him. His palpitations began to rise in desperation as Mubeen entered and walked towards the main attraction, the Sanchi Stupa without Aditya along with him. Suddenly then, he found Aditya standing in queue far in the back, his face betraying every glint of despair and anguish. He was a forlorn figure trudging along in the sea of humanity. He paid his money and walked towards the same attraction site.

The killer then realized it was a standard procedure to avoid suspicion in a public place, probably the brainchild of Mubeen. He was glad Mubeen was there with Aditya else everything would have ended a long time back and things would have been worse, much worse. He began following Aditya, keeping a standard of at least eight to ten people in between so in case he decided to turn around, it would be much harder for him to recognize his uncle in the crowd. Suddenly, he noticed a pen like thing partially sticking out of Aditya's rear pocket. It was perfectly cylindrical but it looked far from anything that resembles a pen. It was probably the clue they found in Rajasthan.

He looked around in the crowd and found what he was looking for. A thin scruffy little boy with another younger kid were milling about in the crowd. They had probably sneaked in and the ancient structure almost obviously held no fascination for them. They needed something that he had a lot of. He looked in their direction until their eyes met and he motioned for the older kid to come up. The kid came up and smiled, and said, '*Namaste sahib!*'

The killer pulled out two crisp hundred rupee notes from his pocket and handed it to him. Ten excited fingers curled around the notes firmly as the killer left those and he pocketed them. Then the killer whispered to him what had to be done and smiled. The boy nodded and went off in Aditya's direction, slipping in and out effortlessly through the crowd. From his vantage point, the killer could clearly see Aditya slowly closing in on Mubeen and the boy darting towards him. The crescendo rose and the boy finally reached Aditya and stood right behind him and looked around casually.

The killer smiled. The boy was good, probably a street professional. Then, rather unexpectedly he twisted around swiped up the cylindrical object from Aditya's pocket with a unique agility distinctive to his age and came running back towards him, the prize in his hands.

Aditya reached up to Mubeen and said, 'Do you remember the last line of the poem?'

'No. You have the poem right?'

'Yes.' Aditya said, his hand reaching out to his pocket only to find it empty. He awkwardly turned his head around to look at his back pocket just to be sure. It was gone!

'I've lost it! Or maybe it had been stolen.' Aditya said, 'Damn! Why do all the bad things have to happen on the same day?'

Mubeen impassively looked ahead, saying nothing. Aditya was becoming more and more like the typical female protagonists of Indian serial shows of the past decade who cried at the littlest and the pettiest of issues inflicted upon them by their mother-in-laws.

'But bearing in mind this premise, I had made a copy which I have in my pocket. And presto! Here it is!' Aditya said, pulling out his prize.

'I knew it.' Mubeen said, as impassive as before.

An ancient monument is what you need to find,

Where the mounds and piles of bricks bury,

The ashes of enlightened one in repose,

When the sun reaches its closest zenith for the day, that which you seek rests

Beneath the shade of the torana of the Vidishas

'*Beneath the shade of the torana of the Vidishas.* Okay. Now do you remember what I had said about Japanese *tors* resembling our *toranas*? Well, cast a careful look at the architraves between the two posts. If you look at traditional *tors*, you'll see the similarity. They look pretty much the same; the only little ignorable difference might be that our architraves do not curve out whereas theirs do.'

Mubeen just nodded, looking about for any suspicious activity. 'Let's go find it.'

80

The killer looked at the object. It was peculiar, made completely of sandstone with a symbol etched on top. The unmistakable *dharmachakra* of Ashoka. The word itself was so ironic. He fiddled with it and finally noticed the line that ran around the body. He pulled from one side and inverted the other and a piece of paper dropped out. He instinctively looked up, locating the place Aditya and Mubeen were minutes earlier but now were gone.

They probably had a copy of the poem and were still on their track. Also, they might have already figured out the clue in the poem. He had expected something else to pop out, something that would stop them in their tracks. Probably they had made a copy, or possibly have it all mugged up. The situation was far from over. He still had to follow them. *But where the hell are they?*

Mubeen and Aditya walked up to the northern gate of the Sanchi Stupa. Mubeen couldn't help but admire the superior craftsmanship and the intricate designs that adorned the *torana*. The architraves balanced over the two pillars showed several cohesive images all combined into one.

'Hey, what do these pictures mean?'

'I cannot say for sure which is which but sources say that some depict tales from the Jataka tales inspired from Gautama Buddha's stories, some others depict scenes from his own personal life giving anecdotes for one and all.'

'Interesting.'

'You know? I am having a feeling of something déjà vu, like I've already been here, a very long time back.'

'Really. Good, then this one must be easy to find. Past life moment recollections are pretty accurate, I guess.'

Aditya looked at Mubeen, his expression sour. 'I'm not talking about past life. I'm talking about this. I feel like I've been here as a kid.'

'Hopefully with your grandfather.'

Aditya turned to Mubeen, this time his face displaying a look of ecstasy mixed with sadness. 'You're right! I had been here with my grandfather when I was about six or seven I guess. Right after my parents died in that plane crash. He had said something to me, standing right here. I still remember the view I had.' Suddenly, Aditya sat down on the rocky pavement leading up to the northern gateway of the Stupa.

'What are you doing?' Mubeen asked, surprised at his odd behaviour.

Aditya's eyes were gleaming. He stood up and sped forward and stood about two feet away from the gate and again squatted down and looked up, moving his head here and there, trying to get some kind of view that nobody else around him were which made him stick out like a sore thumb. A few kids walking by him holding their parents' hands giggled at his ridiculous movements but Aditya was in his own world, too involved to care about these things.

'What are you doing, Aditya?'

'When I was a kid, my grandfather had brought me here.'

'You've already said that. Tell me something new.'

'That day, we had stood right here between these two rounded rocks on either side and he had asked me to remember the place from where I would be able to see the *chatravali* surrounded by the *harmika* on top of the Stupa through the opening between the second and the third architrave of the northern gateway!'

Mubeen looked up in shock. Aditya was right. 'But I don't understand.'

'See. There were three architraves that went across and there were smaller vertical ones forming a sort of crisscrossing on the architraves. On this particular gateway, there were three architraves and the horizontal gaps between the each of the architraves was equally divided into four segments using three vertical pieces, creating a total of eight spaces like that, four between the first and the second and the other four between the second and the third. Now, out of all such gaps one was empty, the rest were filled with designs of men riding atop elephants and horses. Now do you get it?'

Mubeen was awestruck.

'Now, sit down like me, bring your height to about an average six year old kid and try to see through the opening and find the *chatravali*.'

'What's a *chatravali*?'

'It's that disk shaped thing on top of the Stupa surrounded by the railing known as the *harmika*.'

'Okay. I can see it.'

'My grandfather had asked me to remember this place.'

Mubeen looked down and then looked at his watch. It was about fifteen minutes past noon and the sun had begun its slight descent onto the western horizon. There was a shadow that fell very close to his feet, almost right on top. 'See, the poem matches the description too. I'm noticing this about fifteen minutes late but still the shadow wouldn't have moved much from this place in that time.'

'Yes!'

'The question is, do we dig up now? That would look pretty suspicious with such a crowd around us. The last thing I want is to have a team from the terrorist squad hunting us down too.'

81

There they were! Aditya was chattering excitedly while Mubeen was sitting down on the ground in front of the northern gate of the Stupa, moving his head here and there, probably trying to find something. A moment later, he stopped moving and sat fixated at something up at the Stupa, probably the tip with the metal circular disks. *What on earth are they doing?*

He wanted to do something but he was out of ideas. There was no stopping Aditya and Mubeen. They were just too persistent.

'I'm guessing our next clue is under this slab of rock here, because this is where you have to stand to get that perfect angle to look through.'

'I don't know.' Aditya said, losing his initial enthusiasm as his mind drifted back to Rivannah in captivity. Who knew what they were doing with her.

'Come on, Aditya, think! You cannot afford to get distracted now.'

'I said I don't know!'

Mubeen knew there was nothing he could do to help Aditya at the moment. He was too consumed by grief to think straight. He had to figure this one out by himself. Somehow. He looked down at the tile and carefully ran his eyes over the contours. He didn't have to be a historian or an archaeologist to know that if there had been anything written on the upper face of the rock, it wouldn't have survived a year, with the amount of human footsteps trampling all over the place. He carefully studied the edges of the tile, the corners rounded and worn smooth with the passage of time. It looked nothing out of the ordinary, broken edges and specks of red spittle from the mouths of senseless travellers unwittingly destroying their own cultural heritage.

He looked up at the stone gateway, then at the Stupa. Nothing seemed to make sense to him. He squatted down and ran his fingers over the tile, trying to feel the edges, rubbing our mud from the edges.

'When you're trying to find something but you don't know what that *something* is, finding that something can be exceptionally difficult. Unless of course if your luck favours you and you accidentally stumble upon it, things become a lot easier. You know that Aditya, don't you?' Mubeen said.

'Trying to find some stupid piece of paper written a hundred years back is even more difficult when you know for a fact that someone you love is in the hands of someone trying to kill you for quite some time. I hope you get that Mubeen.'

The mud gave way to Mubeen's prying fingers as he tried to feel something that might seem out of the ordinary. Suddenly, he found a gap into which he could slip his fingers in. He gripped it and gave a hard tug. Nothing happened.

'Hey, I think I found something.' Mubeen said.

Aditya, despite his anxiousness rushed over to have a look. There was a ridge that rang diagonally across the rock. Mubeen looked around, to see if there were any inquisitive travellers interested in their find. Finding none so, he gave another tug and the top of the rock tile came off along the diagonal line. There was mud underneath. These were supposed to be solid rocks but here this one was a thin plate over more mud. Something was sticking out right at the centre of the place. Aditya gingerly gripped it and pulled it out. It was yet another cylindrical object, probably with another piece of paper inside.

Looking around, finding no suspicious onlookers in range, Aditya pocketed the object, this time more carefully than the last and Mubeen replaced the rock in its rightful place. Both of them got up, dusted their hands and went off towards the exit. They had yet another work to do.

The killer cursed himself for not thinking of something. They had their next clue and he had no idea what it was and there was no possible way to follow them. He had been overtaken, yet again. And he couldn't do anything about it.

82

The man at the head of the Corporation tapped his fingers on the mahogany table in front of him. When were they going to call? Weren't they taking a little too much time to respond to such news? Even if Aditya had no relationship with Rivannah except that of friendship, he would be scared and would do something.

Also, the killer had gone off the radar for quite a while. He had stopped keeping tabs on him after they last dispute. He picked up his phone and dialled Avinash's tech team leader.

'Hello? Any news on Aditya and Mubeen?'

'No sir. They're still invisible. But our team along with Avinash is ready to pounce the moment they decide to call. From the looks of it, they are using some other source of money that we don't know about. We have all of their official ones under our radar and none of those are being used. But they still are on the run. I don't think they're carrying so much cash. They surely have some outside help.'

'You're right. I hadn't thought about that. Anything else?'

'No.'

'Good. Another thing, if you could manage it, tell me where Pravir is. It has been some time since we last talked.'

'Oh, he's in Sanchi too, didn't you know?'

The man's eyes widened. Pravir was still trailing Aditya and Mubeen to locate the clues so that he couldn't be able to get his hands on them. Secret source of money for the duo. Pravir following them. What was happening? Why were the things again beginning to seem not what they are actually supposed to look like?

'Okay,' he said hurriedly, 'thank you.'

The man hung up and dialled Avinash. It was immediately picked up. 'Why didn't you tell me Pravir is in Sanchi too?'

'I didn't think it was of much significance. What can he do? He has no resources, no backup after he drifted away from the Corporation. You know that.'

'Don't underestimate Pravir. He is intelligent as he is persistent. He won't stop until his objective is achieved.'

Mubeen now set about doing what he had promised. He bought a pair of walkie-talkies from a local electronic store. He also bought a roll of tape, a pair of scissors, a couple of batteries for the walkie-talkies and a set of binoculars. Back in their hotel, Mubeen reviewed his plan while inspecting his props to put up for the show.

'What do you plan to do with these?' Aditya asked.

'Wait and watch.'

Mubeen picked up one of the walkie-talkies and tuned it to a particular frequency and handed it to Aditya. He picked up the second one and again tuned it to the same frequency. He then pressed the button and made a sound which instantly croaked out of the other device. Aditya shook his head, trying to understand what Mubeen had in mind.

He then tore open the tape and wound it tightly around one of the walkie-talkies, pressing onto the button to the microphone at the bottom. Then from his backpack, he pulled out the phone they had obtained and pocketed it. He didn't want to switch it on right now.

'Now, here's the thing. You will go to the ceiling of the building next to this hotel and wait for further instructions okay? In the meantime, I will go to the next building across the road there and set things up, alright? You will have to do me a favour and carry my luggage along with yours since I have to do the running, I cannot afford the extra luggage.'

'Okay. But I still don't understand what you're planning to do. Walkie-talkies? Are we playing a game here?'

'Trust me, I'm playing anything but a game here. You want to hear news about Rivannah? Just wait and watch.'

Both of them left the room together, crossed the reception area and stepped onto the pavement. The afternoon heat was suddenly blistering even in December. They stared walking in opposite direction. Aditya reached his target building first and quickly made his way to the top and waited. He placed the binoculars to his eyes and watched the ceiling of the building in front of him. A minute later, Mubeen emerged from a door and began setting his things up.

He spoke through the walkie-talkie, 'Hey, Aditya. Can you hear me?'

'Loud and clear. But I still don't understand where you're going with all this.'

'I'm buying us some time. This way, we'll be able to communicate but they won't be able to immediately track us down, they'll probably track down the phone location but they won't have our actual location. In that intermediate period of confusion and disparity among them, we'll have a lead. Saw it once on a Liam Neeson movie. Let's try that in real for a change.'

He first found a solid place on which he could place his props. Then, he switched on the phone and placed it leaning against a wall. He then placed the walkie-talkie just beside it, tilted at an angle such that the voice from the phone can be transmitted through walkie-talkie to Aditya.

'Sir! Your phone is back on the radar. They have switched it on.'

Avinash hastily got up from his seat and spoke, 'Call up that phone and patch me through on that line so that I can talk to him.'

'Alright sir.'

Just as he finished adjusting the walkie-talkie, the phone began ringing. Mubeen smiled and said, 'Looks like they're in a hurry. Aditya, I'm going to pick up the call and you start talking. We don't want them to get suspicious of our plot so easily.'

'Okay, go ahead.'

Mubeen picked up the call and the line connected. Then he ran.

Immediately, back on the computers in Mumbai, they had a specific location on their map. 'They've picked up the call. Patch it up to Avinash's current phone now!' the tech lead shouted.

Back in Sanchi, Avinash's phone began ringing. He knew it was the call that he had been patched into. So he started talking. 'Well. I hope this is Aditya on the line, am I right?'

'Yes. Why have you kidnapped Rivannah? You have a rivalry towards me. Why involve her?' Aditya asked, grimly.

'Ah! I like that, straight to the point. No pleasantries. My name is Avinash, by the way. I'm pleased to meet you. I couldn't introduce myself the last time we met so I had to go through the formalities before coming to business.'

'I don't have time for pleasantries. What do you want me to do?'

Mubeen came to a halt panting like a thirsty dog just behind Aditya as he was talking into his walkie-talkie. He knew his elaborate set up would buy him a couple of minutes at the most. Just as he reached, he heard the man on the other side say, 'Ah! I like that, straight to the point. No pleasantries. My name is Avinash, by the way. I'm pleased to meet you. I couldn't introduce myself the last time we met so I had to go through the formalities before coming to business.'

'I don't have time for pleasantries. What do you want me to do?' Aditya replied.

'Nothing too difficult, at least the cost of Rivannah's life is far greater than what you're trying to achieve roaming about in the country. Why don't you give up all you have and we'll let you go free, along with your Rivannah. You just have to give up all you've found so far along with Mubeen.'

Mubeen could see Aditya was beginning to break down. He had to take over immediately. He went in front of him and asked for the walkie-talkie. Aditya shook his head, saying a simple no.

'What are you doing?' Mubeen whispered. 'We don't have time to waste now! They'll be upon us any minute now. Let me do the talking and you do the clue hunting.'

From the other side, Avinash asked, 'What is it, Aditya? Why are you not saying anything? Are you surprised by my graciousness?'

Aditya handed over the walkie-talkie to Mubeen who took it and said, 'I'm sorry, what did you just say?'

'Ah, the great Mubeen Roy at last! You still have to pay me for the phone you have in your hand right now, you know that right? And it is not money that I seek. I seek revenge for the humiliation that you caused.'

'Alright. Come and take it. Just let Rivannah go. She has no involvement in this. She shouldn't be hurt in our fight.'

'But you see the world isn't made of only roses and sunflowers. That cannot happen until you give up all the clues you two have found or take Rivannah's corpse to the morgue. Your choice.'

Mubeen could feel his temper rising. 'Avinash, you don't know whom you're pitching a fight with. You're going to pay with your life if Rivannah gets even a mere scratch or a bruise on her.'

'You see, we are the ones making the deal here okay? So if you don't comply with us, scratches and bruises on her body would be the least of your worries, I can assure you that. That is why I wanted to talk to Aditya. He is so much calmer and intelligent person who knows what the right thing to do in a situation like this is.'

Mubeen could see Aditya's expression becoming more and more

obscure. He could no longer tell what was going on in his mind.

The man sitting beside Avinash spoke up in hushed tones. 'Sir, I have a location.'

Avinash cupped the phone's receiver with his left hand and whispered, 'Take us there quickly. I don't think I can hold them off for any longer.'

'Yes sir.'

'Your empty threats do not frighten me, Avinash. We all know what happened in Kuldhara. How you humiliated yourself. That's what you're capable of. Now why don't we fight like men and leave innocent people out of this mess?'

Avinash paused for a while. Mubeen smiled. He had been successful in irking him. Irking an enemy is one of the best tactics to have a situation in your control even when the opponent seems to have an upper hand. It makes them take wrong decisions at the wrong time. Taunting can work miracles. He wished a miracle would happen for him too. He looked over the ledge behind which they were hiding and saw two black vehicles come to a stop in the middle of the road. This time, a team of seven people jumped out of the vehicles but didn't have any big weapons. Probably they didn't want to hit the news every time they made an appearance.

All of them looked about and then went into the building above which Mubeen had put up the show.

'Mubeen, you don't know whom you're playing your game with.' Avinash said and hung up. He ran up the stairs of the building, checking each and every door in vain. This way, they reach the top floor, tired frustrated and irritated. 'WHERE THE HELL ARE THEY?'

His men remained quiet. 'We check every floor, every home yet he is not here!' Avinash pulled out his phone and dialled his teach team leader. The man on the other side picked up immediately. 'Where are they? I am standing on the top floor of this building after checking each and every flat here and they aren't here. Where are they?' he shouted into the phone.

'They location hasn't changed. They're still there in the building somewhere.'

Suddenly, one of his men pointed to the door leading to the ceiling and said, 'I think that's the only place they might be. It's the only place we haven't checked out yet.'

Avinash hung up and ran up the stairs. He kicked the door and it flew off, breaking away from its hinges. He walked out through the door out into the open. There was nobody around.

'There's no use hiding Mubeen. We're here now and you have nowhere to flee.' But his words were met with the open skies and deaf walls. Suddenly he noticed two black objects in one corner of the ceiling. He ran towards it.

In the meantime, Mubeen and Aditya were running down from their perched location atop the building. Mubeen, just for an added cosmetic effect placed the other walkie-talkie on the ledge they were hiding behind, just to show the fool how foolish he actually was.

Avinash came to a stop right in front of it and was horrified by the utter simplicity of the plan that Mubeen had employed to deceive him. They were actually somewhere else, talking through the walkie-talkie and his old phone was here, set on loudspeaker.

Suddenly, he realized something. They couldn't be too far away from here. Walkie-talkies usually don't have so much of a range. He looked around, scanning the rooftops of the buildings around him. The building on their right across the road seemed the most probable, it was the closest. He ran towards that ledge and tried peering across to find something.

On the ledge there, sat a solitary walkie-talkie.

He looked down from the ledge and saw two people with bags on their backs getting into one of their cars parked below the building. They got in, started the vehicle and rode away.

'Go after them!' Avinash shouted to his men. They all began marching downwards.

Avinash couldn't believe himself. Mubeen was literally mocking him every time they came close to encountering each other. He went over to the place where the phone and the other walkie-talkie were kept. Underneath the phone was a little folded piece of paper. He picked it up. It was a little note.

Thank you for loaning us the phone. Just wanted to say it again, why don't we keep innocents out of this game?

83

'What are you doing Mubeen? They might just go up and kill Rivannah for all we know.' Aditya exclaimed.

'They won't dare.'

'And now you've given up the only thing we had of theirs.'

Mubeen looked towards him and smiled. 'Do I look so stupid to you?'

'What? No. But, what you did-'

'I did what I did because I had a plan in place. I thought it was time to end this mess once and for all.' Mubeen cut in.

'Care to share?'

'Well. It's a long story. The thing is back in Jaisalmer, I had copied down the number of Avinash's phone when I had taken it to a local electronic store where my main purpose had been to buy new SIM cards. It was there I found out that the phone was bugged. That was when a plan began forming in my mind but I had kept it aside when I realized they might try and call you. I had little time to think after I stopped you from talking to your uncle. We were on our heels running to the airport, then the flight to Bhopal during which I was too tired to even talk. But then, yesterday close to midnight, one of my old partners called me. Superintendent Ravi Tandon and told me he had a new case, the kidnapping that had happened a few hours before of Rivannah Shah. At that time, I didn't know she was your girlfriend.

But then, your reaction on hearing the news made me remember the plan that had been lying stagnant in my brain. It was then I began thinking. All the time at the Sanchi Stupa, I was planning. I had already set this plan into motion when we were on our way to the monument. I had called Ravi and asked him to do me a favour and track Avinash's number.'

'What good would that do? Avinash might not even use it anymore.'

'Right. But, he called on this number using a new number. Sophisticated systems now allow us to tap in and know which number is calling our target number. So technically, Ravi has Avinash's new number too and is probably monitoring it too. So the cards are in our hands now. Now, I believe Avinash is not acting on his own. I believe he has a boss over him who communicates with him and gives him orders. He is too dumb to be doing all of this on his own. Now, using the exact same technique used before, Ravi can monitor the calls coming in and going out of Avinash's new number thus he has unlimited access to all the numbers Avinash communicates with and one of which would be the boss. We can then tap into the lines and know exactly who he is talking to, where he is talking from and what is he talking about. So technically, Avinash has fallen into our trap and he is unaware that he is inadvertently working for us and he would be the cause of his own demise, not just in physical terms.'

Aditya looked out of his window, absentmindedly gazing at the passing vehicles. All that information was spinning his brain. He exhaled heavily, shook his head and said in answer was this. 'Damn.'

84

Avinash dialled the head of the Corporation. It was immediately picked up.

'Let me guess, Mubeen escaped yet again,' a condescending voice spoke from the other side, 'you're beginning to irritate me now.'

'Yes.' Avinash replied.

'And you attribute that failure to...?'

'I don't know.'

'I'm giving you one last chance. Get Aditya for me, alive. Do it any way you see fit.'

'Yes sir.'

85

Superintendent Ravi stood before a wooden door, waiting for his turn to go inside. He was in Mumbai's Police Headquarters in Colaba to have a little chat with the Director General. He stood, self consciously, straightening his collar, pulling down his khaki coloured shirt in an effort to make it look even well ironed that it already was. He pulled his shoulder stiff straight and adjusted his badge.

The Director General, Hema Qureshi was a fearsome woman. Strong both in mind and body, she is known to kick some serious stuff up in criminal activities. She was famous for her integrity in the entire country and rumours were running around that she was to receive some award from the Prime Minister soon. Nobody knew the truth but with her popularity in the force, it couldn't be entirely wrong either.

Suddenly, the door in front of him opened and a clerk called him in. He marched in stiffly and looked around at the assembled dignitaries, or the so called protectors of law.

'At ease, Superintendent Ravi. I hope you have something really good for us.' Hema Qureshi said her voice stern.

'There has been a kidnapping of a girl named Rivannah Shah, about twenty, twenty one years of age.'

'Kidnapping is a small issue; we haven't assembled here to listen to that.'

'Yes ma'am. But what I am suggesting is that kidnapping is related to something far bigger. I think I am on the verge of discovering something phenomenal. Something really big is going to go down.'

'Go ahead.'

Ravi took a deep breath in; the tension on his face was palpable. He pulled out a pen drive from his pocket, turned around and inserted it onto a computer near the far wall in the room. The computer was connected to a projector that enlarged the images onto a whiteboard just beside the computer for all of the others to see.

After setting everything up, he turned around to face the crowd and said, 'I hope you all are acquainted with the name Mubeen Roy.'

Hema's lips curled up in an almost a feral snarl but she didn't say anything. It wasn't unexpected for Ravi. Mubeen was popular in these circles but only with the lower circles of police hierarchy. The people in actual power hated him more than anything. He was smart, they knew it but he was the one who did the police's job. He was a military inspector before he decided to quit that job and turn into a private investigator. His reason? It was better to haul huge amounts of money from the private pockets, whom he primarily worked for than to become a liability to the middle class tax payer. So, half of the people in the city preferred to hire him before handing over the matter into official police investigation. His job was much more efficient, more specific and faster. Who doesn't like a quick delivery? Entire multibillion dollar businesses depend and run on the simple act of quick delivery of product to the customer. The police department heads endured him because he helped the police out with certain tricky investigations too, and admittedly he was more than just smart.

'So, about two days back, after the girl was kidnapped and no ransom call came in to the parents, I shared the information with Mubeen. Later the next day, he informed me that the girl who had been kidnapped was the girlfriend of his own client, Aditya Tiwari, grandson of late Mr. Harish Tiwari who had been murdered six days back.'

That raised some eyebrows, just as Ravi had expected.

'Now, I would like to divert from my current story to Mubeen's. The thing is that after Mr. Harish Tiwari's demise, Aditya hired Mubeen to investigate the matter. Two days later, they were on a cross country running spree to evade some people who are desperately trying to kill Aditya too. I began to believe this was some kind of corporate conspiracy to down the opponent which was a safe assumption because Mr. Harish Tiwari, as you all know is or rather *was* very well established in his business, and the name *Tiwari Estates* is actually the foremost name in realty business in the country right now.' Ravi paused for a while to let it all sink in. But he had gotten the Director General interested.

'Go on.' Hema spurred.

'Then, on the day after the girl was kidnapped he called me and said that he had a plan and asked me to track a number. It was switched off for the moment but he had said that he would inform me when it would be active. I naturally trusted him and brought out my most talented team to track down the number. He finally called me three hours later to inform me of the development.

Suddenly, just moments after the phone had been switched on, a call came in and we began tracking it. We even have the conversation transcript. It meant little to me, but I recorded it nonetheless for future references if the need arose, just in case as a backup plan. Would you still like to hear it?'

'If it does pertain to the case, we would all like to hear it but if it doesn't, why waste time?' Hema said with a voice that sounded a little less condescending than usual.

'It might but I do not know yet. It makes no sense to me.'

'Okay, go ahead. Let's hear it.'

Ravi pressed double clicked on an icon on his computer and the speakers came to life.

'Well. I hope this is Aditya on the line, am I right?'

'Yes. Why have you kidnapped Rivannah? You have a rivalry towards me. Why involve her?'

'Ah! I like that, straight to the point. No pleasantries. My name is Avinash, by the way. I'm pleased to meet you.'

'I don't have time for pleasantries. What do you want me to do?'

'Nothing too difficult, at least the cost of Rivannah's life is far greater than what you're trying to achieve roaming about in the country. Why don't you give up all you have and we'll let you go free, along with your Rivannah. You just have to give up all you've found so far along with Mubeen.'

Ravi paused the recording and said, 'That was Aditya Tiwari and a man named Avinash. Our guess is he facilitated or is directly responsible for the kidnapping of Rivannah Shah. But when we tracked down his phone, his location was Sanchi, exactly the same place Mubeen and Aditya were right then.'

'So what does it imply?' one of the men sitting in the crowd asked.

'We do not know for sure but our guess is that Rivannah is nothing but a bait to lure out Aditya. Mubeen has so far been able to protect Aditya from these mysterious pursuers so they finally came upon a more direct solution to the problem. Avinash himself was in Sanchi but he probably had a team under him to kidnap Rivannah. That is just speculation, at the moment. Nothing is for sure yet.'

'Okay. Go on with the recording.'

'What is it, Aditya? Why are you not saying anything? Are you surprised by my graciousness?'

'I'm sorry, what did you just say?'

'Ah, the great Mubeen Roy at last! You still have to pay me for the phone you have in your hand right now, you know that right? And it is not money that I seek. I seek revenge for the humiliation that you caused.'

'Alright. Come and take it. Just let Rivannah go. She has no involvement in this. She shouldn't be hurt in our fight.'

'But you see the world isn't made of only roses and sunflowers. That cannot happen until you give up all the clues you two have found or take Rivannah's corpse to the morgue. Your choice.'

'Avinash, you don't know whom you're pitching a fight with. You're going to pay with your life if Rivannah gets even a mere scratch or a bruise over her.'

'You see, we are the ones making the deal here okay? So if you don't comply with us, scratches and bruises on her body would be the least of your worries, I can assure you that. That is why I wanted to talk to Aditya. He is so much calmer and an intelligent person who knows what the right thing to do is in a situation like this.'

'From this, we can conclude that Avinash is a meticulous and scheming character, probably hired for the very same reason by another really personality whom I will cover a little later. He knows where to prick a person to make him bleed the most. But Mubeen is no less.' Ravi said and smiled as he clicked on the play icon.

'Your empty threats do not frighten me, Avinash. We all know what happened in Kuldhara. How you humiliated yourself. That's what you're capable of. Now why don't we fight like men and leave innocent people out of this mess?'

'Mubeen, you don't know whom you're playing your game with.'

'Something happened in Kuldhara, a place in Rajasthan, that as we have heard before, humiliated Avinash as Mubeen used that point to gain leverage over Avinash.'

'But this all is going nowhere.' Hema said.

'Ma'am, here's the next conversation you would want to hear. From the last call, we tracked down Avinash phone number and began monitoring the calls and messages that went in and out of his phone from that moment on. My team is still hard at work and recording everything that is going on over that line even now as we speak.

He made a call once to a person. I would like you to hear the recording before I reveal the finale.' Ravi said with a smile. He had got them hooked. He would now assuredly have all the resources in the hands of Mumbai police for the case.

'Let me guess, Mubeen escaped yet again. You're beginning to irritate me now.'

'Yes.'

'And you attribute that failure to...?'

'I don't know.'

'I'm giving you one last chance. Get Aditya for me, alive. Do it any way you see fit.'

'Yes sir.'

There was pin drop silence that ensued around the room. Everybody had the same question in their mind but nobody spoke up. Finally, Ravi took the decision to spread the beans he had collected.

'My team, from this call, tracked down the other number. We called in the calling service providers and now we have a name.'

'What is the name, Ravi?'

'The SIM card was registered to the name Dinesh Thakur. And we all know who Dinesh Thakur is, don't we?'

'Founder and chairman of Thakur Group of Companies.' Hema said, almost as if in a dream with her eyes wide open.

'Yup! Another real estate mogul. Actually one of the biggest real estate companies in India – second to none but the Tiwari's.'

Director General Hema Qureshi stood up from her chair; looked directly into Ravi's eye. 'Superintendent Ravi,' she said with fearsome firmness, 'what do you need to unravel this?'

86

Mubeen parked the car in a small alley. 'Okay, bring out the clue,' he said, turning to him, 'let see what it says.'

Aditya leaned towards the door and pulled out the object from his pocket. It was a neat little object, looked much like a pencil, only thicker. It had engravings going over the surface, deep etched but perfectly straight lines. It was heavy, mostly made of metal.

'What is this?'

'I don't know. I only know that whoever made this was obviously very skilled. There's not even a slight flicker in the straightness of the etched marks. I have no idea what it is though.'

'Anything written over the surface?'

'I can't see anything as such.'

'Did we miss anything back at the Stupa? If so, we're doomed. There's no possibility for us to go back right now.'

'I don't think so.' Aditya murmured, gazing at the object intently. 'I think this is some kind of key, the perfect straightness of the lines is indicative of that, their main purpose to turn the rungs of a lock. Again, that is a guess.'

'So where do we go now? I think there's something to it that we're missing. You're grandfather has been pretty meticulous so far. I don't think he would lax down now. I don't have the grey cells to handle this, so it's all up to you.'

Aditya fiddled with it. It was about eight inches long, almost the same as one's index finger, maybe a little more. On the bottom face was the now too familiar symbol of the *dharmachakra*. Holding it like a click pen in his palm, he pressed down on the symbol etched onto the metal surface. Nothing happened. No genie appeared to relieve them of their mess. No mighty sword sprang out to wipe out their enemies.

Out of a hunch, Aditya using his pinkie finger pressed down on the symbol once again, and as if by magic, the surface with the symbol slid in smoothly, rotating. After a complete 180 degree rotation into the object, the side popped off and struck the windshield of the car and came to rest on the dashboard.

Both of them looked relieved as well as crestfallen. The former because they finally had the next clue and the latter because they *had* a next clue and their journey was nowhere near an end.

Several seconds later, both of them peeked in and found exactly what they were expecting to find inside. Yet another piece of paper.

87

Ravi walked out of the room with a broad smile on his face. The first part of his mission was clear and the second most crucial part was about to begin. He reached his chamber, sat down on his seat, picked up the phone and called Mubeen.

'Hello, Mubeen?'

'Oh, Ravi! Yes tell me.'

'You're all set. I have everything in motion for the plan. Hema Qureshi has her thumbs up for this case and you have full jurisdiction to act upon your will. Secondly, you have the entire Mumbai police force behind you, upon orders from Hema.'

There was an expected pause on the side of the line. 'Tell me everything.'

'We did everything as you had planned; we tracked down the number you gave us which lead to a phone whose owner went by the name Avinash. We then tracked into his phone and got another name.'

'Spill it.'

'Dinesh Thakur, of Thakur Group of Companies.'

Mubeen felt like the Greek titan Atlas, after relieving himself from holding the burden of the sky for so many centuries, probably millennia. It was a business conspiracy in an attempt to destroy the strongest competitor. This wasn't the civilized world where debates happened over property and possessions. This was the jungle, where the strongest survived by killing off the competition. Darwinian Theory of evolution. Survival of the fittest had become the motto of businesses. This was evolution.

'Okay. I am going to need some time to process this, Ravi.'

'Alright. But we have to act quickly if we have to nab these tricksters. They think they can do anything they want, kick up any kind of fuss, and go around kidnapping people. They need to know who the boss is.'

Mubeen smiled. Ravi had regained his energetic form. This always happened when he got hooked to a particular case. 'I'll talk to you later.'

Mubeen pocketed the phone and looked towards Aditya. 'What does it say?'

Aditya wordlessly handed the little parchment to Mubeen who took it gently and read the contents out loud.

To an ancient palace you need to go,

In a place named after a beautiful princess it was by a righteous king,

Where hell itself had wrought down even upon the

innocents

On the bank where the two rivers met,

There shall you find the ancient antechamber,

Under the great marked fig tree,

Where when at the time opportune,

The greatest king had sought to give humanity the greatest gift.

'Each clue is vaguer than the previous one. The only thing I can guess is that the king referred to here is Ashoka. Nothing else is striking me as familiar. Can you make anything out of this?' Mubeen asked, his face a picture of clear distaste.

'No. The last line is probably as you said, the meaning of second last line is also pretty clear but the context isn't clear. *Named after a beautiful princess it was by a righteous king;* that means the palace had a feminine name, named after the princess, but whose princess?' Aditya wondered.

'So, the third line should be the focal point of this one. Get that, and you know the entire picture the poem is trying to depict.' Mubeen sat back on his seat.

'You're right. *Where hell itself had wrought down upon the innocents.* A place that was viewed as hell in the eyes of others. Something that probably horrified the people out of their wits. Now what kind of a place might that be?'

'A solitary incarceration, maybe? Torture chambers? But these don't exist anymore nowadays.'

'Yes, but they used to exist and thrive in earlier days. Execution then wasn't like what we have now. A public execution was the tradition for the convicted, torture chambers were part of most palaces, mostly in underground dungeons among other places. But this? I don't know. Coming to my question, why did Ravi call you a while back?'

'Yeah, that. Everything went according to plan and he has a name. But I don't think you will want to hear it.'

'Why?'

'The killing of your grandfather is part of a corporate conspiracy and you being the most favourite descendent of the late Mr. Harish Tiwari. So naturally, you too are a wanted man in those circles. I'm sorry, but this clue hunt has nothing to do with your grandfather's death.'

'WHAT DO YOU MEAN?' Aditya shouted.

'What I'm trying to say is that your grandfather set you on this trail because he probably has something in store especially for you, a legacy maybe but him being murdered is not related to the hunt.'

'Of course it does! You have read the letter that my grandfather had written! You obviously cannot deny that!'

'That is a valid point but my argument is that things and situations lined up in such a way that it seemed that they are. Things are not what they seem to be right now. Dinesh Thakur is after you now and then he probably is going to overtake the company your grandfather built.'

Aditya's eyes widened in horror as he recognized the name. He had even seen the man at several occasions when he as a child had followed his grandfather to important business conferences.

'So what's going to happen next?' Aditya asked, his voice almost a whisper.

'Director General of the Mumbai Police Force is in on this and she is digging into the case with both of her hands. Dinesh Thakur cannot escape the law anymore. He would be convicted for being the brains behind Avinash's brawns on the murder of your grandfather and for several attempts at murder which I myself will confess in front of the court and you will have justice, and that I can promise you.'

'What about this?' Aditya asked, holding up the clue in his hands, 'Was this all a waste of time?'

'I don't know that part yet. For now, while things are being set up back in Mumbai, let's finish this as soon as possible. Dinesh will still be looking out for you. And you need to finish what you have started.'

88

Dinesh Thakur felt the hot water shower down upon him, gently dripping down over his skin, soothing the taut muscles after the strenuous workout at his personal gym in the basement. Things were not going well and he was under a lot of duress. If he couldn't bring things under control, somebody from the government would certainly come sneaking down his backyard and get to know about him. He would be able to bribe some of them off but if suspicion begins to spread beyond a point, bribes won't work anymore and the situation would take an ugly turn. The only solution was to capture them.

But there was Avinash who was failing spectacularly at every opportunity he got. Only reason why he kept up with him was because he was as loyal as a man can get. Mubeen was indeed living up to his name. All through his career, he had tracked down criminals and he knew the ins and outs of the business so it wasn't really hard for him to disappear in a world such as this. Avinash was proving to be completely useless and so was the bait with Rivannah. Mubeen somehow knew that he couldn't kill Rivannah which would only strengthen Aditya's resolve.

Dinesh stepped out of the shower room and quickly dressed up. Suddenly something struck him. Aditya's uncle was still out there following the duo. That meant he probably had some information about where they might be headed next. Dinesh realized one of the costliest mistakes he had made was to break the pact with Pravir. Yet in retrospect, there was no other option. He was becoming completely blinded by his love for his nephew. He had to be discarded. But one thing was for certain. He knew something and so he cannot be ignored. He had to keep a continuous surveillance over him.

He walked out into his room, picked up his phone and called Avinash.

'Hello sir.'

'Avinash. While you search for Mubeen and Aditya, keep your eyes open for Pravir. I believe he knows something and we have to know what he knows. He somehow knew they were going to travel to Sanchi and he might know what their next destination is. I want to know what he knows. Bug him, track him, keep a tail on him, I don't care what you do. I want to know what he knows; I want to know where he is going to go next. Get me everything you can gather. Surely you can manage that much at least?'

There was a pause from Avinash as he digested the little insult. 'Yes sir. I'll get to that immediately.'

Dinesh hung up and suited up in his best Armani. There was a meeting he couldn't afford to miss today.

89

'Any bright ideas?' Mubeen asked after a while, driving towards the airport guided by the GPS on his phone.

'No. But I know who can.' There was a sudden change in Aditya as his eyes looked ahead onto the road but in reality it was somewhere else altogether.

'Who?'

'My maternal uncle, Pravir. I need to call him up immediately. Only he will be able to help us with this.'

'How do you know?' Mubeen asked. 'How can you be so sure?'

Aditya looked at Mubeen, his expression unreadable. 'I just know. I'll tell you later.' He pulled out his phone and began dialling a number he had by heart.

'Aditya, stop. We don't know if your uncle's number is under their radar too. We have changed our numbers but your family members haven't. And our pursuers are intelligent enough to keep their numbers under a tab. The moment you call them, they will probably be able to locate where you are and what you are talking about. We can't take that risk, Aditya.'

'We have to take that risk, Mubeen! For your sake, for my sake and for Rivannah's sake! She isn't safe yet. And I will do everything in my power to make her safe and also make sure she stays safe.'

Mubeen couldn't say anything. He didn't have anything to say in a situation like this.

Pravir sat fidgeting with his phone. He had no way to contact Aditya and so he had no way to communicate and tell him the truth. The Corporation was too at a standstill, so there was some peace in knowing that the worst thing that would happen, whatever that might be, would not involve the Corporation.

Suddenly his phone began to ring. It was from an unknown number. He let it ring for a few times, pondering over who might be calling him but then picked it up.

'Hello?' he asked.

'Uncle? How are you? I couldn't talk to you the last time because something that came up but now I need some help from you.' Aditya said from the other side.

Pravir couldn't believe his luck. God had mischievous ways to align destiny in our lives. He had lost Aditya's number but Aditya himself called him out of the blue to talk to him about something. This was probably why the business of prophecy is such a lucrative one. Everybody wanted to know how their lives were turn out in the near future, nobody liked their current state of prosperity. Everybody demanded more than what they had or deserved in their lives.

'Yes, Aditya. What do you need help with? Anything you need, just ask.'

'When I was a kid, you and grandfather had told me a story of a legend. The legend of Ashoka's palace of torture. Do you remember that?'

The killer paused for a moment. His memory went back to a time ten years back. He clearly remembered that day. It was the day when late Harish Tiwari had suffered his first heart attack. It had been a mild one, so the pain had been intense but not fatal. The day was a memorable one when they had been touring the eastern parts of India and they had stopped over for the day in the city of Pataliputra, the capital of the once all-powerful Mauryan Empire under Ashoka. It was then that Aditya's grandfather had told him about the legend of the Ashoka's torture chamber Pataliputra.

'Yes, I remember that now. But that is just a myth, a legend. No archaeological evidence has been found till now to support the theory. But why are you asking this to me now?'

'Where does the legend say it is situated?'

Pravir was now in a trap of his own making. He was smart enough to realize that there lay the next clue, and Aditya had probably figured the one they had found in Sanchi. The legendary palace of torture was said to be in *Pataliputra* but nothing had been found till now.

But something had led Aditya to question him. He didn't want to tell Aditya the location and he himself could go there instead but he couldn't do anything without the complete clue they found at Sanchi.

'*Pataliputra.*' Pravir replied with certainty.

90

The technician in the offices in Mumbai shakily picked up his phone and dialled Avinash's number. He knew Avinash wasn't in a good mood after Mubeen had tricked him but this was hot news. It was immediately picked up.

'Avinash sir, we have some activity on Pravir's phone.'

'Pravir's? Are you sure?'

'One hundred percent. The next thing is going to shock you even more.'

'Shoot.'

'The caller is none other than Aditya Tiwari.'

'WHAT? Did I hear that right?'

'Yes, you did sir. We now know that he and Mubeen have altered their SIM cards and thus they had become invisible from us.'

'Track down the number and flag it. I want to know everything that goes in and out of that. Alright? Also get a recording of the conversation. I want you to send it to me as soon as possible. Also send a copy to Dinesh Thakur.'

'Yes, sir.'

Suddenly forgetting all about the insult, he picked up his phone and dialled his boss's number. It was picked up after a ring.

'You better give me any more -'

Avinash, surprisingly cut his boss off and began speaking, 'I have better news than you can imagine. Aditya just called Pravir. We also have a recording of the conversation that took place between the two and is on its way to your phone check it out.'

'You bring me good news yet fail to do the necessary work behind it.'

'I will make everything right this time. Mubeen has a lot more to pay than just a phone. They're not slipping out of my fingers anymore now.'

'Good.'

Avinash hung up and quickly downloaded the audio file that came in and then he played it.

'Hello?'

'Uncle? How are you? I couldn't talk to you the last time because something that came up but now I need some help from you.'

'Yes, Aditya. What do you need help with? Anything you need, just ask.'

'When I was a kid, you and grandfather had told me a story of a legend. The legend of Ashoka's palace of torture. Do you remember that?'

'Yes, I remember that now. But that is just a myth, a legend. No archaeological evidence has been found till now to support the theory. But why are you asking this to me now?'

'Where does the legend say it is situated?'

'Pataliputra.'

Avinash smiled. Pataliputra it is.

91

'Torture palace? What am I missing?'

'That is a reaction which is expected from most people who know about Ashoka. All we know about Ashoka that he was the great king, son of *Bindusara*, grandson of the great king *Chandragupta Maurya*, founder of the Mauryan Empire, who conquered the state of Kalinga but that is not everything that he is. Ashoka used to be known as *Chandashoka* or Ashoka the cruel before he converted to Buddhism after the well known war.'

'Cruel?'

'Yes. Did you know in one of his sadistic moments during that time, he wanted to make a palace where people would be tortured, both the criminals and innocents? Modern psychologists would say he suffered some major mental disorder and invent a big fancy name for it. He is also said to have brutally killed all of his brothers, this piece here might be exaggeration but as the saying goes, there's no smoke without fire.'

Mubeen gulped. 'Innocents?'

'Well, that's the story. It is said that he had hired a guy named *Girika*, who also like Ashoka was locally known as *Chandagirika*, or *Girika* the cruel. Ashoka sent his men on a search throughout his kingdom to search for the vilest of men, someone with no sense of conscience whatsoever. He searched for a man who could torture, maim and kill people as easily as he could eat his food. The post of Ashoka's executioner was based completely on merit, and fortunately for him no quotas or reservation system were prevalent during those times.'

At this point, Mubeen couldn't help but laugh.

Aditya continued, 'So this Girika had killed off his parents because they didn't want their son to become Ashoka's pet executioner. He is also said to have killed children, just for the fun of it. And because of these past certificates of achievements in the field, he was awarded the post of the official executioner of the Mauryan Empire. But there were a lot of horribly gruesome work that came along with the job.'

'Okay, so history repeats itself. Hitler may actually be the modern day incarnation of this Girika character. The story is becoming more and more fascinating, did you know?'

'Wait there's more. It was then Ashoka began designing and building the palace. Girika from time to time is said to have given inputs on painful procedures to mete out punishment to the criminals, like pouring molten copper down the throat. I would rather not describe more of his creative genius.

So Girika, upon hearing Buddhist chants describing the five realms of Buddhist hell, had persuaded Ashoka to design the palace in a similar way. The palace was designed in such a way that outwardly it was beautiful beyond comparison. It would a palace with all the external accoutrements of decadence and pleasure, ponds with crystal clear water with colourful fishes frolicking around, exclusive baths, and the exquisite facade would hypnotise the viewer with breathtaking intricate etchings. The very beauty would attract innocent onlookers in venture into the building. The moment they stepped inside, Girika and his personal minions would capture them and ooze the life out of them.'

'Sounds pretty. We're not going there, are we?'

'Of course we are.' Aditya snapped and then continued. 'Now our then sadistic Ashoka had given an explicit order to Girika. Anybody who enters into the palace is to be killed with immediate effect, even if it was the Great Maurya himself. Young, old, rich, poor, man, or woman, nobody was to be spared.

The insides were filled with various torture devices. Some fanatics claimed that Ashoka had even been to the fifth realm of the Buddhist hell to exactly replicate the horrors here on earth. Girika kept providing some invaluable inputs from time. In short, I believe Ashoka was an extremely depressed fellow with little else to do apart from this. His kingdom was now stronger than ever, nobody could challenge his might and superiority except the ill fated kingdom of Kalinga.'

'That's an image of Ashoka I didn't have. I need to thank you for that. This is an entirely new picture. So, uh. Where is this palace of torture?'

'That's the part I still haven't figured out.' Aditya said, carefully unrolling the same sheet of paper.

To an ancient palace you need to go,

In a place named after a beautiful princess it was by a righteous king,

Where hell itself had wrought down even upon the innocents

On the bank where the two rivers met,

There shall you find the ancient antechamber,

Under the great marked fig tree,

Where when at the time opportune,

The greatest king had sought to give humanity the greatest gift

'Okay, so how do you explain the second line? *In a place named after a beautiful princess it was by a righteous king.*'

'Simple. Pataliputra. Traditional etymology states that there was a king named *Sudarshana* who had a daughter named *Patali*. When she bore a son, King Sudarshana named an entire village as *Pataligram* which was later renamed to *Pataliputra*, *putra* meaning son. So the antechamber we have to find is under a great fig tree, which is pretty clear in the second last line. Let's go.'

'I'm going to ask once again. Why do you know all this?'

'I'm going to reveal something to you about me that I've never confided in anyone else. I've always wanted to be an archaeologist. It had also been my grandfather's dream for me.'

'Well that explains it. So what is our next destination?'

92

'Pataliputra.' Dinesh said to himself as he was talking to Avinash. He could have guessed that a clue was hidden there; after all it was the capital of the old Mauryan Empire. This needed to end here and now. He knew he didn't have a lot of time for any more luxuries of having Avinash to do the work. He would now have to dip his own hands into the tar. He needed to have the reins in his hands from now.

'Avinash. Can you do another favour for me and book a flight for me to Patna? I want to be there too this time to see the action happen.'

'I'll do that immediately.'

Avinash hung up and dialled his teach lead. It was immediately picked up. 'Get a flight ticket for Dinesh to Patna immediately. Also get another one in my name and email it to me. Alright?'

'Yes, sir.'

Pravir quickly packed up his stuff, and there was a broad smile on his face. He was back in the game and now he would make no mistakes this time. This might be the last opportunity he had to make things right and he would clinch it tightly. He would get the better of the Corporation who had tricked him into murdering people and see to it that they are destroyed. But that would take time and wasn't on the top of his priority list.

He sped down the stairs of the hotel already plotting his plan. We went to the reception desk, threw over the room key and along with it a large bundle of cash and ran.

The befuddled hotel manager who was sitting at the desk was about to call out, 'Sir, -' But Pravir cut him and shouted back, 'You can keep the change. Thank you for your lovely room. I really enjoyed my stay.'

The manager fingered the crisp notes in his hands and wondered why the man had given him such a hefty tip. Was their service so good? If so, he could increase the rates too. In the midst of his thoughts, the woman receptionist at his side looked up to him and said, 'That man didn't even stay for a day! He came in last night, according to the register and is leaving now, barely completing twelve hours.'

The manager smiled and looked at her. 'He said I can keep the change. So I'm keeping the change.'

The woman opened her lips to say something but then decided not to. She certainly didn't want to lose her job.

Outside, Pravir hailed a cab, jumped in. 'Raja Bhoj Airport,' he said, quite out of breath and placing another wad of cash on the front seat, 'as fast as possible, okay?'

93

About two hours later, a gloomy dusk had fallen over the city of Bhopal but there was merriment in the air. The next day was going to be a special one for everybody. It was the Christmas Eve and the next day children were going to wake up with gifts beside them. It was the international festival of joy.

Mubeen and Aditya dumped their vehicle in some corner of the street, leaving the key in the car for some lucky thief to pick it up. *When you have the resources, why not use it to help others in need?* Mubeen mused. The airport was sparsely populated and so the queue was small. They quickly bought their tickets to Patna and sat down to wait. They couldn't afford to be captured now yet they were sitting ducks in a place like this. But there was no other option either. Plane companies with their stupid rules and functionalities.

'So where exactly are we going in Pataliputra?' Mubeen asked looking around for suspicious faces.

'We have to do a little bit of digging around there. I cannot get anything more out of the poem.'

'What about the line which says, *on the bank where the two rivers met.*'

'The two rivers are probably the Ganga and Son rivers and our location is probably on the bank of the confluence.'

'But isn't building something on the bank of a water body difficult? I mean the soil is softer because of the higher moisture content and naturally wouldn't be able to hold out against the weight of an entire palace.'

'True. But the Taj Mahal was built on the back of river Yamuna, wasn't it? It's undoubtedly still standing with no chance of sinking and breaking down.' Aditya said, then with a momentary pause of introspection, he continued, 'though Delhi's pollution might be the reason for its destruction in the not-so-distant future.'

Mubeen sat back, inhaling the cold air conditioning of the airport and said nothing. It was true. Pollution levels in the country were on an all time high people were doing deplorably little to handle the issue. One cannot blame the Prime Minister to cleaning up Mumbai's streets! Of course not! In a country of 1.2 billion, a staggering seventeen percent of the world population, what could one old man sitting in an air conditioned room of 7, Race Course Road in Delhi do? The responsibility rested in the hands of the common people staying in the country. But unfortunately most remained blissfully unaware of that very fact and continued to what they have been doing all this time.

Shaking these thoughts out of his head, he looked around, keeping up his surveillance of the airport. For all he knew, Avinash and his goons were already on their way to the airport or better still, waiting at the airport in Patna to abduct the two of them just as they stepped out of the airport.

'You want coffee?' Mubeen asked, looking around for a café and found one.

'Sure.'

Mubeen got up and walked towards a café and ordered two lattés and paid the money with the credit card. Several minutes later, after a lot of grinding and shaking noise two cups were placed in front of him, the hot drinks sending dense steam into the air conditioned atmosphere.

Not so far behind him, Pravir entered, eyeing the seating area and spotted Aditya sitting alone in one of the seats and Mubeen bringing two cups with him. He quickly turned their backs to them. It wasn't yet the right time to display his actual visage. He booked his tickets to Patna and sat down in the farthest corner possible from the duo.

But he was elated. His situation was back on track. This time, they would not escape his grasp.

94

About five hours later, changing planes because of the connecting flights and the waiting time in the interim, they reached Lok Nayak Jaiprakash International Airport. Mubeen and Aditya were travelling light, with barely a few days worth of clothes and nothing apart from that. They had a laptop but it had become pretty much redundant in the past couple of days.

Just as they stepped out of the airport, Mubeen asked, 'So where exactly are we going?'

'To the confluence of the rivers Ganga and Son.' Aditya said, his eyes gazing forward at the empty parking lots.

Suddenly a man came up behind them. A familiar voice spoke up behind them. 'Unfortunately, I heard that.'

Mubeen's eyes widened in shock and he tried to turn around but Avinash continued, 'Uh. I wouldn't do that if I were you. I have over fifteen guns pointed straight at you two and several others at Rivannah back in Mumbai.'

Mubeen pressed his jaws and looked at Aditya, infuriated. And now, Aditya was no more the angry young man but a frightened, whimpered soul desperate for some help. His eyes were filled with apology and guilt. He looked around the parking lot and found a couple of men walking about randomly, most of them were travellers but some of them had restricted movements, as if they were waiting for something. How couldn't he have noticed them just as they walked out?

'So, if you want to survive and see to it that Rivannah is well, which she is till now, you will have to come along with us. And no abrupt movements okay? I won't tolerate that any more. And no more of your stupid tricks, I've had enough of that back in Kuldhara and Bhopal.'

'Stupid they may be, but they were enough to fool you weren't they?' Mubeen taunted.

Avinash grunted and punched Mubeen in the back. Mubeen couldn't do anything in return. There were too many people against two, out of which only one had any experience in situations like these.

'Okay, we're going with you.'

'Good choice. Now give me your gun. I wouldn't take the risk of letting you keep your gun with you. Come on, hand it to me, slow and steady.'

Reluctantly, Mubeen pulled out the gun from his backpack and handed it to him.

'Now, do you see that red vehicle coming towards you? Well, I want the two of you to get into the back nicely and slowly. Alright?'

The car came to a halt in front of them. The duo got in and Avinash took the seat beside the driver. It seemed like a local guy, not one of Avinash's armed thugs.

Avinash turned around and asked Aditya, 'Where did you say we are supposed to go? Careful, yours and Rivannah's lives may depend upon what you say when I ask you the questions.'

Aditya closed his eyes and a moment later he replied, 'The confluence of Ganga and Son rivers. That's where the next clue lies.'

'But the poem says that the location is the place where the three rivers meet, not two, right?'

'Some geological changes might have taken place that might have caused the rivers to change their paths but this location was the city of *Pataliputra*.'

Suddenly Mubeen opened his mouth to say something but closed it. It wasn't the right time yet. The driver nodded when he heard the instructions and gunned the engine. He knew where they had to go.

The traffic was light and the location wasn't too far away from the airport. It was about a thirty minute ride and they reached the location. They were finally in Patna, under which lay the ancient city of *Pataliputra*. Aditya stepped out of the car and looked around. The immense Ganga flowed with her usual ferocity and the Son River flowing into the goddess from the south west. It was a beautiful scene if it were not polluted by the humans. It was no wonder that the men of ancient times revered Ganga as a mother, as an all mighty goddess.

But Aditya couldn't find what he was looking for. There weren't fig trees around and the two rivers. All there was to see, was the barrenness, sandy bank of the river and the roaring peal of the mighty river flowing down.

Suddenly, Aditya turned around and faced Mubeen. 'You were right! How could I be so wrong this whole time?'

'Who... wait what? Me?' Mubeen asked, befuddled. All he knew was that Aditya was onto something concrete this time.

'The confluence of the three rivers!'

Mubeen realized it was the time to act. 'Aditya, don't say anything.'

'That isn't a wise decision.' Avinash said, as another car pulled up behind the one they were travelling in. Avinash pulled out his own gun from his waist holster and pointed it at Aditya. 'Spit it out!'

Dinesh Thakur stepped out of the car and walked towards the spectacle.' Avinash, lower your gun. Let's talk this through peacefully.'

Avinash's eyes widened but he couldn't say anything. Dinesh had personally come into the situation so he had to settle into the position of the second one in command.

'Well, well, well! Who do we have here! Mr. Dinesh Thakur himself!' Mubeen exclaimed with fake excitement in his voice.

Dinesh finally laid his eyes on Mubeen, the famed Mubeen who had been able to thwart each and every one of their efforts to stop them. He looked at him closely. 'So you're Mubeen. I'm glad that I was lucky enough to see you before you die.'

Mubeen shrugged. 'Lucky you.'

'So why don't you want us to proceed with this? The more time you waste, the more Rivannah suffers. Your choice.'

'We wish, in fact he wishes to talk to Rivannah right now, to know if she's okay and in the condition you mention. If she is anything apart from that, we will not cooperate, that I can assure you.'

'Alright. That doesn't sound too harmful. Avinash? Will you do the honours?'

It was now Aditya's turn to look befuddled. What was Mubeen

doing? Having a talk with Rivannah? He couldn't do that right now. But as he looked into Mubeen's eyes, there was firmness in the sight which told him that he had something in his mind. Avinash walked up and handed the phone to Aditya after dialling a number.

'Who is this? Is that you father?' Rivannah called out from the other side of the line.

Aditya closed his eyes in an attempt to stop his barrage of tears that was about to follow. Rivannah was going through all this just because of him. Just because Dinesh had a personal feud with him, he had kept Rivannah prisoner.

'Father? Is that you father?' she asked again.

This time, Aditya spoke up, his voice barely a whisper. 'Hello Rivannah, this is Aditya, not your father.'

'Thank god, Aditya! Wait a minute. I don't understand why-'

'I'm sorry Rivannah, all of this happened because of me. Only I am to blame for this. Please forgive me. I promise you no harm will come to you till I am here.'

Dinesh rolled his eyes as he admired the ferocious beauty of Ganga as he shut his mental ears to block out Aditya feeble attempts to pacify Rivannah. Boys these days couldn't even court a young woman properly. Then he laid his eyes on Mubeen. There was something about him, something that made his stand apart in a crowd. But suddenly he noticed something. Mubeen was nodding his head, as if affirming something and Aditya was talking on the phone for way too long. There was something going on between the two of them.

'That's enough! Avinash take back your phone. Too much freedom can be harmful sometimes.' Dinesh ordered, and then turning to Mubeen he asked, 'Are you completely satisfied now?'

Mubeen looked back at him and replied, 'Yes.'

Turning to Aditya he asked, 'Now take us where the next clue leads us else you know the consequences.'

Aditya swallowed, looked down for a moment, debating whether to spill the beans or not and a few seconds later he made up his mind. 'I need a map. A detailed topographical map of the region. Immediately.'

'Why do you need that?' Avinash asked suspiciously.

'Will you do something that you're told to do for once?' Aditya shot back.

Avinash bit back his tongue to control himself and looked towards Dinesh. Dinesh looked back at him and nodded his head. From the back of the van, he brought out one of those humongous ten inch iPad and held it out to Aditya. Aditya opened up the map and turned on the location of the device. Several silent seconds passed by as the network patched up to the GPS of the closest satellite via the internet. Then the map automatically located the device position and zoomed in on the place.

Aditya placed the tablet of the bonnet of the sedan they were sitting in a while ago and began searching for something. Mubeen peeped over his shoulder and glanced at the map. Through the middle of the map ran a thick blue line with several curves and disturbances all along.

'This one here is the Ganga River.' Aditya began, pointing at the screen. Dinesh came over along with Avinash to inspect. For the entire time, Avinash kept his hands on his gun safely in his holster. One wrong move and he would take them down.

'And this one here,' Aditya said, pointing to another river that merged up into the Ganga, is the Son River. This is our location now.'

Aditya then pulled out the piece of paper that had the clue written on it and placed it above the tablet for everyone to see.

To an ancient palace you need to go,

In a place named after a beautiful princess it was by a righteous king,

Where hell itself had wrought down even upon the innocents

On the bank where the two rivers met,

There shall you find the ancient antechamber,

Under the great marked fig tree,

Where when at the time opportune,

The greatest king had sought to give humanity the greatest gift

'Those pretentious bastards.' Dinesh murmured under his breath.

Aditya looked at Dinesh after hearing his comment. Then he continued, 'The fourth line mentions our destination is a place where the two rivers meet.

'Which two rivers? We have a lot of rivers coming and joining the Ganga.' Mubeen asked, looking at the map.

'No, there isn't. But there was. In the past, during Ashoka's reign.'

'What do you mean?' Dinesh asked. Aditya could clearly see the contempt in Dinesh's voice as he uttered the name of Ashoka. Personally, Aditya felt like choking Dinesh with his bare hands but now wasn't the time. That man had conspired to kill his grandfather and he wasn't going to let him go so easily. He also needed to find who actually did the deed. But for now, he would have to wait for his time.

'Historical books written by Greek traveller to India during that period of time, named Megasthanes state that the three rivers, Son, Ganga and the Gandak River up here met almost at the same place, making it a confluence of the three rivers. ASI or the Archaeological Survey of India also had found definitive geological proof of the Son River's earlier path which ran parallel to the Ganga before meeting up with the latter.'

'So where are we actually going now?'

'*Pataliputra* excavation site under the ASI. I firmly believe that's where we'll find what we seek.'

95

Ravi was calmly dozing away on his desk when one of his men walked up to him and said, 'Sir!'

Ravi jumped up in surprise. 'Oh, you. Yes, tell me. What is it?'

'We've got some activity on Avinash. We have the call recorded and also we have located the call origin and destination.'

'Tell me more.' Ravi said, standing up from his chair.

'The call originated somewhere in Patna.'

'Patna?'

'Yes and the destination is here in Mumbai. After listening to the call transcripts, I realized that Rivannah is still here in Mumbai and I know her location.'

'How so?'

'The call was made from Avinash's phone which you had instructed us to flag. It was to another unknown number which too we now have under my radar. Anything that goes in or out of that phone, we'll be the first ones to know. So, my conclusion from the call is that the man speaking on Avinash's phone is Aditya and the on the other side was Rivannah. So, basically Aditya had asked for proof that Rivannah was still alive and well. Perhaps that's why the call was made.'

'So that means Aditya and Avinash have been captured by those thugs. That does not bode well for the mission. Anyway, I need you to track down Dinesh Thakur for me once again. I need to know where he is. Check everything on the internet that has his name on it. If you get a plane booked anywhere near Patna, call me immediately. If I don't pick up my phone, radio me, understood?

'Yes sir.'

'So where have these goons hidden Rivannah?'

'Tardeo, Mumbai. One of the most expensive residential addresses in the whole on Mumbai.'

Ravi looked at him as if he was struck by thunder. 'Are you a hundred percent sure about the location?'

'The call didn't last long enough to trace it down to a particular location but we do have a region of radius of a kilometre or so.'

'Good job my friend. That should be enough for our police to find the actual location. I'm even thinking of giving you a citation in the report or something for this.'

'Thank you so much sir!' The man was literally overjoyed. He couldn't believe his luck.

'Okay. Now keep your team on the alert. I want to know everything you get to know while I'm in the field, alright? Anything new comes up, you call me first. In the meantime, I'm going to leave my phone here in case Mubeen happens to call. If he does, track down his phone location precisely and report to Hema. She'll know what to do.'

'Yes, sir.'

Ravi placed his ochre cap on his head, adjusted his shirt and his waist holster gun. It was finally the time to start the action.

Ravi knocked and entered Hema Qureshi's room. She looked up, her eyes inquisitive. 'What is it Ravi?' she asked.

'We've found her. She's somewhere in Tardeo.'

'What do you need?'

'A warrant and a squad of forty Force One officers in plainclothes under me.'

'You want to go under disguise?'

'I don't want them to flee as the sight of our khaki uniform. We have to grab them when they're least expecting it. From what I know, things are going well with them and both Aditya and Mubeen have been captured in Patna. I suggest we should inform the local police to beef up as soon as possible.'

'I'll do that. You do the work of getting Rivannah out of their hands safe. I'll also inform her grieving father of this news.'

Ravi nodded stiffly. 'Yes, ma'am.'

Forty five minutes later, Ravi and his team of officers in plainclothes were on their way to Tardeo in eight white Mahindra XUV's. All of them were wearing Bluetooth speakers for constant communication between the team. Things could get sour any moment and all of them had to react quickly. Each member of the team had a Glock 19 on their bodies, armed, safety off, ready to fire. For a last choice back-up option or if they went low on ammunition, they had Brügger and Thomet MP9 or the machine pistol 9mm in the back of their cars and under their seats to hide them from plain sight. These Swiss guns can literally rip through obstructions like butter.

The eight groups had split up and had decided to cover the entire area from eight different attack points. They would first do a visual reconnaissance of the area and slowly moving inwards. Each team had a coordinated GPS system which indicated each other's positions live on the map and also the target area was also loaded onto each one of those. This would ensure each knew where the other was at any point of time, again for quick reaction to an emergency situation which may turn up.

Those scoundrels wouldn't have any chance of escaping. These men under Ravi were part of the legendary Force One segment of the Mumbai Police. They were trained specially under the lines of the NSG or the National Security Guards, one of the most elite in the country, to respond to immediate terrorist situations spanning the entire Mumbai metropolitan area. It had been created under the Mumbai Police after the 2008 Mumbai terror attacks. They were highly trained and skilled to respond to any and every situation possible.

If there was going to be a war, they were going to be prepared for it.

96

Again in the back seats of the cab, Mubeen and Aditya sat staring at the roads outside. People walking around oblivious to their surrounding, completely in their own worlds lost from everything. For a moment, Aditya began envying them, remembering his old times when he had been one such until the murder of his grandfather which shook him out of his beautiful tapestry of life. Knowing probably the very man in the car behind theirs was the one who had conspired to kill his grandfather.

Then his thoughts drifted back to the moment when Dinesh Thakur had said, *those pretentious bastards*. Things were becoming more and more unambiguous to him. The Council of the Nine was real. And his grandfather played some really important role in the organisation. And they had a secret which they strived to protect even at the cost of their own lives. Something Dinesh would kill to obtain. And obviously, he had some personal enmity with the Council.

Mubeen on the other side was thinking about ways to get Ravi to know about his location. If Ravi had been going according to their plans they had decided on, he would probably be on his way to rescue Rivannah. That done, he himself could handle the things here. Rivannah was a fulcrum that could bend either ways but he didn't want to take any chances with situations. He had had enough of those. If he were to get down on the situation and save himself and

Aditya, he couldn't do it even with the slightest possibility of Rivannah getting killed. He couldn't do that to Aditya. He had taken several chances at it and his luck had favoured him.

Forty minutes had passed since Aditya had talked to Rivannah. Ravi should be onto something by now.

'Hey, Aditya,' Mubeen asked, 'are you sure we're going to the right location.'

'Quite sure.'

'But?' Mubeen asked.

'But this entire mess is confusing me. What did my grandfather actually want for me? What am I to do now?'

'You've gotten this far. I know this will end well.'

'Not with that idiot sitting on our shoulders. Also they have her.' Aditya wiped a tear off his face.

'Leave those two to me. I'll handle them. You just continue what your grandfather planned for you. Okay?' Mubeen whispered under his breath.

'What are you two talking about? Avinash asked, turning around and smiling like a lunatic.

Mubeen shook his head pitifully and said, 'Why do you need to interfere in everything? Why don't you wag your tail like Dinesh tell you to?'

This finally pissed him off. Avinash pulled out his gun and leapt back and held the gun to Mubeen's forehead. His right hand was shaking with fury but his mind was still deciding whether or not to shoot him. Mubeen took advantage of that got hold of his right hand.

Within a fraction of a second, he twisted it hard in a direction it was never supposed to turn thus freeing the grip. Then with one smooth manoeuvre, the gun was in his hand, pointed directly at Avinash's forehead, the muzzle this time pressing into the skin.

Avinash couldn't even utter a shout by the time the gun was pointed towards him. His wrists still hurt from the wrench and he sought to massage it but he dared not move a muscle.

'You do know about Rivannah, right? The situation in which she is in? One phone call and she'll be dead.'

'In that case, let me give you back this gun.' Mubeen laughed and handed the gun back. Avinash's short temper was ridiculously funny when instigated.

Avinash turned around and sat back on his front seat, fuming. Mubeen was crossing every limit imaginable. But he needed to focus. Their job wasn't done as of yet. He knew for a fact Pravir would soon be in their company.

Today, Aditya would probably receive the worst shock in his life.

Several kilometres away from there, in a small police station in Patna, a phone rang loudly, cutting through the otherwise silent office. Additional Director General of Police in Bihar of the Patna zone picked it up and spoke into it huskily, 'Hello?'

'This is Hema Qureshi, Director General of Mumbai Police speaking. Who are you? Identify yourself.'

'I am the Additional Director General of Bihar Police. What do you need?'

'I need all your units to be on the alert, especially in the Patna region near a place called Pataliputra. I have information from my associates under me that something is going to go down there.'

He knew who Hema was but he wasn't going to accept everything she said at face value. He had to probe further. 'Why? Who all are involved? My men are on duty in their respective places and I need to see concrete evidence something big is going to happen else I find no purpose in disturbing my usual discipline.'

There was a palpable pause from the other side. 'It is a matter which involves Dinesh Thakur and Aditya Tiwari, grandson of late Harish Tiwari. It is a business feud and we need to stop it before the situation goes out of hand. I hope you understand that.'

That was enough. 'I'll alert my units right away.'

'Thank you.'

97

Pravir fiddled with a pen in his hands as his driver drove through the thin lanes following the two cars, the latter among which contained Aditya.

How did the Corporation come to know about this? Pravir had been thinking. Then he had realized. *They probably have my phone bugged. How could I have been so stupid?*

Fortunately, his driver was an experienced one, who knew the streets well. Pravir looked out at the raging Ganga towards his left. No matter how many times one looked at it, its magnificence never seemed to diminish one bit. Her calm, serene yet powerful demeanour only made people unable to tear their eyes off it. He cast his eyes back on the road in front of him, keeping his focus on the car in which he had seen Aditya get in. There wasn't anything he could do to stop the Corporation now. They had the two of them right under their noses now.

Suddenly he saw the two vehicles come to a halt on the side of the road. About three hundred metres away from them, Pravir asked his driver to stop. He threw in another wad of cash on the front seat and asked him to wait. The amount of money he had in his hands was usually the month's driving fee. The driver was ready to wait all night if need be.

Just as he was about to go ahead, he bent down and said, 'What place is this?'

'This is the *Pataliputra* excavation site *Kumhrar*.'

'Okay. Wait for me okay?'

'Yes sir.'

Pravir slowly walked forward. He could see a couple of men, one of which was a man whose face he knew but couldn't quite place and the other beside him was Avinash. Aditya and Mubeen stood at the forefront of a garden that sprawled out in front of them. Red coloured bricks piled on top of each other random rose up from the ground among the foot long ferns that grew alongside. To any layman, this would rather look like some abandoned housing plot but it was the ancient city of *Pataliputra* under the ground there, probably waiting to be discovered.

Huge figs and other trees populated the area among the ruins of the ancient city. *Kuhmrar* had once been looked into but further archaeological digs were not performed in the place. Reports said that the still standing structures were reburied in sand so that they can be protected from the passage of time and not erode away. Most of the item unearthed from the region were on display in a museum in the park.

'So where is your marked fig tree?' Dinesh asked.

Wait a second. Pravir thought to himself. *That is Dinesh Thakur, a real estate mogul, one of the best after my father-in-law. Why is that man here? Is Avinash reporting to him?*

Then it struck him. The pure horrors of what he had done.

Everything he had ever known, or ever made to believe – a lie.

98

'Ravi sir, team five has completed search of sector five. Nothing out of the ordinary has been found. We are ready to proceed towards The Imperial. Awaiting command.'

Ravi nodded to himself and replied, 'Team five, report acknowledged. Please stand by for further instructions.'

'Yes sir.'

Soon, more and more of these messages started dropping in their search reports. Each and every one of them had the same content. The central point of their radius of search area had been The Imperial twin tower residential skyscraper complex. Their plan had been to search the surrounding areas and then converge in on the centre where the signal had most likely originated.

Twenty minutes later, all the teams stood in their designated places around one of the most coveted and costliest residential addresses in the city. The Imperial.

'What are we to do sir?' someone asked.

'We have to check each and every floor of both the buildings. According to my knowledge, each building has about 60 floors making it a total of 120 floors to be covered. We are a total team of forty. So basically, each one of us has to cover at least three floors. I propose we go in the order of teams. Teams one, two, three and four will infiltrate building one. I along with the remaining four teams will infiltrate the second.'

'But wouldn't that impose a risk upon us. If, say one of us does find the kidnappers, assuming that the number of kidnappers is more than one, won't that man be compromised and his life at risk?' somebody chimed in.

'That is a risk we have to take but we'll have to ensure is any such things happen, we have measures to not let those men out of the building because they will be automatically alerted of our presence. My plan is that whoever finds them immediately shouts out the flat number and floor so the others close by in the same building are alerted. The ones on the other building will immediately rush down and secure the perimeter of the building in which the kidnappers are. That way, we'll have twenty working on finding them in the building and another twenty, seeing to it that they do not escape.'

'Sounds like a plan, Mr. Ravi.'

More comments of appraise and approvals dropped in. Five minutes later, all the men parked their cars just outside the building complex and walked in. They all came in one by one at different timings so nobody would be alerted. They couldn't be seen talking to each other or else the whole plan fails. Each member of the team took different elevators. Luckily, there were seventeen of those providing a lot of option and would also provide for the deftness to respond quickly in case the kidnappers are found. Walking down a sixty storey building is never a wise option, except probably when there's a fire.

The men went to their respective locations and started their work. They were a highly trained and coordinated squad and they worked their ways up for each of their respective floors. Ravi himself set to work when suddenly his radio gawked. Ravi instantly reduced the volume and then spoke into it, 'What is it?'

'I have new information. Over the communication line, you said that you didn't find anything in the search area and only on place is remaining. The Imperial twin towers. So I did a little snooping.

Dinesh own an entire floor there on building 2. This is just a speculation from the recent turn of events, so may not be entirely right. But I have a feeling that Rivannah might be there.'

'Alright. Which floor?'

'60th floor, the topmost. I wonder how much it might have cost.'

'These real estate moguls are filthy rich and most of it from sources we have no clue about or probably never will.'

'All the best, sir.'

'Thank you.'

Ravi replaced the radio in its original position, pressed a button on the communication device and spoke into it.

'I have news. Dinesh Thakur owns the entire 60th floor. I want all the members assigned to building 2 to meet me on the seventeenth floor. From there we will approach the 60th floor together. Your orders are to shoot to frighten. If the kidnappers fire back, shoot to kill but not one stray bullet must touch the victim. In the meantime, the remaining units set up a perimeter around the building and stop everyone from moving out. You have the official orders, so don't worry. Understood?'

Everybody replied in unison. 'Yes sir.'

99

'So where is your marked fig tree?' Dinesh asked once again.

Aditya was looking around the entire park. 'We need to spread out. There's a lot of area we have to cover in a short time.'

'I'm not doing anything. You have to get to the bottom of this alone. You came along alone this far, why not a little more? You do remember that Rivannah's life hangs in the balance here so you should do as I say.' Dinesh replied and looked at Mubeen from the corner of his eye. He had a little twitch on his lips, the tiny smile of mischievousness. *What could it be?* Dinesh thought to himself.

Aditya looked at him, his eyes piercing. 'If you really want what you have come here seeking, then get to work.'

It was probably the first time anybody had spoken to him like that. He flinched at Aditya's gaze and then set about ordering his men into action.

Suddenly a man jumped out from behind the bush, swiftly pulled out a gun from one of men and held it to Dinesh's temple. 'That's it. Everything stops NOW!' Pravir shouted, 'Do you remember the time when you said you had another plan to accomplish your goal, one which I wasn't a part of. Well, I couldn't help but be back in the game.' Almost instantly, all the remaining men pulled out their own guns and pointed towards him.

Aditya and Mubeen whirled around to face their new visitor. Aditya's jaws dropped open as he recognized the man. 'Uncle Pravir?'

Mubeen gaped at the new visitor. It was none other than Aditya's own maternal uncle pointing a gun to Dinesh's head. *What is going on?* was the question that came to Mubeen's mind. The pieces didn't quite fit together in the puzzle suddenly as Aditya's uncle jumped into the scene. It was like the entire jigsaw puzzle was falling off yet again.

Avinash looked around scared.

Mubeen couldn't understand what made up that expression. Something was in the air and he had no idea what was going on. That was something he wasn't quite used to.

Pravir held the gun firmly; he had no problem with that. The only problem is that his true identity would be revealed if Dinesh wanted it to. He didn't want to let that happen. But he also had to do something to stop Aditya from finding the clue and handing it to Dinesh.

Suddenly Dinesh spoke up, 'Killing me won't serve your true purpose, would it?'

'It might.'

'Well, let's see. Why should Aditya trust you? After all, you -'

'STOP!' Pravir shouted. Then he breathed in heavily and clenched his jaws.

'After all what? Tell me!' Aditya exclaimed.

Dinesh head turned to face Pravir. His expression seemed to say, *he asked for it, now I can't say no, can I?* Coughing a little to clear his voice, he said, 'After all, you killed his grandfather, in cold blood.'

Pravir cringed, but his razor sharp eyes bore into Dinesh. It was perhaps with a superhuman effort that Pravir was able to control himself from firing the gun in his hand. Everything he had ever strived to achieve had been shattered with that one sentence.

'WHAT?' Aditya tried to shout but all that came out was a bare whisper.

Mubeen couldn't believe his ears. His entire case was falling apart. Aditya's uncle killed Aditya's grandfather? He knew that Pravir was a maternal uncle so might have his eyes on the property but even murdering wouldn't serve the purpose. The property and business would be handed down to the next living blood relative if else otherwise specified, which he was sure wasn't.

It was then that Dinesh resumed speaking, this time to Aditya, 'Your uncle Pravir is a murderer. Did you hear about another man who was murdered recently in the country? In fact another one was in Switzerland. But all of them had one common denominator. All of them were of Indian origin. Hiren Patel, the biggest media personality in the country, Teddy Kapoor, member of the CERN. Did you know who killed them?' Now turning towards Mubeen, he said, 'I am making your work easier on this one. I present to you, the new crazy fanatical serial killer, Pravir Varma!'

Aditya stood rooted to his place, unable to think, move or use any other physical faculty he previously had control over. He looked at his uncle, trying to determine his expression as to what it tried to say, so that perchance it could say that Dinesh was lying and he had done no such thing. But the expression of Pravir's face was clear enough.

There was no denial.

Only regret.

Pravir was in no mood to talk. All the beans that were to spread had been spread. There was nothing to be said anymore. But he had a little question that lingered in his mind. He knew he wasn't going to leave this place alive, or without chains so he had only this one opportunity to know it.

'And this Corporation? Was this all a lie too?'

'Ha! The Corporation. It is a fancy name indeed. Well, sorry to beak it to you but this was a lie too. There *is* no Corporation! There was always just me, me and me haunting you, destroying you. Using you. I am in it for the money. I'm going to get what I am here to get. All you're going to get it a free ride to heaven, or hell, as the case may be. I don't know, neither do I care.' Pravir shrugged.

Pravir's heart skipped a beat. Not in love, but in desperation. He had been the instrument of his own destruction, Dinesh had successfully used his emotions to control him and use him.

His mouth opened, his mind was reeling, and his head was all woozy. He couldn't think straight any more. Everything in his world had been a lie. What he had sought to achieve had been for the good of the entire world yet all he actually did was to gift wrap that exact thing and given it to the devil to misuse. All that knowledge, all that information would now rest in the hands of this man. And he couldn't do one damn thing about it.

'I tried really hard but I couldn't save you. I'm sorry Aditya, but I have no other choice left in my hands anymore apart from this. But I have to do this. Else I won't die in peace.'

'NO!' Aditya shouted, tears flowing from his eyes. He rushed ahead to stop his uncle but Mubeen refrained him.

Pravir inhaled and as he exhaled heavily, as he pointed his gun down at Dinesh's stomach and fired.

100

Instantly, a fusillade of bullets poured down on Pravir. The force of the bullets forced him to move back and fall on his back. Time seemed to move slowly for Aditya as his uncle fell to the ground dramatically before his eyes, his face expressionless. There was no fear, pain or anguish written on his face. Blood flowed freely from the multiple bullet injuries throughout the body. In a span of several seconds, his clothes were drenched in blood completely.

As the shooting stopped, Aditya rushed forward and fell down on his knees beside his once beloved uncle.

'Please...' Pravir said, swallowing painfully, 'forgive me. I did it all just for you.'

Aditya wiped his tears and refrained himself from breaking down even more. 'Did you kill my grandfather?'

'Aditya, this is much bigger than you can ever -'

Aditya cut him off. 'Did you kill my grandfather? Yes or no.' Aditya steeled himself for the answer. He knew Dinesh had spoken the truth but he wanted to hear it from his uncle's own mouth.

'Yes. But-'

Aditya didn't stay beside any longer to listen to anything else. He got up before his uncle could complete his sentence and walked away to mourn his loss.

Mubeen felt sorry for the young man. Aditya was so young, yet he had lost so much of his family and of himself. He never felt the kind touch of a mother's palm on his forehead or the surprise gifts from his father. His grandfather had been his entire world for him and his uncle had been the father who he never was. Now, all of a sudden, in a span of a little more than a week, he lost them both under gruesome circumstances.

Any man under such a situation might lose all sense of hope, belief and trust. The entire world would become a game for him, a game of deceit, murder and malice. Every look would become an intention to kill; every smile would become a deception.

But something surprised Mubeen. Aditya wasn't in fact mourning or crying away in the corner. He was looking around, searching. He realized now was the time to bring in the big guns. He stood at an angle, pulled out his phone and dialled Ravi's number.

Official systems had to interfere in this now. There was no way he could handle this alone anymore.

101

Back in the Mumbai Police Headquarters, a phone began ringing. It was Ravi's. He had intentionally kept this back in case Mubeen called. The man on duty instantly connected the necessary wires and picked it up. He tried speaking but no reply came, only the line maintained its connection. Its purpose was clear.

Find me.

The man immediately set about tracking it. Three minutes later, he had the exact location in Patna. He took a printout of the report and rushed to the Director General's office.

'Ma'am, I have some news.'

'Who are you?' she asked, her voice condescending as usual.

'Ma'am, I work under Superintendent Ravi in the tech department.'

This got her attention. 'What do you have for me?'

'I have found Mubeen's and in turn Aditya's location precisely. Here's the report. Ravi Sir said you would know what to do with it.'

Hema took the paper from the man and nodded. 'Yes, I do. You can leave.'

Just as the man left, Hema picked up her phone and dialled Bihar Police number. It was picked up after a ring.

'Hello? This is Director General of Mumbai Police, Hema Qureshi. I have the exact locations and I need your force to reach the location as soon as possible. We have no idea what is going on down there, anything might have happened. You need to act quickly on this one, sir.'

There was a pause on the other side as the man weighed his options.

'Alright. Fax me the details of the location right now. I'll send in my units there immediately.'

'I will do that right away.' Hema smiled. Mubeen was indeed a resourceful and a useful man in times such as this. He had the courage to place a call at a time when he was probably a captive. And it was because of his courage that filthy rich malefactors like Dinesh Thakur can be put behind bars and become a source of inspiration for the likes.

102

'What is it Aditya?'

'I think I know where it is.' Aditya replied quietly and started walking into the park. He stepped over the long weeds growing profusely beside the partially unearthed brick structures jutting out from the ground. 'This is a part of the *Sri Arogyavihare Brikshusamghasya*.'

'Wha... what's that?' Mubeen asked, dumbfounded by the illogically difficult name.

'An ancient hospital, for short. That was what was written in Brahmi Script on an inscription made on a terracotta seal unearthed nearby.'

'Couldn't you say this at the first time? Now don't tell me you know the doctor who sat here too.'

'I do. The name is *Dhanvantareh*. But these were items from the Gupta period, about seven centuries after Ashoka. So it doesn't really concern us.'

'Okay.' Mubeen said, frowning. Aditya was taking him deep into the park. The foliage around was increasing but there was a certain certainty in Aditya's stride that made his fell that Aditya wasn't lost as he was. Suddenly, he swerved off the contructed pathway leading throughout the park and went into the trees to his left.

'Hey, where are you going?'

The only reply he got to his question was silence. Aditya was in his own world now. Suddenly, he came to a halt in front of a fig tree. It was a thick one, with hundreds of roots hanging down from the stems. The leaves were a tender green and a serene coolness seeped into the atmosphere under the tree.

Aditya stood gazing at it for a second then went close to it and started to feel its texture. His hands moved tenderly over the bark of the tree, over the rough waves and dunes of the surface. Mubeen stood at a distance and looked on. There was something uncannily familiar about the tree. The shape, the way it stood. Everything about it seemed eerily familiar. But nothing seemed to strike him.

'Why does this tree seem so familiar?' Mubeen asked, voicing his thoughts.

'I believe you have seen pictures of the *Bodhi* tree, the tree under which *Bodhisattwa* or *Gautama Buddha* himself sat.' Aditya said without even looking back.

Then it struck him. 'Yes! You're right! This tree is an exact replica of the pictures drawn for representation!'

'This is not a replica, my friend. This tree is an offspring of the actual *Bodhi* tree that existed during *Buddha's* times.'

'What do you mean?'

'The noble lineage of the *Bodhi* tree had never been broken. When the actual tree in *Bodh Gaya*, with the passage of time had been on the verge of dying, a sample had been taken and planted here to that the noble lineage of trees would not die. It was hidden from the eyes of the public, only the one at *Mahabodhi Temple* would remain open for public, which too is a descendent of the actual tree. Two more of these exist, one in Sri Lanka and another one I don't remember where.'

'Even trees have stories to say. How intriguing!'

'Everything has a story to say, a history to be learned and a lesson to be taught. The thing is that we have forgotten to learn from the past, which is in reality one of the most important teachers who can teach us anything and everything we want. Our now so called "modernism" in the 21st century promotes the fact that future is the only way forward but is it really so? History has so much in store for us yet we ignore it, oblivious to the unlimited possibilities and ideas it can offer for our societies and communities.'

'You have some really strong opinions which are an antithesis of the general belief of the masses.'

'My opinions are mine alone and no one can take those away from me.'

'Anyway is this the marked tree which is mentioned in the poem? From my standpoint, I don't see any resembling marks. The heart shaped leaves of a fig tree are pretty normal as far as I know. The bark of the fig tree looks relatively normal apart from the uncanny familiarity of the entire tree itself.'

Aditya walked up to him. 'That's the point. You're looking too closely. Look at the big picture. The tree itself is the ancient marker; I realized the point when you mentioned to me that the tree looks familiar. So for uncovering this clue, I have you to thank.'

'Oh, please don't.'

Several metres away, Dinesh was lying on the ground holding his injury and Avinash by his side.

'Where did they go? Dinesh asked through clenched teeth.

'I don't know, somewhere off into the woods.' Avinash replied.

'Also call your men and tell them to kill Rivannah. Tell them to kill Rivannah in the worst possible way imaginable. And then ask them to make it go viral, this should hit the news. I don't want the Tiwari family to survive. I want to live to see to it that the family withers away. A part has broken away with the death of Pravir. Now I want the entire family to rot away and then finally cease to exist.'

'Yes sir.' Avinash replied nervously as he pulled out his phone. He dialled the last number he had called a while back.

'Hello? Kill her as slowly as possible. Then make it viral. Make sure she is recognizable. It should make the police and everybody else look bad. Do it as soon as possible, alright?'

'Yes sir' came a reply from the other side of the line, 'with pleasure.'

103

'Everybody ready?' Ravi asked, standing in front of the door, his gun gripped tightly in his hands.

'Yes.'

'Let's do it.' Ravi took a careful aim at the doorknob and fired one shot. He knew he would have only one chance at that shot to have the element of surprise. So his first shot would have to suffice. He then kicked the door with all his might and it came open.

'FREEZE!' Ravi shouted.

All the men were too stunned to react. Only one of them held a gun to Rivannah's thighs and a phone in his hands. Rivannah herself was on a chair in the middle of the room, hands tied behind her back and legs tied to the legs of the chair. Her eyes were filled with fright and dark circles under them, a cumulative of her couple of days in captivity.

'Looks like we're here just in time.'

The man with the gun composed himself quickly and said, 'Move and I will shoot her.'

'Okay.' Ravi said, and before the man could think of anything else, he fired. The head exploded and spread crimson goo everywhere as the bullet found its mark perfectly on the forehead.

'So, uh how was this man killed?' Ravi asked, nonchalantly to the men standing behind him.

'Collateral damage sir, there was a lot of crossfire and the man happened to be at the wrong place in the wrong time. One bullet found its mark and we are sorry for the loss. Of course, the version depends on the cooperation of the remaining men.'

'Yes. If you do cooperate and agree to give up who you're working for, we are probably looking at three or four short years in jail. If not, well you know.' Ravi said, smiling. These men were amateurs. Their appearances were big and all buffed up but on the inside, they were whimpering. A few minutes of awkward silence would ensue after which full cooperation was guaranteed. This was what the police liked to call an open and shut case, nothing could come in to break the shell.

Finally the men gave up. They threw up their hands, and Ravi motioned for his men to cuff them. He personally went ahead to untie Rivannah. He first untied the cloth covering her mouth. He then went on to untie her hands and legs.

'I have a question.'

That came as a surprise. Usually kidnapping victims didn't ask a lot of questions until a very, very long time. They usually are too traumatized to even talk. And now she's here, asking a question.

'What is it?'

'How is Aditya involved in all of this mess?'

Ravi raised his eyebrows in befuddlement. He surely didn't even have a remote expectation of a question such as this. 'Well, how did you know Aditya was involved? I mean, you were here, right?'

'Something had happened and Aditya had gotten an opportunity to talk to me. Now answer my question.'

That was it! How could he have missed that? 'Uh, yes. That is a part I personally still haven't figured out. Probably when you meet Aditya, you could ask him. I only know that he is somewhere near Patna with a man I can trust with my life who goes by the name Mubeen Roy and I suggest you can trust him too.'

'I want to talk to him. As soon as possible.'

'I'll do that as soon as I get hold of him.' Ravi said, nodding. Rivannah was one strong woman.

104

'Sir, Rivannah has been rescued.' Avinash said, horrified.

'WHAT?' Dinesh couldn't understand anything.

'My man hadn't hung up on the call when I heard a loud shout and the sound of the door breaking open. After that, the man in charge of the police team said something in reply to which my man replied with a threat. In answer to that, I heard another shot and the sound of the phone itself hitting the floor. Soon, the remaining men gave up, from the looks of it.'

Dinesh couldn't believe it. How could that have happened? His perfect plan had ended in a disaster from every direction. At one point, he thought he had everything. He thought he had everything in his hands. Aditya and Mubeen had walked into his trap. Or did they?

Desperation led to fear as he began to imagine the consequences of his deeds. As he recollected what all he had done and had been an instrumental part of, a part of his breath left him, never to return. But how could his carefully constructed and fool proof plan have succeeded? He didn't even know what he had missed, what all had happened behind the curtains to bring him down. Whose plan was this? It was as if the person who had plotted his downfall had known all his steps long before even he himself had thought of them.

Suddenly he could feel his senses slip out of his grasp. His vision began to blur, his hearing began to dull and his head began to ache. *Massive blood loss from the bullet wound is probably causing this.* Dinesh thought to himself.

Suddenly, he heard the wail of a police siren. Out of the corner of his eye, he saw the blinking of red and blue lights as a couple of cars came to a harsh halt at the mouth of the Kumhrar Excavation Park.

In desperation, he lunged up at Avinash and said, 'Find them and strike them down. I don't want them to get anywhere near the clue. Do it! This is my last work for you before I die. Do this for my sake.'

'Yes sir. I'll get to it right now.' Avinash said, looking at the police and then towards Dinesh.

Then he quickly motioned to his men and ran off into the woods in pursuit of Aditya and Mubeen.

105

'The clue says that whatever there is to find lies under the marked tree. So do we have to dig?' Mubeen asked.

'I think so, yes.'

'Then let's get to it. I don't think we have a lot of time in our hands. Where should we begin?'

'As the poem suggests, it should be right under the tree, waiting for us to find it. Let's begin near the roots. My guess is that it will not be too deep. But I had a question before we got down to it. What is going to happen to Rivannah?'

'By now, she should be in the safest of hands, maybe in the hands of her parents.'

'Don't joke with me, what do you mean?'

'When I forced Avinash to give his men a call to let you talk with Rivannah, it was not just to check if she was alive and well. It was because we had Avinash's phone number and if we could track down the other number, the Mumbai Police can do the rest. I'm sure my good friend Ravi is handling this according to our plan and she should be safe. And if she isn't yet, she is soon going to be, that I can promise you.'

Aditya suddenly turned and hugged Mubeen. It was a rough bear hug but the meaning was clear. Aditya had no words to express his heartfelt thanks to Mubeen for doing so much for him.

'Alright, alright. That's enough for now. Let's find what you grandfather had in store for you.'

Both of them kneeled down on the ground and began patting the mud here and there, sometimes pulled out a fistful or two to see if there was anything underneath. Aditya took the help of a few sharp rocks to do the digging. Mubeen adopted the idea too. Suddenly Aditya's rock hit against something hard. A metallic clang resounded through the serene woods. They looked at each other, their eyes clearly portraying excitement. Both of them moved to the same place and then began to manually shift the mud from the place.

As the mud shifted, something metallic golden in colour began to emerge from within. Soon, they found the edges. It was a rectangular box kind of object, hollow from the inside, a conclusion based on the sound produced. The body was pink golden in colour and the edges were silver. Mubeen was having some second thoughts. These things could be made of real gold and silver. Who knew? He even considered the option of knocking out Aditya and running away with the box. But then he dismissed the idea as some kind of tomfoolery. But again, if it was really gold, it was worth a fortune, more so if he could prove its antiquity.

'What do you think?' Mubeen asked.

'This might be it.' Aditya said, a smile adorning his lips after a very long time.

They began clearing away the mud from the place. After a while, when all the mud had been cleared, they knew it was what they were looking for. At the very centre of the box, etched into the gold was an intricate *dharmachakra* at the centre of which was a hole. It was a very small hole, about the diameter of an average index finger. The twenty four spokes were beautifully and exquisitely engraved with accurate design and not one single flaw visible to the naked eye.

'What is that hole for?'

'It is a keyhole. And I believe we already possess the key.' Aditya said, pulling out the little object within which they had found their clue, from his pocket. Aditya slowly and steadily brought the key near the keyhole. About ten centimetres away from the keyhole, the key slipped out of Aditya's fingers and lodged itself into the hole, completing the perfect symbol.

'Wait, did you do that?' Mubeen asked.

'No! It just slipped out of my hands like it was being pulled or something. The mechanism inside must be magnetic I think. Else I have no explanation how this took place.'

Aditya, out of pure chance looked up at the woods behind Mubeen. What he saw shocked him. Avinash and his gang of goons were two feet away Mubeen's back. As Avinash realized he had been spotted, he began running towards them. Aditya in a desperate attempt to save Mubeen lunged at him but was a fraction of a second late and the butt of Avinash's gun hit the back of Mubeen's head, tearing the skin and drawing blood.

Mubeen let out a loud scream as he fell down on his back, clutching his head in his arms, his fingers slowly turning crimson from the blood. Seconds later, he was out cold.

Everything to Aditya seemed to be happening in slow motion. Avinash had his gun pointed at Aditya, two feet away from his face. All the remaining men too had their weapons pointed at him. Aditya had closed his eyes, bracing for the inevitable to happen. But just as he was about to close them, from the corner of his eye he saw several men wearing khaki uniforms and weapons in their hands emerge from the woods.

Then began the firing. The police immediately shot down two of the goon and while that distracted Avinash, Aditya quickly covered up with mud what they had found underneath the ground. That would have to wait for a later time. Aditya knew better than to stand up. The safest, most reliable option to save your life during a gun fire battle was to lay flat on the ground. And that's exactly what Aditya did.

In the rapid crossfire, another bullet struck Avinash in his thighs and he fell down shrieking. The bullet had torn through his shins, probably shattering his bone for a lifetime. In a matter of thirty to forty seconds, the police had overpowered the men and minutes later had all of them cuffed up.

One of the police men came up him and said, 'We want to congratulate you young man. You helped us in nabbing these criminals.'

'I didn't do anything. He did. And he needs help right now!' Aditya exclaimed, pointing at Mubeen lying on the ground, still out cold. Instantly two of the policemen carrying a stretcher kneeled down beside the lying figure of Aditya and gently placed him on it.

'Don't worry Mr. Tiwari, he'll be fine. We have paramedics with us.'

'Thank you, sir.'

'Now I believe you have to go back to Mumbai, there are a lot of legal formalities you have to undergo. But come back soon. I promise you, your next trip would be a far peaceful one.'

Aditya smiled politely and looking at the place he had covered up he said, 'I surely will come back. I have a little work to be finished.'

The police smiled genially and nodded. He didn't want the name of his own state rot because of some idiotic yet filthy rich man who decided to break hell throughout the beautiful state.

EPILOGUE

Mubeen Roy's phone rang loudly from his bedside table. His eyes flung open as the piercing sound of his cell phone reached his ears. Then, as he realised it, he took up the phone. The call was from an unknown number. He rubbed his aching temples. Frustrated, he picked up the call.

'Hello?'

'Good to see you're finally awake Mubeen! You've been in and out of consciousness for the past five days.' Ravi said from the other side of the line.

'Wait... what? Where am I? Five days?'

'Try and find out for yourself.'

Mubeen rubbed his eyes and looked around. The place seemed vaguely familiar, something out of an old, once forgotten dream. The colour of the room, the texture of the bed sheets, the view outside the window, everything seemed to be familiar yet he couldn't quite place them all in his mind.

He stood up and looked about; he noticed the doorstep menu pamphlet bear the words *HOTEL MARINE PLAZA, MUMBAI*.

Slowly, realisation dawned upon him. He was back in the hotel he had been before he took up Aditya's case. In fact, it was the exact same room! As he sat up, his suspicions were slowly proved. Suddenly, as he sat up he felt something behind his head. His hand went up to feel it. He rubbed his fingers over the area and realized it was cotton, a bandage. The whole back of his head had been cleared right off to bandage a wound.

But the question is, when did I ever get that injury? Then he remembered Ravi's words. *You've been in and out of consciousness for the past five days.* FIVE *days?!*

He threw off his sheets and tried standing up on his own feet. Almost instantly, as he tried to stand up, the feeling of having a lead ball inside his head came up and he began to feel woozy. He sat back down.

'I must have taken a pretty hard impact there.' Mubeen said to himself, rubbing his temples.

Right then, he found a letter lying at the edge of his bed. It was an unmarked one so probably it was hand-delivered. He opened it up and pulled out a piece of paper from within. In that sheet of paper was a letter.

Dear Mubeen,

I hope this letter finds you in good shape. If not, take some rest. Now as you read on, I will tell you of the things you have missed in the days you were sleeping away in the hospital.

Firstly, I am sorry I couldn't save you from Avinash's hit. I had seen him at the last moment so I tried but couldn't do anything. I doubt you'd remember any of that. Anyway, you do remember the clue, right? Well, it had been the last clue. Inside were documents and another set of instructions I set myself on the very day I was free from all the legal procedures. Within the three or so days I had, I embarked upon the mission to complete the final set of instructions. It led me to a place where all my doubts were resolved.

Each clue had a purpose, a deeper meaning. Now you must be wondering why only four of these clues. Well, in simple words, Ashoka was a big fan of Buddha and Buddha had four principles of set down by Him or the Four Noble Truths he had realized when he gained enlightenment. From the day I was born, my grandfather had been preparing me for this journey. He taught me everything I know, spurred within me a fire of interest in subjects like these.

Remember the photo we had when we opened the very first clue? If we had looked closely, it was a picture of me in my grandfather's arms and in the backdrop was the statue of *Vivekananda* of the Vivekananda Rock Memorial, taken from the exact place we found our entrance into the cave underneath the Kanyakumari Temple. The clue in Kuldhara had been our effort entirely. In the third, you would remember that I had already been there when my grandfather had asked me to remember that place. And with the fourth clue too, he had shown me that place several times. I always knew where to look; I just had to figure out which one was which.

In conclusion, I would like to say one thing. Everything makes sense to me now. My grandfather's murder was not just a murder. It had been a long standing plan that my grandfather had cooked up and it began its action when he was murdered. It had been an elaborate plan to rat out a mole. Now I think you can guess who the mole was. Yes, it was my uncle. He had been fevered by an idea that caused him to track down and kill members of successors of Ashoka's Council of Nine.

Now you must be thinking where I fit in. Remember the analogy of the Bodhi Tree I had told you about? Keeping up the ancient gene to uplift the sacredness of the line of descendents. Same thing is with me. I am a descendent of an ancient line, an ancient line of kings, and a bloodline that has remained with humanity throughout the past two millennia. I presume you can guess the rest.

Lastly, I would like to thank you for all that you have done for me for the past few days. I have no words to express my gratitude for all you have done and sacrificed. As a curt note, I also want to add that the conspirators in my grandfather's murder are going to get nothing more than some time in jail. That's it. Now, if they turn up dead in their jails, I request you *not* to look into the matter. Also I hope all that I have betrayed to you today will remain with you. These are the last requests I want to make.

Also the most stunning piece to the puzzle is yet to come. Even you were a part of his plan. Remember that newspaper I had shown you which featured an article on you? My grandfather had specifically asked me to remember that a few days before the murder happened.

Thank you so much once again, Mubeen. You have been and always will be one of my best friends who stood with me through the worst of times.

Ah! Also, get well soon!

Yours dearly,

Aditya.

Mubeen could believe what he read the first time. He went through the letter two more times before he actually came to the conclusion that he wasn't hallucinating because of the head injury.

It was as if late Mr. Harish Tiwari knew it all along. Yet he didn't do anything to prevent that. What could have been the reason for that? Did he know already who was plotting to kill him?

Whatever the reason might have been, Mubeen would never know.

All he knew was one thing.

There can be no smoke without a fire.

Life went on normally for Mubeen as he recovered. He was back in the limelight with his recent wondrous accomplishment of solving the murder case of Mr. Harish Tiwari, resolving the "corporate conspiracy" between the real estate dynasties of the Tiwari's and the Thakur's. It wasn't the first time a business had resorted to violence to eliminate competition but this surely was one of the biggest and the deadliest.

Time was going so well for Mubeen that the Mumbai Police Department offered him the post of the Commissioner of the Crime Branch of the Department which he politely refused in a written statement which mentioned that he would like to help out only on the basis of his own decision and not governmental forces.

Dinesh Thakur was thrown in jail after a weeklong court case that he was bound to lose. In fact, the case went on for a week because of the monumental number of proofs and evidences that the opposition had against him. He was sentences to life imprisonment along with the members of his illustrious team of killers spearheaded by Avinash. Several months later, these inmates were mysteriously killed.

Again, Mubeen was called in to look into the matter but he again politely refused, stating that he had recently recovered from a serious injury and he required his own "down-time".

ABOUT THE AUTHOR

Indrashish Mitra is an 18 year old student of Mass Media at KC College, Mumbai. Before this, he has published three short stories and a poem on popular online literary journals. Alongside Mass Media, he is also doing a Diploma course in Creative Writing from the prestigious Indira Gandhi National Open University (IGNOU). He is also a freelance editor which he runs through his website; two of his edited novel manuscripts have hit the markets and are doing reasonably well.

To know more about him or his work, visit his website – www.indrashishmitra.com or email him at indrashishmitra@ gmail.com To connect with him, Facebook handle – AuthorIndrashish Instagram handle – @ indrashish.mitra Twitter handle – @ indrashishmitra